Jaci Burton i. a *New York Time* ... Oklahoma with her husband and ... who are all scattered around the c ... lover of sports, Jaci can often tell ... being played. She watches entirely ... unhealthy amount of reality TV. Wl ... deadline, Jaci can be found at her local casino, trying to become a millionaire (so far, no luck). She's a total romantic and loves a story with a happily ever after, which you'll find in all her books.

Find the latest news on Jaci's books at www.jaciburton.com, and connect with her online at www.facebook.com/AuthorJaciBurton or via Twitter @jaciburton.

Praise for Jaci Burton:

'A wild ride' Lora Leigh, No. 1 *New York Times* bestselling author

'It's the perfect combination of heat and romance that makes this series a must-read' *Heroes and Heartbreakers*

'Plenty of emotion and conflict in a memorable relationship-driven story' *USA Today*

'Strong characters, an exhilarating plot, and scorching sex . . . You'll be drawn so fully into her characters' world that you won't want to return to your own' *Romantic Times*

'A beautiful romance that is smooth as silk . . . leaves us begging for more' *Joyfully Reviewed*

'A strong plot, complex characters, sexy athletes, and non-stop passion make this book a must-read' *Fresh Fiction*

'Hot, hot, hot! . . . Romance at its best! Highly recommended!' *Coffee Table Reviews*

'Ms Burton has a way of writing intense scenes that are both sensual and raw . . . Plenty of romance, sexy men, hot steamy loving and humor' *Smexy Books*

'A wonderf ... l!' *The Romance D* ...

By Jaci Burton

Hope Series
Hope Smoulders (e-novella)
Hope Flames
Hope Ignites
Hope Burns
Love After All
Make Me Stay
Don't Let Go

Play-by-Play Series
The Perfect Play
Changing The Game
Taking A Shot
Playing To Win
Thrown By A Curve
One Sweet Ride
Holiday Games (e-novella)
Melting The Ice
Straddling The Line
Holiday On Ice (e-novella)
Quarterback Draw
All Wound Up
Unexpected Rush
Rules of Contact

Don't Let Go

Jaci BURTON

headline
ETERNAL

Published by arrangement with Berkley,
an imprint of Penguin Publishing Group,
a division of Penguin Random House LLC

First published in Great Britain in 2016
by HEADLINE ETERNAL
An imprint of HEADLINE PUBLISHING GROUP

1

Cataloguing in Publication Data is available from the British Library

ISBN 978 1 4722 2829 1

Offset in 12/12.80 pt Times LT Std by Jouve (UK)

Printed and bound in Great Britain by CPI Group (UK) Ltd, Croydon, CR0 4YY

MIX
Paper from
responsible sources
FSC® C104740

Headline's policy is to use papers that are natural, renewable and recyclable
products and made from wood grown in well-managed forests and other
controlled sources. The logging and manufacturing processes are expected
to conform to the environmental regulations of the country of origin.

HEADLINE PUBLISHING GROUP
An Hachette UK Company
Carmelite House
50 Victoria Embankment
London EC4Y 0DZ

www.headlineeternal.com
www.headline.co.uk
www.hachette.co.uk

This is dedicated to all the dreamers out there.
Write them down, wish them, follow them,
and never, ever give up on them.

Chapter 1

BRADY CONNERS WAS doing one of the things he enjoyed the most—smoothing out dents in a quarter panel of a Chevy. As soon as he finished, he'd paint, and this baby would be good as new.

It wasn't his dream job. He was working toward that. But with every day he spent as a mechanic at Richards Auto Service, thanks to the shop's owner, Carter Richards, he was pocketing money. And that got him closer to his dream—opening up his own custom motorcycle paint shop.

Somewhere. Maybe here in Hope. Maybe somewhere else. Probably somewhere else, because the town of Hope held memories.

Not good ones.

A long time ago—a time that seemed like an eternity now—he'd had plans with his brother, Kurt, to start up a business together.

That dream went up in smoke the day Brady got the call that his brother was dead.

He paused, stood, and stretched out the kinks in his back,

wiping the sweat that dripped into his eyes. He took a step away and grabbed the water bottle he always kept stored nearby. He took a long drink from the straw, swallowing several times until his thirst was quenched.

Needing a break, he pulled off his breathing mask and swiped his fingers through his hair, then stepped outside.

It was late spring, and rain was threatening. He dragged in a deep breath, enjoying the smell of fresh air.

He really wanted a cigarette, but he'd quit a little over a year ago. Not that the urge had gone away. Probably never would. But he was stronger than his own needs. Or at least that's what he told himself every time a powerful craving hit.

Instead, he pulled out one of the flavored toothpicks he always kept in his jeans pocket and slid that between his teeth.

Not nearly as satisfying, but it would do. It would have to.

He leaned against the wall outside the shop and watched the town in motion. It was lunchtime, so it was busy.

Luke McCormack, one of Hope's cops, drove by in his patrol car and waved. Brady waved back. Luke was a friend of Carter's, and while Brady wasn't as social as a lot of the guys he'd met, he knew enough to be friendly. Especially to cops.

Samantha Reasor left her shop, loading up her flower van with a bunch of colorful bouquets. She spotted him, giving him a bright smile and a wave before she headed off.

Everyone in this town was friendly. He mostly kept to himself, did his work, and then went home to the small apartment above the shop at night to watch TV or play video games. Some nights he did side work painting bikes. He had one goal in mind, and that was to save enough money to open his business. He saw his parents now and again, since they lived in Hope, but the strain of Kurt's death had taken a toll on them.

Nothing was the same anymore. With them. With him, either, he supposed.

Sometimes life just sucked. And you dealt with that.

His stomach grumbled. He needed something to eat. He pushed off the wall and headed up the street, intending to hit the sandwich joint on the corner. He'd grab something and bring it back to the shop.

He stopped suddenly when Megan Lee, the hot brunette who owned the bakery, dashed out with a couple of pink boxes in her hand. She collided with him, and the boxes went flying. She caught one, he caught one, and then he steadied her by sliding his arm around her.

She looked up at him, her brown eyes wide with surprise.

"Oh my gosh. Thank you, Brady. I almost dropped these."

"You okay, Megan?"

"Yes. But let me check these." She opened the boxes. There were cakes inside. They looked pretty, with pink icing on one and blue on the other and little baby figurines in strollers sitting on top of the cakes. There were flowers and other doodads as well. He didn't know all that much about cake decorations. He just liked the way they tasted.

"They're for Sabelle Frasier. She just had twins." She looked up at him with a grin. "A boy and a girl. Her mom ordered these for her hospital homecoming. I spent all morning baking and decorating them."

He didn't need to know that, but the one thing he did know was that people in this town were social and liked to talk. "They look good."

She swiped her hair out of her eyes. "Of course they're good."

He took the boxes from her. "Where's your car?"

"Parked just down the street."

"How about you let me carry these? Just in case you want to run into anyone else on your way."

Her lips curved. "I think you ran into me."

He disagreed, but whatever. He figured he'd do his good deed for the day, then get his sandwich.

He followed her down the street.

"I haven't seen much of you lately," she said.

He shrugged. "Been busy."

"I've been meaning to come by the shop and visit, but things have been crazy hectic at the bakery, too." She studied him. "How about I bring pastries by in the morning? And I've never brought you coffee before. How about some coffee? How do you take it? Black, or with cream and sugar? Or maybe you like lattes or espresso? What do you drink in the mornings?"

He had no idea what she was talking about. "Uh, just regular coffee. Black."

"Okay. I make a really great cup of coffee. I'm surprised you haven't come into the bakery, since it's so close to the auto shop. Most everyone who works around here pops in." She pressed the unlock button on her key fob, then opened the back door and took the boxes from him.

Man, she really could talk. He'd noticed that the couple of times they'd been together in social situations. Not that it was a bad thing, but for someone like him who lived mostly isolated, all that conversation was like a bombardment.

But he liked it. The one thing he missed the most since his self-imposed isolation was conversation. And Megan had it in droves. He just wasn't all that good at reciprocating.

After she slid the boxes in, she turned to him. "What's your favorite pastry? You know, I've dropped cupcakes off at the auto shop. Have you eaten any of those?"

He was at a loss for words. He always was around her. A few of his friends had fixed the two of them up before. Once at Logan and Des's dinner party, then again at Carter and Molly's wedding. They'd danced. Had some conversation. Mostly one-sided, since Megan had done all the talking.

He wasn't interested.

Okay, that wasn't exactly the truth. What heterosexual male wouldn't be interested in Megan? She was gorgeous, with her silky, light brown hair and her warm chocolate eyes that always seemed to study him. She also had a fantastic body with perfect curves.

But he was here to work. That was it. He didn't have time for a relationship.

He didn't want a relationship, no matter how attractive the woman was. And Megan was really damned attractive.

"Brady?" she asked, pulling his attention back on her. "Cupcakes?"

"What about them?"

She cocked her head to the side. "Oh, come on, Brady. Everyone has a favorite pastry. Cream puffs? Donuts? Scones? Cakes? Bars? Strudel?"

He zeroed in on the last thing she said. "Apple strudel. I used to have that from the old bakery when I was a kid."

She offered up a satisfied smile. "I make a killer apple strudel. I'll bring you one—along with coffee—in the morning."

He frowned. "You don't have to do that."

She laid her hand on his arm and offered up the kind of smile that made him focus on her mouth. She had a really pretty mouth, and right now it was glossed a kissable shade of peach.

He didn't want to notice her mouth, but he did.

"I don't mind. I love to bake. But now I have to go. Thanks again for saving the cakes. I'll see you tomorrow, Brady."

She climbed into her car and pulled away, leaving him standing there, confused as hell.

He didn't want her to bring him coffee. Or apple strudel. Or anything.

He didn't want to notice Megan or talk to Megan or think about Megan, but the problem was, he'd been doing a lot of that lately. For the past six months or so he'd thought about the dance he'd shared with her. The laughs they'd enjoyed together and her animated personality. She had a sexy smile—not the kind a woman had to force, but the kind that came naturally. She also had a great laugh and she could carry a conversation with ease. And that irritated him because he hadn't thought about a woman in a long time.

Ever since his brother had died, he hadn't wanted to think about anything or anyone. All he'd wanted to do was work, then head upstairs to his one-room apartment above the auto shop, eat his meals, and watch TV. And on the weekends he'd do custom bike painting. Keep his mind and his body busy so he wouldn't have to think—or feel.

Women—and relationships—would make him feel, and that wasn't acceptable. He'd noticed that right away about Megan, noticed that he liked her and maybe—

No. Wasn't going to happen—ever. He needed to get her out of his head.

He only had time for work and making money. He had a dream he was saving for.

And now he barely had time for lunch, because he had a Chevy to get back to.

Chapter 2

MEGAN GRABBED HER purse and the cupcakes she'd made
for tonight's book club meeting. She was already late because
she'd had so much baking to finish for tomorrow, and she'd
lost track of time. Then she'd had to shower to clean off the
bakery scent—a flour, sugar, and butter combo.

Though the girls probably wouldn't mind that.

She drove over to Loretta Simmons's bookstore, noting
that the street was filled with her friends' cars and she was
the last to arrive. Typically, she was early. Her pulse raced as
she got out of her car and pushed through the door.

She loved this bookstore, which took up the entire first
floor of the renovated old mercantile in downtown Hope.
Loretta had returned to town after her divorce last year
and had leased the first-floor space in the historic building
Reid McCormack had gutted and rebuilt.

Now it was the Open Mind bookstore, and lately it had
become her favorite hangout. It not only had tons of books,
but also coffee and tea, plus wireless and an electronic bar
for people who had e-readers or laptops and wanted a quiet
place to work or study. It was perfect for voracious readers,

and with the local college nearby, it was also a great place for the students to come by at night to read or study.

Megan wandered to the back and found her friends set up at their regular spot.

"Hey, sorry I'm late," she said.

Her best friend, Samantha, looked up from the book in her lap, her long blond ponytail twirling back and forth as she lifted her head. "You made it."

"Yes, finally." She laid the boxes on the round table in the center. One of the things she loved was all the comfortable seating areas, spaces where groups could come together to meet. This one had several cushioned chairs, a sofa, and a table.

"We're so glad you're here," Loretta said. "And not just because of the cupcakes."

"Well, sort of because of the cupcakes," Chelsea said. "But I brought wine, so we'd have survived if you hadn't made it."

Megan laughed. "I'm sure you would have. But I never miss book club."

She unpacked the cupcakes from the box and arranged them on a plate.

"What have we got tonight?" Molly asked.

"Dark chocolate cupcakes with vanilla buttercream frosting."

Chelsea poured the wine. "Which goes perfectly with zinfandel."

Emma, who was eight and a half months pregnant, laid her hand on her lower back. "I miss wine."

"Your doc said you could have a glass, didn't he?"

"Yes, but I think I'll opt for tea."

Megan looked around. "Where's Des?"

"Opting out tonight," Emma said. "She said she'll see us all at the baby shower this weekend at the ranch, providing she doesn't have the baby before then."

Megan went over and grabbed one of the glasses of wine Chelsea had poured. "Who do you think will go first, Emma?"

Emma delicately lowered herself into one of the chairs. "I'm hoping me."

Molly laughed. "I'm hoping it's you as well. I have tomorrow on the office pool."

Emma arched a brow. "There's an office pool on my due date?"

"Honey, the entire town has pools for your and Des's delivery dates," Sam said. "With both of you due at the same time, how could we not?"

"Well, I have a couple of weeks left, so I don't know what you were thinking, Molly."

Molly shrugged. "That first babies sometimes come early. Though I have you two weeks late on another pool."

Emma rubbed her belly. "My poor baby being gambled on." She paused for a few seconds, then said, "Is it too late to get in on the action?"

Megan laughed. "I don't know, Emma. I think you might have insider information."

"Oh, please. I wish I knew when this little one was coming out. And hopefully it's soon."

While everyone played guessing games about Emma's due date, Megan wandered over to Sam, who was making herself a cup of coffee. "How's the new house coming along?"

"It's hit-and-miss. We got the foundation poured before winter set in, and they're working on plumbing, electrical, and getting the walls and the roof up. But you know they're dancing around the weather, and early spring has been rainy, so we're hoping that calms down somewhat so we can make some headway. In the meantime, we're living at my house. The yard is big enough for Not My Dog, who's perfectly happy as long as he's with Reid and me."

Megan smiled. "And of course he goes to work with Reid every day anyway."

"This is true."

"How's Grammy Claire?"

Sam's smile faltered. "About the same. She has her good days and bad days. Some days she recognizes me, some days she looks at me like she doesn't know who I am."

Megan squeezed her arm. "I'm sorry."

Sam nodded. "We're prepared for it. Physically she's still doing well enough to stay at her home, thanks to Faith, Grammy Claire's best friend, living there with her. I don't know what we'd do without her help. And the nursing staff who come in for regular visits have been lifesavers."

"It also helps that you and Reid are just across the street."

"Yes. We stop by every day and check on her."

"And maybe someday the two of you will have a honeymoon."

"Oh, we don't need that. It was enough that Grammy Claire was able to be at our wedding, and that she had full cognitive function at the time."

Megan saw the tears welling up in her friend's eyes, and knew how much it was hurting her to slowly lose her grandmother to Alzheimer's. "But you two are still newlyweds, so anytime you need my help with anything, all you have to do is ask."

Sam hugged her. "Thank you. I know I can count on you. But speaking of all things love, I haven't seen you dating anyone lately. What's up with that?"

"Oh, well, you know how it is. The bakery keeps me busy."

Sam slid her a look. "And that excuse is getting old. How did things go with that date you had last week?"

"The one with the guy from the newspaper?"

"Yes, that one."

Megan gave her a blank stare. "He was . . . nice."

Sam wrinkled her nose. "Nice? That's it?"

"Yes. That's it."

Sam sighed. "So, in other words, no spark."

"What are we talking about sparking?" Chelsea asked. "Not that I'm eavesdropping, but . . . okay, I'm eavesdropping."

"We're talking about Megan's date the other night."

"Ohh, you had a date?" Chelsea asked, pulling up a spot next to Sam. "Spill the details."

If there was one thing their hot redheaded friend loved, it was gossip. And Megan knew Chelsea had opinions, especially on men and dating. "Unfortunately, nothing to spill. Nice guy. Good job. Great manners over dinner. He was polite, made decent conversation and all, but I felt . . . nothing."

Chelsea's hopeful look disappeared. "Oh. That's unfortunate. As someone who dated more than her share of men in the past—"

"Like the entire male population of Hope," Sam said.

Chelsea shot Sam a look. "Hey. Not the entire population. Maybe half."

Megan laughed.

"Anyway," Chelsea said, "I can attest to the fact that sometimes the chemistry just isn't there, despite how good a man looks on paper."

Megan folded her arms. "Says the woman who landed the hottest bartender in Hope."

Chelsea graced them all with a well-satisfied grin. "I did, didn't I?"

"And she's smug about it, too," Sam said.

"I am, aren't I?"

Megan shook her head. "No cupcakes for you."

"Megan," Chelsea said, looking shocked. "You wouldn't do that."

"A few more bad dates and I might just consider it."

"But you wouldn't deny Sam, who just married the hottest architect in town."

Sam gave Megan an apologetic look and took a sip of her wine.

"Hmm, you have a point, Chelsea. Maybe I'll just keep all the cupcakes for myself."

"Or maybe you should consider dating more," Sam said.

"Okay, there's that. But even Chelsea can attest to the fact that the pickings are slim."

Loretta came over and sat on the edge of the sofa. "What are we picking?"

Sam leaned her head back. "Dates for Megan."

"And I mentioned the prime pickings among men are slim," Megan said.

Loretta nodded her head. "I can see how it would be hard to date in a small town."

"You have a point there," Chelsea said. "However, I think my problem was that I was extremely picky. Now that I've had an opportunity to take a step back and reflect, I can assure you that there are several good-looking and eligible men in Hope."

Megan wasn't buying it. "Name three."

"Jeff Armstrong, Brady Conners, and Deacon Fox."

Leave it to Chelsea to rattle off three names without even hesitating. Jeff was a very attractive doctor, Brady worked at Carter Richards's auto shop, and Deacon owned a construction company. Deacon had also been Loretta's high school boyfriend. She tilted her gaze to Loretta, who seemed to show no emotion when Deacon's name was mentioned. Though she wondered how Loretta felt about Deacon now after all these years.

Sam laughed, then laid her hand on Megan's shoulder. "She's got you there."

"I tried dating Brady," Megan said. "That didn't work out."

Chelsea frowned. "You and Brady dated? When?"

"Okay, so we didn't actually date. We had a couple of fix-ups where we were sort of pushed together."

"Which is not at all like dating," Sam said.

"No it's not, but he never asked me out."

"I haven't seen Brady go out with anyone since . . ." Molly let the sentence trail off.

"Since his brother died," Chelsea said. "Yes, I know. All that hot studliness going to waste. You should go after him, Megan. Are you interested?"

"She's definitely interested," Sam said.

Megan shot Sam a mind-your-own-business look.

"Oh, I see. So it's a lust thing," Chelsea said. "Well, who wouldn't lust after that man? If I wasn't already taken by a hot guy of my own, I'd be all over Brady Conners. Tall, well-muscled, rides a motorcycle, and that man just exudes sex."

Megan looked over at Chelsea, who shrugged.

"What? Just stating the facts. Come on, Megan, surely you agree."

She couldn't deny it. "I do agree. But I don't know. It seems like a waste of my time to chase after a man who isn't interested."

"I've seen him around town," Loretta said. "Chelsea does have a point. He is fine-looking."

"Maybe you're not dangling the right carrot," Chelsea said.

"I don't think many of Hope's citizens would appreciate me showing up at Carter's shop naked."

Sam snickered. Chelsea laughed. Loretta smiled over the rim of her wineglass. Molly and Emma smiled.

"Not exactly what I meant, Megan," Chelsea said. "You have to make yourself irresistible to him."

"I actually ran into him earlier today. Or, rather, he ran into me and my two boxes of cakes. I talked to him about baked goods."

"That would have gotten Reid's attention," Sam said. "Then again, he's a sucker for a good cinnamon roll."

"All men love sweet things," Emma said. "If you know what I mean."

Megan knew what she meant.

"So bring him some baked goods. And while you're at it, flash him some cleavage."

She looked down at her T-shirt and jeans. "Sexy is not my persona, Chelsea. That's more up your alley."

Chelsea grinned. "Ooh, well thank you. But you don't have to change your appearance, Megan. We love you just the way you are. Which, by the way, is absolutely beautiful."

Considering Chelsea was stunning, with her gorgeous red hair and stylish clothes and beautiful smile, Megan took that as a compliment. "Thank you."

"But how does he react around you?" Chelsea asked.

"Like he's interested. And annoyed about it."

"Hmm," Loretta said.

"That's a very good sign," Sam said.

"I agree," Molly said. "Men aren't like women. They keep their emotions close."

"And you know, Loretta," Chelsea said, "there are plenty of eligible men out there for you as well."

Loretta looked none too happy that the conversation had steered over to her.

"Oh. Um, I'm not interested."

"In men?" Chelsea asked.

Loretta laughed. "I like men very much. But after the divorce, I'm concentrating my efforts on the new business here, and on Hazel. I think that's enough for now."

Megan's gaze drifted to where Loretta's nine-year-old daughter, Hazel, was reading on the floor in the corner of the bookstore, completely oblivious to their conversations. She was such a cute kid, with her jeans and her T-shirt and her ponytailed hair pulled through the back of her baseball cap.

"She's so adorable, Loretta," Megan said.

Loretta sighed, then smiled. "Thank you. I think so, too. Should we start?" She held up the book club selection, Shannon Stacey's newest book. Megan was so excited about this one, since Ms. Stacey was one of her favorite authors. She loved everything she wrote.

Megan poured another glass of wine, and Chelsea pulled her aside.

"Seriously, Megan. You have nothing to lose with Brady, and everything to gain. The man sounds interested. So give him a little shove in the right direction."

She shrugged. "I'll try, but I don't know. He doesn't seem to want to be shoved."

Chelsea laughed. "They never do. Then again, men can often surprise us."

If Brady even once asked her out, Megan would be more

surprised than anyone. But she had promised to bring him coffee and something from the bakery tomorrow, so she'd start there and see if anything came from it. The man was hot and sexy and worth pursuing, so why not?

She'd give it one shot—and one shot only—and then see what came of it.

Chapter 3

ANOTHER RAINY DAY. Brady cursed the weather, because it
would be that much longer before the paint dried on the Buick
he'd worked on late last night. It also meant he'd have to leave
the bay doors closed today. He stepped into the office and
was greeted by Megan Lee, who nearly ran into his chest.

He took in the sight of her. Today she wore her hair in
a high ponytail, which accented her cheekbones and her
mouth. Her lips were painted some pretty shade of pink.

He tried not to look at her mouth.

"Oh, hi, Brady. We almost ran into each other. Again."

"Morning, Megan. Are you looking for Molly? I think
she's in a meeting with Carter."

"Actually, I was looking for you. I promised you coffee
and apple strudel."

He remembered that conversation from yesterday. How
could he not, considering he thought about Megan all the
time? He didn't actually believe she'd show up before six
thirty in the morning with a cup of coffee and a box in her
hand, though.

"I'd love to stay and talk, but I've got customers, so I

have to run. I hope you stop by the shop and let me know what you think."

With a short wave in his direction, she walked off. He stood there, holding the coffee and the box, watching the way her hips moved in those tight jeans she wore.

How could a woman wearing jeans, a pink polo shirt, and canvas tennis shoes look so damn sexy?

Ignoring his wayward thoughts, he took the box into the break room and opened it.

Sure enough, there was an apple strudel. His stomach growled. He popped the lid off the coffee, watching the steam rising from the cup. He inhaled the scent of the fresh roast and took a sip.

Damn good, and a hell of a lot better than the sludge he made from that ancient coffeemaker upstairs in his apartment. He lifted the apple strudel out of the box and took a bite.

It melted in his mouth, the taste of apples and sugar exploding all over his taste buds.

He wanted to savor it, but he devoured the entire thing in a minute. He even licked his fingers and searched the box to see if maybe she'd put two in there.

Sadly, she hadn't, so he finished off his cup of coffee, then dumped the containers in the trash and headed toward his work bay.

On the way, he looked out the window to see that the rain had finally stopped and the sun had emerged. It would help to dry the car he had painted, so he pushed the button to open the bay door, pulling off the tape and paper that covered the unpainted part of the Buick. He headed toward the Dumpster outside to dispose of the trash when he saw something dark scurry behind the Dumpster.

What the hell was that? Probably some kind of rodent.

But he heard whimpering, and rodents didn't whimper.

He bent down to investigate. An animal was wedged in between the Dumpster and the wall of the building. It was too big to be a rabbit or a cat, so it had to be a dog. It wasn't growling, so that was a good sign.

But it was shaking.

"Hey there, buddy," he said, using his calmest voice. "Whatcha doing back there?"

It wouldn't come out and was obviously scared to death. Not surprising, considering it had been thundering during the storm, something that scared a lot of dogs.

"I'm gonna reach back there and pull you out, okay? Don't be afraid. And don't bite me."

He didn't know why he was talking to the animal, but he kept his voice low and easy so the dog wouldn't be afraid of him.

As slowly as possible, he slid his arm toward the shivering dog. Not an easy feat, because there wasn't a lot of space between the wall and the Dumpster, and with the dog wedged back there, he could barely fit his hand. But the tiny being wasn't trying to shy away from him, and he kept talking to him as he got ahold of his fur and managed to pull him out from his hiding spot.

"There you go. Now you're free."

He picked up the dog, who couldn't weigh more than ten pounds. If that much.

Jesus, what a mess. He was wet, covered in mud and filth, and, Christ, did he stink. He couldn't even tell what kind of breed the dog was since he was so muddy. All he knew was it was small. And kind of furry—maybe. And matted. And stinky.

But he was shivering, no doubt cold and scared. Brady pulled the dog against his chest.

"Come on, you wet thing. Let's get you someplace dry."

As he was holding the dog, he realized he didn't have a lot of options other than the supply closet. But it was ventilated, and at least it was warm and dry. He grabbed a few shop towels and spread them on the floor in there, placing the dog on top of the towels. The tiny fur ball turned around several times and curled up in a tight circle, promptly going to sleep.

With a shrug, Brady closed the door, went into the break room to grab a bowl and fill it with water, then opened the door to the supply closet and put the bowl next to the dog. He barely opened his eyes to peer up at Brady, then went back to sleep.

"Traumatic morning, huh, buddy?" Brady asked before shutting the door behind him.

He figured he'd check on the dog in a little while, but for now, he had to get some work done.

After finishing up two vehicles, he checked on the dog, who was still asleep. Some of the mud had dried on him, but damn, that dog was a mess. On his lunch hour, he dashed to the pet store to pick up some dog shampoo and flea dip, along with dog food, a harness, and a leash, though he had no idea why, since the dog probably got loose from someone's yard in the rain and this would all be a waste of money. But whatever, he couldn't have the thing be dirty and hungry. He ran back to the shop and opened the door to the closet. The dog had been asleep, but when he heard Brady, he sat up on his blanket of towels and wagged his tail.

"First things first, Killer. You need a bath."

He scooped up the dog and deposited him in the over-sized sink in the garage, rinsed off the caked mud, then lathered the little guy up with shampoo and rinsed it off. After that, he gave the dog a flea dip, though he hadn't seen any fleas when he washed him. But better to err on the safe side. He grabbed clean towels to dry off the dog, only to discover "he" was a "she."

Well, hell.

He picked her up and stared down at her now-exceptionally cute, fluffy face. His parents had only had one dog—Benjie—and they'd gotten him when Brady was a teen, so he hadn't grown up around animals, even though he'd always wanted one when he was little. And he'd always been on the go as an adult, so getting his own dog hadn't been an option for him.

"What's a girl like you doing wandering the alleys and getting all muddy?"

No response, but she did lick his nose.

"Yeah, don't get too attached. We're not going to be lifelong friends."

She was damned adorable, with brown-and-white-tipped fur and the cutest ears. He had no idea what breed she was, but she sure was cute. And who would let a dog like her outside without watching her?

He put on her harness and attached the leash. "How about a walk?"

She wagged her tail, but she balked when he started outside the garage bay doors. She'd only walked about two feet when she parked her behind on the asphalt and refused to budge.

Brady looked down at her. "So, we're not leash trained, huh? That's okay. We can work on it."

He realized he was already planning on training her, as if she was his. Which she wasn't. No doubt she'd gotten loose and her family was looking for her.

But what the hell. He had to wait for the primer to dry on the car he'd worked on, so he might as well spend some time leash training her. He let her know who was the boss, and he figured she probably really wanted to pee, so he led her over to the grass. With a great amount of reluctance she cooperated and they ended up on the grass, where she did her business. Then it was time for a return trip, only this time he walked her around toward the front of the building, where he ran into Megan heading down the street.

"Oh my God, Brady, I didn't know you had a dog."

"I don't. She wandered into the shop this morning after the rainstorm. She was a muddy mess, so I cleaned her up and gave her a dry place to sleep."

"Awww." Megan bent down and picked up the dog. "Aren't you just adorable?" She lifted her gaze to Brady. "Do you think she's abandoned?"

He shrugged. "No idea. She wasn't wearing a collar or any form of ID on her, but she probably belongs to someone. Though she was a mess, and it didn't look to me like she was just out in this morning's rain."

Megan wrinkled her nose. "That's sad. And makes me angry. People should take better care of their fur babies."

"Yeah. I'm going to run her by Emma's vet clinic this afternoon to see if she has a microchip identification on her."

"Good idea. If she doesn't, will you keep her?"

"I don't know. I'm not much for taking care of anything."

"Seems to me you've already done a great job of taking care of her. You've given her a bath and a warm place to recover from the storm. Next step is giving her a home with you."

Brady looked down at the dog, surprised to find himself feeling attached to the dog already. And he wasn't one to attach himself to anyone or anything. "I don't know, Megan. We'll see."

She leaned into him and laid her hand on his arm. "Everyone needs someone. This little cupcake down here seems like she's perfect for you."

He gave her a dubious look. "I don't know why you'd think that."

She lifted her warm brown eyes to his. "I guess because lost souls sometimes have a way of finding each other."

He had no idea what the hell she was talking about. The dog was lost. He wasn't. Needing to change the subject, he said, "Oh, thanks for the coffee and strudel this morning."

"Did you like them?"

"Megan, they were great. I might actually stop by your bakery for coffee now. That crap my coffeemaker makes isn't going to cut it anymore."

She grinned. "Good to know. That's how I wrangle in customers, you know. Give them a little tease, then pull them into the bakery."

"So it's like confection crack?"

She tilted her head back and laughed, and he enjoyed the sound. "Something like that. So I'll see you tomorrow morning?"

He wasn't one to commit, but he could already smell that coffee and something sweet. Or maybe it was Megan who smelled sweet. He resisted the temptation to lean in and take a deep breath, just to see if that sweet scent was her.

"Sure."

"Good. And I'd really like to know how little cupcake down there does at the vet's office. Will you text me and let me know?"

"Uh, I don't have your phone number, Megan."

She cocked her head to the side and smiled. "And why is that, Brady?"

He frowned, and she laughed.

"Do you always have to look so painfully serious, Brady? I can fix the phone number problem. Give me your phone."

He dug it out of his pocket and she typed in her name and number, then handed it back to him and pulled out her phone. "Now I'll need yours so I know it's you when you text me."

He wasn't sure how they had gotten around to exchanging numbers, but it was good for the dog that she had people who cared about her, so he gave Megan his number.

"Thanks," she said, slipping her phone into the back pocket of her jeans. "You know, if you—and the little cupcake—aren't busy tonight, I'm trying out some new bakery recipes at home. I could use some unbiased judgments. And I could provide dinner before the dessert. I don't know if you already have something in mind for dinner . . ."

Dinner was typically fast food or a sandwich, which he ate alone in his apartment above the shop. "Uh, no. No plans."

Her smile brightened. "Great. Come have dinner with me. Bring the little cutie with you. Then instead of texting me, you can tell me all about the vet, and your plans for her."

"Um . . . okay."

"I'll text you the time. I really have to go now, Brady." She bent down and ruffled the dog's fur. "See you later, little cupcake."

She wandered past the shop, and Brady wondered how an innocent conversation had turned into dinner with Megan tonight. Not that he minded a home-cooked meal, because he got very little of that, but he was wary of spending time with her.

She was a damned good-looking woman, and he was attracted to her.

Brady didn't want entanglements or to get involved with anyone, so spending any time at all with Megan was never a good idea.

Still, it was just dinner. How involved could that be?

He looked down at the dog, who stared up at him, waiting for his next move.

She really was cute.

"Come on, Killer. Back to work."

Chapter 4

NOW THAT MEGAN had invited Brady to dinner, she had to figure out what she was going to make. She knew he was single and lived alone and likely didn't have home-cooked meals all that often, so she decided to fix something nice and substantial. Fried chicken and mashed potatoes should do it, along with green beans and bacon. Oh, and fresh-baked rolls.

Her stomach growled just thinking about dinner, but before that she had to tackle her baking. First she made mini chocolate mousse cakes and set those aside before starting on a caramel cheesecake. She was always happy the bakery closed early in the afternoon, which gave her time to grocery shop and head home to start working on her dessert projects.

Baking was never done. At least not in her mind. She loved to experiment, even with desserts that might not ever appear in her bakery.

When the doorbell rang, she wiped her hands on a towel and went to answer the door. Brady was there, and at his feet sat the pup.

She couldn't help the grin on her face. "I see you brought your dinner companion."

He frowned. "You told me to bring her. Is that not okay?"

"Of course it's okay. Come on in."

She shut the door behind him. "I'm working in the kitchen. Follow me."

She led him through the living room and into the kitchen. "Take a seat on the barstool. Would you like a beer or a glass of wine? I also have iced tea."

"A beer would be good. Thanks."

She pulled a beer out of the refrigerator and handed it to him, then got out a bowl and filled it with water, setting it down next to the peninsula so the dog could have something to drink.

"Did you take her to the vet?"

"Yeah. Stopped by Emma's clinic after work. The doc there who's taking over for Emma while she's on maternity leave said the dog doesn't have a microchip. Leanne, the vet tech, said she hasn't seen the dog there before. She took a picture and sent it to the clinic north of town, and they said they didn't recognize the dog, either."

"Huh." Megan took a sip from the glass of wine she'd poured earlier. "So no one knows her, at least not from the clinics."

"No. Doc there said she looks young, less than a year old. He went ahead and gave her puppy shots and meds and they put her picture up on the bulletin board, but he said judging from what I told him about her condition it's likely she was abandoned or ran off from someone."

"That's so sad. So are you keeping her?"

He shrugged. "I guess so, unless someone claims her. I'll put up signs in the neighborhood and we'll see what happens."

"Poor little cupcake."

"I was thinking of calling her Killer. Or maybe Thing."

Megan gave him a horrified look. "Those are awful names for such a cute little dog. Cupcake fits her better."

"A guy can't have a dog named Cupcake."

"And why not?"

"I don't know. It's not a dude name."

"You're a dude. Your dog is not. She's a girl and she should have a girlie name. Like Cupcake. Isn't that right, Cupcake?"

"Cupcake isn't a girl name."

"It most certainly is."

"Well, I'm not calling her that."

Megan rolled her eyes. "Fine. Then you should name her Tulip."

"That's even worse."

"Sassy."

He grimaced. "God, no."

"Fancy."

He cocked his head to the side. "You're joking, right?"

"Biscuit."

"Woman, please. Killer is sounding better and better all the time."

"You are hard to please." She looked at the dog, then smiled. "Roxie."

He opened his mouth to object, then paused. "Okay, that might work. It's tough, but still a girl's name."

"It's cute. I think it fits her."

"Well, Killer fits her, too."

Megan laughed. "No, it doesn't. I'll bet she couldn't even kill a bug—could you, Roxie?"

Brady cast a disgusted look at her. "Roxie, huh?"

The pup barked.

"Aha," Megan said. "I'd say she's chosen her own name—haven't you, Roxie?"

"Roxie it is, I guess. I need another beer."

Figuring she'd won that round, she grabbed another beer from the refrigerator and handed it off to Brady.

"What are you fixing?"

"Fried chicken, mashed potatoes, and green beans with bacon, along with rolls. Does that sound all right?"

"Anything that doesn't come from a microwave or a sandwich shop sounds all right to me."

"You're easy."

"Not the first time I've heard that."

For some reason, his reply felt sexual, and it made her stomach tumble. And things south quiver.

"Is there anything I can do to help?"

"No, but thank you."

"So I'm supposed to just sit here and watch you do all the work?"

"Does that bother you?"

"Yeah. Kind of."

She laughed. "Okay. Come over here and wash your hands and I'll put you to work."

She liked that he wasn't happy about doing nothing, but she sure wasn't used to having a man work side by side with her in her kitchen. She'd cooked for guys before at her house, but she couldn't recall ever having one help her.

A first.

He washed up, then came over to stand beside her. "Okay, what do you need from me?"

She looked over at him, studying how tall he was standing next to her. His jeans were loose, his gray T-shirt clean and stretched tight over some very fine muscles. She let her gaze travel over his forearms, where dark hair covered his skin. And those tattoos made him look tough. Sexy. Edible.

She wanted to climb all over him.

His chest was wide, and she wondered if he worked out or if his physique was a product of the work he did. He had a broad nose and full lips, and he wore his raven hair short. His green eyes had a magnetic quality, as if he could read her mind.

She hoped not, because right now her mind was awhirl in very dirty thoughts.

"Megan."

She blinked. "Yes?"

"Where do you want me?"

She supposed "In my bed" would be an inappropriate response, though she wondered what his reaction would be if she said that.

Instead, she handed him a stack of potatoes. "Peel these."

"I can do that."

While he peeled the potatoes, she breaded the chicken, then set the pieces in the fryer to cook while she prepped the green beans and took the potatoes Brady had peeled and put those in the boiling water.

"Now you can fry up some bacon to go with the beans," she said to him, pushing the bacon over toward him, along with a pan.

She had to admit it was nice to have some help in the kitchen. She cooked and baked all the time and always had meals under control. She was good at time management and multitasking, but that didn't mean she didn't appreciate assistance, and with Brady handling some of the tasks, it made the meal prep go a lot faster. Before she knew it, the potatoes were done and Brady was mashing them, so she finished off the beans and bacon and pulled the now-cooked chicken out of the pan.

"With your help, that didn't take as long," she said. "So thanks."

He looked over at her. "You're welcome."

"Now we can eat."

She had already set the table, so she placed all the food on serving platters and they carried them into her dining room.

"You know, we could have just eaten at the island," Brady said as he held her chair out for her.

"Thank you. And I often do that when it's just me. But when I have company over, I like to make it special by eating in the dining room."

"I'm not company."

"Sure you are." She poured from the pitcher of iced tea she'd made, filling his glass, then hers. "I invited you to dinner, so that makes it special."

For the first time since he arrived at her house, his lips ticked up into a smile. "Okay, then."

She paused, staring at him. "You should do that more often."

"Do what?"

"Smile."

That smile disappeared, his signature frown taking over. "I smile."

"Rarely. Usually you look like you just ate something that didn't taste good."

His brows furrowed even farther toward each other. "I do not."

She laughed. "Yes, you do."

"Fine. I'll show you." He took a forkful of potatoes and slid them into his mouth, chewed, swallowed, then graced her with the fakest grin she'd ever seen, even pointing to his mouth.

"See? Smiling."

She rolled her eyes. "It's better when it's genuine, Brady."

He raised his hands. "I give up."

Brady didn't know what to make of Megan, or of her comment that he never smiled.

He smiled plenty, goddammit. Or at least he thought he did. But her comment stung, and maybe there was some truth to it. He'd internalized his grief about Kurt for so long that he'd become a recluse. This was the first time he'd been out alone with a woman since before his brother died. Maybe he should try being civil.

Since she was the one who usually initiated conversation, he could start there.

"This is really good fried chicken."

Megan smiled, and her smile came naturally. "Thank you. I'm so glad you like it."

Everything was good. He'd been eating microwaved and take-out food for so long that he'd forgotten how good home cooking was.

"Thanks for inviting me over."

"You're welcome. I have to admit I had ulterior motives."

He arched a brow, curious as to where this conversation was headed. "Yeah? And what would those be?"

"I live alone, so I eat by myself most nights unless I

have something planned with my friends. So you're kind of my savior tonight."

He'd never been anyone's savior, and he sure hadn't been there when it had counted for his brother. "Glad I could be here for you. And you're saving me from another night of bland pot roast or my millionth turkey sandwich of the week."

"What about your parents? They live in town, right?"

"Yeah, they do."

She waited a beat, and when he didn't say anything more, she followed up with, "Oh, you know you could always eat at Bert's diner. The food there is awesome and is the closest thing to home cooking as you can get."

She'd grabbed a clue really fast that he didn't want to talk about his parents, which he gave her credit for.

"I eat there once in a while. But mostly I just head upstairs from the auto shop to the apartment."

She took a sip of her tea and studied him. "Why is that?"

He shrugged. "I guess I just want to be alone."

"In the bell tower."

"Huh?"

Her lips curved. "You've kind of garnered a reputation around town as a recluse, Brady."

"I have?"

"Yes. You don't hang out with the guys. You don't date. You don't socialize, period. So people have made up stories about you."

He laid his fork down. "Is that right? What kinds of stories?"

She lifted her eyes as if she was trying to remember. "Well, let's see. One has you cooking meth up there. Another I've heard is that you're into BDSM and you've set up your secret bondage club in the apartment. Oh, and another says you're Hope's newest mobster, running your money-laundering operation from your lair above Carter's shop."

He hadn't heard any of this. Then again, he rarely talked to people, so where would he hear it from?

"Meth? Really? Bondage? And a mobster? People have good imaginations."

"You know where we live, Brady. People will gossip."

"And yet you trusted me enough to invite me over for dinner."

She shrugged. "I don't tend to pay much attention to gossip. Plus all of those ideas are ridiculous."

He studied her. "Which means you have one of your own."

She took a sip of tea, smiling at him over the rim of her glass. "Of course."

"Which is?"

"That you're secretly a Russian spy, on the run and in hiding from your country's assassins, who know you've turned double agent and you're selling intelligence secrets to the US. But you can't blow your cover and come out with your intel until the superassassin who's after you has been flushed out and taken down."

Brady arched a brow. "Watch a lot of TV, Megan?"

She shrugged. "I read a lot."

He finished off his chicken and pushed his plate to the side. "I think I like your scenario best."

She grinned. "Thanks. I thought it was a good one."

He leaned back and took a couple of long swallows of tea, trying to digest both his meal and the information Megan had given him about what the town thought of him.

Okay, so maybe he'd pushed people away after Kurt's death. And maybe he'd been more than a little reclusive. But damn, the gossips had been working overtime on him, hadn't they?

Though he'd been honest when he told Megan hers was the best. She had a decent imagination.

"Ready for dessert?" she asked.

"You mean there's more?"

She stood and grabbed her plate, looking down on him as if he'd just asked the dumbest question ever. "A meal isn't complete without a good dessert."

"Okay, then. Bring it."

He went into the kitchen and laid his dinner plate in the sink, then watched in awe as Megan brought forth two desserts.

"Is that cheesecake?"

She nodded. "Caramel."

He was already full, but no way would he turn down cheesecake.

"Cheesecake is my weakness."

Her lips curved. "I'm making a mental note of that."

Roxie—God, was he really going to name her that?—had followed them into the kitchen.

"Maybe she needs to go out," Megan said.

"I'll take care of that. I'll be right back."

"Plenty of room for her to do whatever needs done out in the backyard."

He nodded and attached the leash to Roxie's harness. The dog promptly parked her butt.

Megan laughed. "Not fond of the leash, is she?"

"It's a work in progress. Whoever had her before obviously didn't leash train her."

He gave her a tug and she reared back. He pulled, but it was like dragging a tiny furry mop across the floor.

With a roll of his eyes, he scooped her up and carried her out back, Megan's laughter ringing in his ears as he opened the door.

"You're making me look bad, Roxie," he said as he deposited the dog on the grass. She promptly walked out three feet and did her business, then stepped out of the grass and sat at his feet.

"Got that part down, don't you?" he asked with a sigh, then gave a quick tug on the leash so they could head back to the house.

She sat.

"Heel," he said, giving the command for her to walk.

She looked up at him, giving him the I-don't-think-so look.

He shook his head. "We're going to have to work on this, and by 'we,' I mean 'you.' But right now there's cheesecake in that house, and I'm not in the mood for leash-walking lessons."

He picked her up and carried her into the kitchen, depositing her inside the back door and disconnecting the leash from her harness. She trotted over to the bowl of water Megan had set down for her and took several messy drinks.

Megan bent down to run her hands over Roxie's fur, giving Brady a fine view of Megan's backside. He decided to just stand there and watch while she picked up the dog and cuddled her close to her chest. She turned around and smiled at Brady.

"Everything go okay out there?"

"Everything except her walking with the leash attached."

Megan kissed Roxie on the head. "I'm sure she'll learn. She's very cute and smart—aren't you, Roxie?"

The smart part was debatable, but she had the cute part down.

After Megan put the dog down on the floor, she washed her hands, then went back to the island. "I made chocolate mousse cake and cheesecake. I'd actually like for you to try both of them if you don't mind."

"I'm never going to mind eating dessert."

"You say all the right things, Brady." She served up one of each onto his plate. "Coffee?"

"Sure."

"I made a fresh pot while you were outside with Roxie."

She really did think of everything. "I'll get the plates. You bring the coffee."

He carried the plates into the dining room, and she came in with a tray bearing two cups of coffee and a carafe.

"In case we want refills on our coffee."

"You must entertain a lot."

She picked up her fork and sliced off a bite of cheesecake. "Why do you say that?"

"I don't know. Everything you do just seems . . . perfect and organized and so well thought-out. If you had dinner at my place—"

"Spy headquarters?"

He laughed. "Yeah. Spy headquarters. You'd have gotten microwaved meals eaten on tray tables in front of the TV. Or, if I'm feeling like going all out, maybe takeout from Bert's."

"Nothing wrong with that. I like the food from Bert's. I do draw the line at microwaved meals, though. And I'm sure with a little effort you could probably cook."

"I can toss stuff on the grill. Throw a salad together. And make eggs and bacon. That's the extent of my cooking prowess."

"You can survive on that."

He dug in to the cheesecake first, and he had to bite back a groan. It was so damn good he wanted to dive face-first into the entire thing, gobble it up, and then grab the whole cheesecake and run out the door with it.

"Damn, Megan."

She'd been watching him. "So it's good?"

"Uh, yeah." After he finished the cheesecake, he sampled the chocolate mousse cake.

Sonofabitch, it melted on his tongue like a chocolate orgasm.

He lifted his gaze to hers. "Why don't you have a boyfriend? Or a husband?"

She frowned, then wiped her lips with her napkin. "Excuse me?"

"I mean, you're hot as hell and you make great food. Not to mention these desserts. Why hasn't some guy carried you off and married you?"

He saw her cheeks blush crimson. "Oh. You think I'm hot?"

"Sure." He waved his fork at her. "Soft hair, pretty eyes, sexy mouth, great ass. What's not to like?"

She laughed. "As far as compliments go, that was pretty good. So, thank you."

"You're welcome." He busied himself with polishing off the rest of the dessert, and even contemplated asking for seconds, then decided he'd regret that later when he was trying to sleep tonight.

He went into the kitchen and helped Megan with the dishes, despite her trying to push him away. It was the least he could do to thank her for a home-cooked meal that came with the best damn desserts he could remember having.

After her earlier nap, Roxie busied herself running back and forth from the kitchen to the living room to the dining room, her feet occasionally tumbling out from under her, so she'd go *splat* on all fours. Then she'd get up and scramble and do it all over again.

Megan laughed at her as they stood at the sink. "She's got some energy—that's for sure. But she needs some chew toys to help her burn off that energy."

"I guess so. I'll look into that."

After they finished the dishes, they took their glasses of iced tea and moved into the living room. Megan took a seat on the sofa. Brady picked the comfortable-looking chair next to the sofa. Roxie tried to claw her way onto the sofa, so Megan scooped her up and set her on her lap.

"Would you like a beer or some wine?" she asked.

"No, thanks. I'm good with the tea."

He grabbed a flavored toothpick out of his pocket and slid that in his mouth.

"I have some floss in the bathroom if you have something in your teeth."

"Some—oh, no. Nothing in my teeth. This is to keep me from wanting a cigarette."

She frowned. "Oh. You quit?"

"Yeah."

"How long ago?"

"About a year or so."

"Well. Good for you."

"Thanks. After dinner is always when I get the toughest cravings."

"I never smoked, so I wouldn't know. Your brother did, though."

He stilled, pulled the toothpick out of his mouth. "You knew Kurt?"

"Sure I did. I dated him for a while."

His head felt fuzzy and full. "When?"

She lifted her eyes to the ceiling. "Let's see. It was about two years before he died. We dated about six months or so."

"I didn't know that."

She shrugged. "No reason for you to. You weren't around then. He told me you were working in . . . Memphis, I think?"

"Yeah." He'd been off learning his trade, working for a great body painter, riding his bike all around Tennessee. And pissed at his brother because he couldn't get off the drugs.

If only he'd come home. If only he'd been here, maybe things would have been different.

"So what happened?" he asked.

"What happened? Oh, between Kurt and me? He was nice. We had fun together, but the chemistry between us just wasn't enough to sustain the relationship, so it was a mutual breakup. I didn't know about the drug thing back then. He hid it well."

Brady looked down at his shoes. He never wanted to talk about his brother, never wanted to relive the pain and the guilt he felt. "Yeah, he did that well."

"None of us knew. Not until a lot later."

He finally lifted his gaze to hers. "I knew. I knew for a long time."

She gave him a sympathetic look. "But you couldn't have fixed him, Brady. No one could have. Surely you understand that."

This wasn't the first time someone had tried to hit him with understanding and sympathy. The problem was, no one understood the deep bond he'd shared with his brother. They'd been tight since they were kids, and no matter what had gone down, they had always been there for each other.

He should have tried harder to reach him, should have pushed harder for another shot at rehab for Kurt, instead of shrugging and staying out of town, hoping like hell his brother would see the light this time and climb out of his heroin addiction.

Instead, he'd let it go. And his brother had died as a result, because he hadn't cared enough to push one more time.

He stood, realizing he needed to get out of there before he drowned in the thick fog of painful memories. "I need to go."

Megan frowned. "Are you all right?"

"Yeah, I'm fine. I just have an early day tomorrow."

"Oh, of course, sure."

He scooped up the pup, then turned to Megan. "Hey, thanks for dinner tonight. I really appreciate it."

"You're welcome." She walked him to the door and opened it, then grasped his arm. "Brady."

He turned to face her. "Yeah."

"If you ever need someone, I'm here for you."

Same thing he'd told his brother during one of the many times he'd thrown out the lifeline. Only Kurt hadn't grabbed it. "Thanks."

He looked into Megan's warm brown eyes, and on impulse, grabbed her around the waist, needing that contact of another human being, something he'd denied himself for far too long.

Just for one damn second. He tugged her against him and his lips met hers in a crashing thunder of hot passion. She moaned against his lips, grasping his shirt in her hands, and for just a few seconds, he felt wildly alive again.

And damn, it felt good.

Roxie squirmed between them and he backed away. Megan licked her lips and he felt a moment of regret for leaving.

But he had to get away.

"Night," he said, then turned and walked to his truck, feeling more regret now than ever before.

* * *

MEGAN WAITED AT the door until Brady pulled away. She was certain she didn't exhale until she saw his truck turn the corner.

Then she remembered to breathe.

"Wow," she whispered to herself as she closed and locked the door.

That had been some kiss. Passion and need had been wrapped up in Brady's kiss, along with a desperate longing that had surprised and touched her, awakening a hunger within herself she hadn't even realized she had.

She knew Brady had taken the loss of his brother hard, but until now, she hadn't understood how hard. She'd thrown out the comment about dating his brother in an offhanded way, not realizing how difficult it was going to be for him to even hear his brother's name mentioned.

As she picked up the glasses and carried them to the sink, she thought about how reclusive Brady had been since he'd come back to Hope. He hadn't been super outgoing or friendly, and he certainly hadn't been dating anyone. Frankly, it had happily surprised her that he'd even agreed to come over for dinner tonight.

The man had some demons, and she was beginning to understand why. But she had a lot more to learn about Brady Conners. She wanted to know more, and she wanted to help him in any way she could.

And if there was a way, she wanted a lot more of that passionate kissing he'd laid on her.

Because . . . wow.

TOO PENT UP to sleep, Brady headed down to the paint shop that night to work on a custom bike job.

It was a beauty of a Harley that a guy wanted painted. He'd given Brady a photo of what he had in mind, but Brady always did his work freehand. He'd applied the black layover paint earlier, and now he was adding the design.

He'd painted zombies before, and he liked making each bike unique. He visualized how he wanted the gas tank picture to look, then started to paint, adding the features and distorting them.

Once he started a design, it always seemed to flow out of him and onto the bike, a rhythm that kept him going for hours.

The small paint gun was an extension of his hand as he let the art transfer from his mind to the bike. This was where he could relax, where he could reach his zen. It was quiet here, only the sound of the paint spraying onto the bike. He didn't even have to think, only visualize what was in his head and get it onto the metal.

Just the way he wanted it, a mindless melding of his hand and the bike, and no other distractions. He went at it for a few hours, then finally took a step back to check the work.

Yeah, that was perfect. He was sure the client would be happy with the result. The guy would have some undead on his bike. He'd finish it off tomorrow night.

Kurt would have loved the scene he just painted. They'd played zombie killers all the time when they were kids, and had always talked about painting zombies on their own bikes someday. They'd spent hours and days coming up with zombie paint schemes, envisioning all the different ways they'd use their ideas at their custom bike shop when they went into business together.

That had never happened, because Kurt had totally fucked up his life.

And then he'd overdosed and died.

Brady wiped his hands and tossed the rag in the corner. He washed up, then reached for a toothpick, shoving it in his mouth when all he really wanted right now was a goddamn cigarette.

But he was stronger than his urges.

Too bad his brother hadn't been.

Brady wished he could go back in time, back to right after high school when he'd found Kurt snorting coke in his room. He'd ignored it then, shrugging it off as something his brother was just messing around with.

A passing phase, he'd figured. He'd even asked Kurt about it, and Kurt had said it was just partying. No big deal.

But it had been more than partying. It had become more and more frequent, and coke had turned to meth, and meth had turned to heroin.

Brady had tried time and time again to get Kurt to stop. Kurt had told him at first that he had it handled, that he could get off of it at any time. And eventually, he'd just stopped telling him that and told him to go away, to leave him alone.

Brady stepped outside to draw in a deep breath of night air, and stared up at the moon, wishing he could somehow fly up there to get far away from those memories of Kurt that had settled over him tonight and refused to let go.

He walked up and down the alley, willing something—anything—to enter his mind other than his brother.

But he could see Kurt's face right now, and that was all he could see, his memories firmly implanted in the past.

There had been a few arrests for possession, and Kurt had even stolen money from him.

Their parents had intervened, and Brady had gotten involved. They'd all begged Kurt to go to rehab, to get help. Brady had never been a demonstrative kind of guy, but he'd flat out told his brother that he loved him one night, that he was afraid he was going to lose him. He'd told him he'd be there with him every step of the way if he'd just get clean.

Kurt had laughed at him.

Wasn't the last time, either. Then there were the overdoses. Those he just couldn't handle. After the last one, Brady had had enough and left town. He couldn't bear to watch the slow disintegration of the brother he'd worshipped.

Shaking off the dark thoughts and the road he'd unintentionally gone down, Brady cleaned up his supplies and surveyed the work he'd done.

Yeah, Kurt would have loved this bike. He'd have laughed at the horror of it.

God, he missed his brother's laugh. They'd laughed so much together, all the damn time. Brady could still hear the echo of that laugh even now, especially at night when he worked alone and the silence was like a deep, dark cave.

It never freaked him out, though. He liked that it was here in the dead of night when he could still hear Kurt's laughter, could still hear his brother's voice.

It was the only thing about his brother that was still a comfort. And that kind of comfort was so damn rare.

He put his supplies away, stared at the bike one last time, then turned off the light and locked the door.

Chapter 5

MEGAN STOPPED BY Carter's auto shop the next day, ostensibly to talk to Molly, but also because she had a gift for Roxie. It turned out Roxie was occupying Molly's office, because Brady was painting and he didn't want the puppy exposed to the fumes.

She laid her bags down on the chair in Molly's office, then bent to scoop up the dog.

"She's kind of adorable, isn't she?"

Molly nodded. "She's made friends with everyone, from the office staff to the guys in the shop. She has a way about her."

Megan scratched Roxie behind the ear. "Now you need to teach that making-friends thing to Brady."

Molly leaned back in her chair and tucked her chin-length dark brown hair behind her ears. "Isn't that the truth? Carter and I have tried to engage him in activities, invited him to our place and out to the bar. We thought maybe we could get him to come out and play more often. So far, no luck."

Megan laid Roxie on the floor and took out the little stuffed chicken she'd gotten at the pet store. She handed it to Roxie, who sniffed it, grabbed it in her mouth, and went to her blanket in the corner. Megan took a seat in the chair. "I had him over for dinner at my place last night."

Molly's bright blue eyes looked at Megan with interest. "Really. That's amazing. How did you manage that?"

She shrugged. "We'd been talking about Roxie and then it just came up and he agreed."

"Huh. So what happened?"

"Fried chicken happened."

Molly laughed. "You know that's not what I'm talking about, Megan."

"I know. Dinner was nice. We talked. He kissed me."

Molly blinked. "Wait. What? He kissed you?"

"He did. It was a sudden thing. We were talking about his brother. I mentioned offhandedly that Kurt and I dated, and I think bringing up the subject of his brother upset him. He decided to leave, I walked him to the front door, and he grabbed me, kissed me, and then left."

Molly leaned back in her chair. "Unbelievable."

"I know." She was glad to know someone other than herself saw it as a big event.

"So what does that mean?"

"I have no idea. I'm a little confused. But I brought him baked goods."

She laughed. "Of course you did."

The door to the painting bay opened and Brady emerged. Megan sucked in a breath as Brady, all sweaty, walked down the hall and into the break room.

"Oh, you are so interested," Molly said.

Megan tore her gaze away from the hallway and put it back on Molly. "Is it obvious?"

"You might want to wipe the drool from the corner of your mouth."

"Oh, stop it. I am not drooling." But she did swipe at the corner of her mouth anyway.

Brady came out with a large bottle of water and headed toward Molly's office. As if she could sense Brady, Roxie scrambled off her blanket and rushed toward the doorway, her chicken toy still firmly planted in her mouth.

"Hey," Brady said, scooping Roxie up in his arms. "Whatcha got there?"

"A gift from Megan," Molly said.

Brady glanced over at Megan. "That was nice of you."

"We had talked about her needing some toys and I happened to drive by the pet store on my way out to lunch today, so I stopped in."

"Thanks." Brady set Roxie down.

"I also brought you something from the bakery."

Molly grabbed her laptop and got up from her desk. "If you'll excuse me, I need to run these invoices into Carter's office and have a chat with him. I'll talk to you later, Megan."

"Oh, sure. See you, Molly."

Megan stood. "I didn't mean to interrupt your workday." She smiled at Brady.

"You didn't. I'm on a break after doing a paint job. I came in to take Roxie outside. You could come with me."

"Sure."

He pulled the leash out of his pocket and attached it to Roxie's harness. As soon as he did, Roxie sat. He tugged, and Roxie resisted.

Megan's lips quirked. "She's still not in love with the leash, I see."

"Yeah."

"Mind if I give it a try?"

He handed her the leash. "Give it your best shot."

She took the leash, letting it go lax. "Let's go for a walk, Roxie. Come on, baby, let's go."

Roxie wagged her tail and followed Megan out the door, her stuffed chicken toy still in her mouth.

"Well, sonofabitch," Brady muttered as he followed behind them.

Roxie was a little awkward, trying to walk ahead of her,

but Megan gave a slight tug on the leash, and the dog stayed in step next to her as they made their way up the street to the park.

"Care to share your secret?" Brady asked.

"No secret. Just give the leash a little slack, raise your voice in an excited manner, and she'll follow you."

"Uh-huh." He took a toothpick out of his pocket and slid it in his mouth.

Of course, that made Megan focus on his mouth, which reminded her of the way he kissed her last night, which made her stomach tumble and her body heat up. So instead, she turned her attention on the dog.

"She apparently likes that toy you got her."

"I guess she does. I'm glad. There are a few more in the bag in Molly's office."

"That was nice of you. And thanks for the baked goods. You didn't have to do that."

She turned to face him. "I know I didn't have to, Brady. I wanted to."

He looked down at the grass, then back up at her. "About last night. I'm sorry."

"About what? About kissing me?"

His lips curved, and when the man smiled it was devastating to her libido.

"No. Definitely not sorry about that."

"Good. Because I'd have been disappointed if you were going to apologize for kissing me."

"I meant about leaving so abruptly. It was rude."

"No reason to apologize."

"We'll have to try it again."

Now she smiled. "The kissing thing?"

He sucked in a breath. "You're very tempting, Megan."

"Am I? Good."

He stepped closer, as if he was going to try the kissing thing right there on the street. But then a horn honked and he took a step back.

"I should get back to work," he said.

"Okay. Oh, are you coming to the McCormack ranch shindig this weekend?"

He frowned. "I have no idea what you're talking about."

"There's a big baby shower for Des and Emma McCormack."

"Definitely not going to that."

"Everyone's invited. I'm sure you are, too. Carter and Molly are going. It's a coed celebration, just a big party."

"Yeah, I think I'll pass."

"No. You won't. I'm inviting you as my date."

He gave her a curious look. "Are you?"

"Yes. So please come with me."

"I don't do baby showers."

She laughed. "Trust me—it's not a girl thing. It's all their friends, including the ranch hands and their families—basically everybody."

"Do I need to bring a gift?"

She shook her head. "Their families already had their baby shower, and Des and Emma said they have everything they need. This is just for fun."

He paused for a few seconds, then finally nodded. "Okay."

She grinned. "Awesome. Now get back to work. I'll text you with the details about the weekend."

"Sure."

She laid her hand on his forearm. "Oh and don't forget to grab those baked goods from Molly's office before Carter finds them."

He frowned. "He wouldn't steal those from me, would he?"

She shrugged. "You never know. See you later, Brady."

Brady watched as Megan gave Roxie a quick pat, then wandered off down the street, her ponytail swinging back and forth.

He hadn't expected to find her in Molly's office when he'd come out of the painting bay. Nor had he expected to feel the excited twinge in his gut when he'd caught sight of her.

And now he was going to some party at the McCormack ranch this weekend.

But whatever.

He looked down at Roxie, who looked back up at him, that weird yellow stuffed chicken hanging out of her mouth.

He shook his head and bent down. "Ready to go back to the shop?"

He started walking, leaving the leash lax like Megan suggested.

Surprising the hell out of him, Roxie followed.

Okay, so that worked. When he got back to the shop, he cleaned up his tools while Roxie ran up and down the halls. He was grateful Carter and Molly didn't mind Roxie hanging out there. Otherwise, he would have had to keep her upstairs in a crate, and he really didn't want to have to do that. She seemed happy to be around people.

His phone buzzed and he pulled it out of his pocket, frowning.

He punched the button.

"Hey, Mom."

"Hi, Brady. We haven't seen you in a while."

"Been busy with work and stuff."

"Of course you are. I was wondering if you could stop by after work and take a look at your father's car. It's making a strange noise."

"What kind of noise?"

"I have no idea, since I'm not a car person. Your father said it's a grinding noise."

"Dad could bring it over to the shop here and one of the mechanics can take a look at it."

Her mother gave a short laugh. "I mentioned that to your father, but he said there's no reason to do that when we have a mechanic in the family."

He sighed. The last thing he wanted to do was visit his parents, but he also didn't want his father driving around with a screwed-up car. "Sure. I'll stop by."

"I'm so glad. We're looking forward to seeing you."

He heard the neediness in her voice and it pained him, but he still didn't want to go over there. For so many reasons.

"I'll see you after work, Mom. I gotta go."

"Okay, Brady. Love you."

"Love you, too, Mom."

For a day that had started out all right, he already knew it wasn't going to end well.

Chapter 6

BRADY HAD DEBATED on whether it was a good idea to bring Roxie with him to his parents' house, but in the end, he figured maybe they'd focus more on the dog and less on him, which would be ideal, so he slid her into his truck and drove over to their place.

He pulled the mail out of the mailbox and shook his head, going through it as he went to the door. Everything was for Saul and Rita Conners, just as he expected. He walked up to the front door, wishing there were a couple of pots of flowers like Mom used to keep out there years ago. Anything to brighten the place up. Instead . . . nothing. Just the old green door, which could use a coat of paint.

When his mother opened the door, her eyes widened. "You got a dog? Why didn't you tell me you got a dog?"

"It just happened. She wandered into the shop a couple of days ago."

"Oh, she's precious." Her mother held her arms out and took Roxie from him.

"Her name's Roxie."

"Well, hello, Roxie. Aren't you just the sweetest thing?"

Grateful not to be the one to be smothered in the hugs and kisses his mother was currently bestowing on Roxie, he walked in and shut the door behind him.

His mother had already disappeared with his dog, so he followed the sound of cooing and excited talking. He heard his dad's voice, so he figured his mother was showing off Roxie to his father.

Maybe he could just leave Roxie with his parents for a few hours, come back later and pick her up, and then he wouldn't have to endure—

"Oh, Brady. There you are," his dad said.

Or, maybe not.

He walked over to his dad, his hand outstretched to shake his father's hand.

His father pulled him into his arms for a tight hug.

Brady closed his eyes and endured it, knowing his father needed this.

When his dad pulled back, he smiled. "You look good."

Brady smiled back. "Thanks. So do you."

He was lying. His dad was still too thin. So was Mom. They'd both lost weight since Kurt's death. And not the "Hey, we've been exercising and eating right" kind of weight loss. They were both pale and thin.

"So what's going on with the car?"

"Oh. Some kind of grinding noise. Might be the brakes or something. Not sure."

His dad had never been a car kind of guy. He was an accountant, not a man hardwired for mechanics.

"Let's go take a look. Hey, Mom. Keep an eye on Roxie?"

His mother had Roxie on the sofa and was playing with Roxie's chicken.

"Of course. You two go ahead."

They went out the side door to where his father's eight-year-old Tahoe was parked in the carport. His father handed him the keys and Brady started it up, listening to it idle. He didn't hear anything, so he gunned the engine. Still, nothing.

"Let's take it for a drive," Brady said. His father climbed

in, and they fastened their seat belts. Brady put it in gear and pulled out, taking it around the block a few times, then out onto the main road, making sure to hit the brakes hard at each stop.

He didn't hear any grinding noise, so when he pulled back into the carport and put the car in park, he left the engine on and looked over at his dad.

"Seems to be running okay, Dad."

He got out of the SUV, opened the hood, and checked out the engine. Nothing was loose and it all sounded normal. He went over and shut off the engine and pulled out the keys, handing them over to his father.

"Brakes feel fine. Everything looks and sounds normal."

His dad shrugged. "That's strange. I could have sworn I heard something for the past week."

Uh-huh. He wasn't buying it.

"Come on inside and we'll get something to drink," his father said.

They went into the house, and his father pulled out two glasses to fix them iced tea.

His mom was in the kitchen, and something was cooking on the stove.

"I made stew," his mother said. "You'll stay for dinner, right?"

"Sure." Somehow he got the idea this had all been planned. Something wrong with the car. Dinner already on the stove. But whatever. He was here. He could put up with dinner.

"Harold, go play with the dog," his mother said. "She's just so sweet."

There'd been no dogs since their dog Benjie had died eight years ago. He wasn't sure why his mom and dad hadn't gotten another dog.

Maybe it was because they'd been too busy focusing all their time and attention on Kurt.

While his mom worked on dinner and his dad played with Roxie, Brady took his glass of iced tea and wandered into the living room. He went over to the mantel above the fireplace, where the family photos still stood untouched, as if no time had passed. There had been no new memories made since Kurt's funeral. No marriages, no grandkids, nothing new to replace the ones that stood there now.

There were photos of him and Kurt as kids, the typical sports shots from baseball and soccer. The grade school and high school photos had been framed as a collage, but the ones of Kurt were lined up on the piano like a goddamn shrine. He wandered down the hall and into the bedrooms. Mom had finally turned his room into a sewing and craft room. Kurt's room, though, still had his old bedspread and twin bed, and all of Kurt's trophies and ribbons and posters were preserved as if they expected him to walk through the door at any moment and hop into that twin bed.

Hell, Kurt had long ago stopped coming by the house, hadn't stayed in that room for years before he'd died, and his parents had still held out hope that they could somehow reach him, could somehow entice him to come back home, as if they could rehabilitate him on the strength of their memories of their sweet young son alone.

Yeah, that hadn't worked. And keeping this nauseating shrine wasn't helping them move on, either.

Not that he had much room to talk, since he wasn't exactly the world leader of the moving-on movement.

He went over to the small desk, remembering coming into Kurt's room to ask him for help with a math problem.

His damn brother had been a math genius. He could have done anything with his life. Kurt had decided against college, had gotten a job as an auto mechanic in Tulsa. It had been a good job, too. Until he'd lost it because he'd missed so much work due to his drug use. Then he'd wandered in and out of jobs. Hell, he'd mostly wandered, disappearing for days, sometimes weeks, only to resurface to hit up their mom and dad for cash.

At first they'd given him money, and he'd stay at the house for a while. Until he'd abruptly disappear again. Brady had told them to stop giving him money, that he was using it for drugs. He'd argued multiple times with his parents about that.

He stared at the blue ribbon Brady had won for track his senior year of high school. He remembered cheering on his brother at the finish line.

He sighed. That was so long ago.

He flipped on the desk light in Kurt's room, remembering the night they'd found him passed out on the floor in here.

Mom had hollered and they'd all come running. She said they had to help him, that they had to rally around him and let him know they were there for him. Anything to keep him home, that he couldn't live on the streets.

Christ. What a clusterfuck that had been.

They'd gotten him into rehab once. He'd cleaned up after that for a few months, even gotten a job. He'd talked about going to school, getting a degree.

It had all been useless. He could have been anything. Instead . . .

With a disgusted sigh, he turned off the light and left Kurt's room, running into Roxie. He grabbed her stuffed chicken out of her mouth and tossed it for her. She dashed down the hall after it.

He smiled, then looked up at the hallway walls. It was like the Walk of Kurt, his brother forever memorialized. More photos. Everywhere he turned, there were reminders of his brother.

How did his parents survive a day in this fucking house? It was like a mausoleum in here, stuffy and filled with memories of the dead.

His mother came around the corner.

"Oh. There you are. Dinner's ready. You should wash up."

He nodded, then ducked into the bathroom, partly afraid he'd now find photos of his brother stuck to the bathroom mirror.

He washed his hands and went into the kitchen. His father was already at the table, and his mother had set bowls of steaming hot stew at each place. He was surprised she didn't set a place for his brother.

Okay, maybe that was a step too far.

"Smells good," he said, offering up a smile for his mom.

She smiled back at him. "Thank you. You know how much your father likes stew, and before the weather gets too warm I figured I'd better serve it up at least one more time."

He settled in and took a taste. It was hot, but damn good.

"How's work?" his father asked.

"Busier than I thought it would be."

"That's wonderful," his mom said. "Have you found a more permanent place to live yet?"

"No. The space above Carter's shop is working fine for me right now."

"But it's not long-term," his father said.

"No. It's not long-term. I'm just saving up money by staying there—the rent's cheap."

"You could move back home and stay with us," his mother said.

"Thanks, but no. I'm a little old to be living at home."

His mother looked disappointed—just like she'd looked disappointed every other time she suggested he move home, and every time he declined her offer.

"Well, you know the door is always open."

"Thanks, Mom."

He ate in silence for a few minutes longer.

"Anything new on the dating front? Are you seeing anyone?"

And that was a topic he would not get into with his parents. "No. Just focusing on work right now."

"And your new dog," his dad added with a smile.

He looked down at Roxie, who lay at his feet. "Yeah. She was unexpected."

"She's very adorable," his mother said.

"You two should get a new dog," Brady said.

"Oh, well, I don't know about that," his dad said. "I'm

not sure any dog could compare to Benjie. He was one of a kind."

"Still, it would give you two something to focus on. Dogs can breathe some new life into your lives."

His mother glanced at his father, the two of them sharing a look.

"Oh, I think we're doing okay just as we are," his mother said.

He wanted to shake both of them, to tell his mother to put the pictures of his brother away and start living again. She had stopped working after Kurt died, and he'd bet she didn't leave the house other than to go to the grocery store and to church. He wasn't even sure she went to church anymore.

And all his father did was go to work, come home, sit in his chair, read his paper, and do the crossword puzzles until he fell asleep in the chair at night, then shuffle off to bed.

It was as if when Kurt died, they had, too.

Brady might not be the life of every party in town, but at least he had continued to live after his brother had died. He got up every day and showered and worked and goddamn functioned. He couldn't say the same about his parents, who were like walking zombies.

And every time he came over here he felt like he was being pulled down into this well of grief with them.

It suffocated him.

He couldn't even talk to them anymore, because it was always small talk about his life and his work and they never talked about the giant dead elephant in the room that was his brother.

He might not like talking about Kurt, either. He got it. His brother had died and it sucked.

But the living had to keep on living. Or at least function at a normal level.

He really should say something to them.

But he didn't. Instead, he ate his dinner and made small talk, and then sat in the living room with them for an hour or so after dinner until he could make a polite excuse and get the hell out of there.

And then he had to face the disappointed and sad looks on their faces when he said he had to go, which was always so goddamn gut-wrenching and left him with a sense of guilt that pissed him off.

"Are you sure you don't want to stay for pie?" his mother asked. "I bought a nice pecan pie at the store."

"No, I really can't."

"Well, if you can, stop by again soon," his father said, his face sagging with grief and sadness and looking older than it should for his age.

"Yeah, I'll do that."

He hugged his parents and scooped up Roxie, then made a beeline for the front door, dragging in a breath of fresh air when he stepped outside, as if he'd just escaped a deep, dark oxygen-sucking cave.

He climbed into his truck and started it up, staring at his childhood home, which seemed more like a prison now.

It wasn't his fault his brother was dead, and he wasn't going to be his parents' lifeline. He couldn't save them. Just as he hadn't been able to save Kurt.

He put the truck in reverse and backed out of the driveway.

Chapter 7

MEGAN HAD BAKED two cakes for Des's and Emma's baby showers, and pink and blue cupcakes as well. She was going all out for this event, but then again, two of her closest friends were having babies. She wanted this to be special.

The main cakes were vanilla and chocolate, with yellow and green frosting. Since for some odd reason both Des and Emma had decided to be surprised about the sex of their babies, she couldn't have a definitive coloring on their main cakes. Their decision, of course, and it gave her more leeway on decorating. Des liked chocolate, and Emma liked vanilla cake, so there would be something for everyone. Plus, she'd used pink and blue on the cupcakes.

After finishing up the fondant bows on the cakes and icing the cupcakes earlier this morning, she'd set them all in the refrigerator so she could run home and shower. When she'd texted Brady last night he'd told her he'd pick her up, but since he had a truck and she had the car, she said she'd rather drive, since she had more room for all the cakes. So she stopped at the auto shop first.

He was standing outside with Roxie. She couldn't help

but smile at the picture the two of them made. Tall, gorgeous hunk of man wearing jeans and a dark long-sleeved Henley. And a tiny dog on a leash, said dog with a yellow stuffed chicken hanging out of her mouth.

So incongruent, yet so perfect together.

She stopped at the curb and he climbed into the passenger seat, putting Roxie on his lap.

"Hey," she said.

"Hey yourself."

"I need to stop by the bakery and load the cakes, then we'll be on our way."

She pulled up to the back of the bakery and popped the trunk of her car.

"I'll be right back," she said. She got out and went to the back door. She unlocked it and went inside, surprised to realize Brady was right on her heels.

"Figured you might need some help carrying all of whatever you have there out to your car."

"Oh. Okay. Thanks."

She had a huge refrigerator, and once she opened the door, it took up a lot of space, especially with Brady and her both in the small bakery kitchen. She'd stored the cakes and cupcakes down on the bottom rack, so once she bent over to retrieve them, her bottom rubbed against Brady's— legs? Or maybe that was his . . .

Something else that she was having a fun time imagining.

"Oh. Sorry," he said, and then his back was draped over hers. "Let me get those."

Talk about intimate. Not that she minded having his body all over hers. Except she'd spent all yesterday making these cakes and cupcakes, and she was totally distracted having her butt nestled in between his very hard thighs.

Distraction was never a good thing when she was holding a cake in her hands.

"I'm going to hand this one up to you. You can pack it in the trunk."

"Got it."

Then his forearm brushed against her hair as he lifted the cake out of her hands. She breathed in his freshly showered scent, and all her synapses started firing in the "Hey, Brady, let's have fast, hot sex in the bakery kitchen" direction when she should be focused on the "Hey, Megan, let's not drop the cupcakes, okay?" direction.

But they finally wrangled everything into the trunk and were off to the ranch, much to her libido's utter disappointment.

And now her nerves were a jangled mess. Not only was she worried about the cakes and cupcakes being perfect but she was trying not to focus on Brady's long legs stretched out in the passenger seat of her car or the way he kept running his fingers over Roxie's back, wishing it was his hands on her.

She decided to keep her attention on the road.

"So . . . cakes, huh?"

She nodded. "Yes. Cakes."

"What kind?"

"Chocolate for Des, vanilla for Emma. And the cupcakes are a mix as well."

"Sounds good."

She wanted to cringe at the small talk. "How's Roxie doing?"

"Pretty good, actually. She's walking well with the leash."

"I'm glad to hear that."

"Now tell me about this baby shower thing. Are you sure the guys are going to be there?"

She gave him a quick glance. "Of course. It's actually an excuse for a party. With Des and Emma both due soon, it'll be the last chance to get everyone together before their babies arrive."

"When are their babies due?"

"In a few weeks, actually. We tried to organize the baby shower last month, but had to cancel due to the storms we had, so this is the best date they could come up with that everyone was available. It's cutting it pretty close to their due dates. Fortunately, neither Des or Emma has gone into labor yet."

"That's good news."

"Is it?"

"Yeah. Those cakes look good. I wouldn't have wanted to miss out on that."

She laughed. "You'll enjoy the rest of the food, too. There are a lot of people coming and everyone's bringing a dish, plus there will be barbecue."

"And now I'm hungry."

They arrived at the ranch. Megan pulled up in front and parked. Emma's sister, Molly, and their mother, Georgia, came outside to help carry the cakes in, where Martha, the ranch manager, was waiting for them.

Brady had let Roxie out of the car. Minus her favorite chicken.

"Don't want the other dogs taking that away from her. It's her favorite toy."

"Is it?" Megan asked.

He gave her a smile. "Yeah. She loves that damn thing. Carries it everywhere with her."

Roxie immediately ran off to join all the other dogs on the ranch.

"Oh, these look amazing, Megan," Martha said, giving her a big hug. "Des and Emma are going to love them."

"Where are they?" Megan asked.

"They're upstairs. Des is getting dressed. They should be down shortly."

"Martha, you know Brady Conners, don't you?"

Martha smiled. "I sure do. You've been here before. Nice to see you again."

Brady nodded. "Ma'am. Thanks for having me here today."

"You're very welcome. There's beer in the cooler outside, and iced tea and lemonade in the pitchers here on the counter. Megan, there's also wine and sangria."

"I'll have a glass of sangria," Megan said.

"The guys are all outside over by the barbecues," Martha said to Brady.

Brady nodded. "I think I'll see what they're doing."

"Okay."

While Megan poured herself a glass of sangria, the front door opened and Samantha and Reid came in.

She loved her best friend, Sam. Since Sam and Reid had gotten married and moved in together, Megan hadn't had a lot of time with her. Plus, Sam's grandmother's Alzheimer's had advanced, taking up a lot of her time. She understood family came first, so she'd backed away, knowing Sam needed space not only with her new husband, but also to take care of Grammy Claire.

But now she went over to Sam and hugged her. "I've missed you."

Sam smiled. "I've missed you, too."

"How's Grammy Claire?"

"Having a good day today. I spent over an hour with her visiting, and she was fully aware the entire time."

Megan squeezed her hand, knowing how precious those moments with her grandmother were to Sam. "I'm so glad."

"Me, too. So what's to drink?"

"I'm having a sangria."

"That sounds amazing. I'm going to have that, too."

Reid walked by and brushed his lips across Sam's. "I'm heading outside to find the guys."

"Okay, bye," Sam said, then went to fix herself a glass. "Where are Des and Emma?"

"Slowly making our way down the stairs," Emma said.

Megan smiled as she watched Des and Emma coming toward the kitchen. At nearly nine months, both of them were the blooming vision of impending motherhood. Emma had her hair pulled to the side in a blond braid, while Des had her dark hair piled high on her head in a messy but oh-so-attractive bun. They both wore maxi skirts and short-sleeved blouses that barely covered their protruding bellies.

And she'd never seen two women look more gloriously beautiful.

"What would you two like to drink?" Martha asked.

"Just water for me," Emma said, rubbing the small of her back.

"I'll pass for now," Des said.

"Hi, honey." Georgia Burnett came over to pull Emma into a hug.

"Hey, Mom," Emma said.

Georgia gave Emma a quick up and down look. "Baby has definitely dropped."

Emma laughed. "That's what the doctor said this week. He thinks I might go early."

Des sniffed. "My doctor did not say that, unfortunately. I'm ready for this to be over with."

"It'll be over with soon enough," Martha said. "Just not today. We have a party to get to. Now it's a beautiful day outside, so you two go sit and get some sun."

Emma held up her hands. "As if *I* have any control over what this baby wants to do."

Georgia looked over at Martha and smirked. "She's grouchy today."

"I heard that, Mom," Emma said as she and Des retreated out the front door.

Megan looked at Sam and Molly, and the three of them grinned.

"Glad it's them and not me," Sam said.

Molly lifted her glass. "I'll drink to that."

Megan followed the women out to the large front patio, where Logan, Des's husband, and Luke, Emma's husband, had set up cushioned chairs with footrests for Des and Emma. There were folding chairs for the rest of the non-pregnant women, so Megan pulled up a chair and sipped her sangria and listened to Emma and Des talk, learning way more about pregnancy than she ever wanted to know.

She grimaced and shuddered, listening to their talk about hemorrhoids and mucus plugs and Braxton Hicks contractions until one of the women—Megan thought her name was Shelly—leaned forward.

"I take it you haven't had any kids yet?" Shelly asked.

Megan shook her head. "Not yet."

"Wait until after those babies pop out," she said. "Then you get to hear the horror stories about labor and child-birth, and the oversharing of intimate information gets worse."

"Really?" She couldn't imagine it could get much worse than this. She'd tried to be stoic about this. She'd never been pregnant, nauseous, or swollen, so she couldn't be empathetic to her friends.

Shelly nodded and gave Megan a sympathetic look. "It's just what we moms do. Sorry about that."

"Well, I guess by the time I get around to having a baby, I'll be fully informed."

Shelly laughed. "And you'll do the same thing. Trust me. Whenever a mom starts talking about pregnancy, we all chime in with our own stories. It's just a natural thing."

"Sure. Of course it is." And Shelly was probably right, though Megan had no idea if that would ever happen to her, since pregnancy wasn't anywhere on her radar in the near future.

First, she'd have to get married, which wasn't looking to be anytime soon.

Actually, she'd be happy enough just to find a stable guy to have regular sex with.

That thought made her smile.

Babies were down the line somewhere later.

She could just imagine Des and Emma holding their babies. And maybe at some point she'd get a chance to babysit. That was as far as she wanted to project her future.

Marriage and babies for herself? Yeah, someday.

But at the moment, after hearing those horror stories? That someday could definitely wait.

* * *

BRADY HUNG OUT with the guys near the barbecue. He kept one eye on Roxie, who seemed to be having a great time mixing it up with the other dogs. Good thing they were all friendly so he wouldn't have to worry about her today.

He drank beer and Logan and Luke and Reid talked about the ranch—and about babies, since that seemed to be the topic of the day.

Though, fortunately, they switched pretty quickly from babies to baseball. He currently sat between Carter and Logan, who were arguing baseball teams.

"Haven't heard you weigh in yet," Logan said.

Brady shrugged. "I'm a St. Louis fan. Always have been."

"Ha," Logan said to Carter. "Another one on my team."

"You're fired, Brady," Carter said, shooting a glare in Brady's direction. "Everyone knows Kansas City is the better team."

Brady's lips lifted and he took a long swallow of his beer. "Yeah, I'll pack up my things and move out as soon as I get back today."

"Okay, so you're not fired," Carter said. "But I seriously question your loyalties."

Logan slapped him on the back. "Don't worry, Brady. If Carter's too stupid to realize your value, you can come work for the McCormacks."

"Hey, I didn't say I was a St. Louis fan," Reid said.

"You didn't have to say it," Logan said. "All the McCormacks are."

"Yeah, but I lived in Boston for all those years."

"Don't even try to tell us you switched loyalties while you lived there," Luke said.

"I didn't say that." Reid offered up a smirk. "But I did go to some games in Boston."

When Reid's brothers gave him looks, Reid laughed, then added, "With clients. For business purposes only. Promise."

"You're lucky you added that 'business purposes only' in there, kid," Logan said.

Brady enjoyed this brotherly exchange, but it also gave him a twinge in his gut. He and Kurt used to argue baseball all the time. Hell, as kids, they'd get in fights about whose team was better. His brother was a die-hard Kansas City fan, and Brady loved St. Louis. So he understood the back and forth about team loyalty.

It made him miss his brother.

"Thinking about Kurt?" Carter asked.

His boss was astute. "Yeah."

"Sometimes that's not a bad thing, especially if it's a good memory."

He looked over at Carter. "I guess so."

"You ever want to talk about it, you know I'm right here."

"Thanks." That was the problem. He never wanted to talk about it. Because talking about it, or even thinking about it, made him remember Kurt. And even if they were good memories, they inevitably led down the road to the bad ones.

"Food is ready," Logan said. "Let's take it inside."

Brady's stomach grumbled, and he had to admit he was more than eager to eat, especially if it meant no more conversation about his brother.

They all gathered inside and scooped up piles of barbecued chicken and more side dishes than Brady could count. He had potato salad, beans, corn on the cob, and coleslaw, along with garlic bread—at least to start. There was seating inside and outside, so he found Megan and they decided on a spot at one of the large picnic tables outside with several of the other couples.

"When Bash and I have kids, we're having all girls," Chelsea said.

Bash rolled his eyes. "First, honey, let's get through the wedding. And second, I intend to have all sons."

Chelsea let out a snort. "We'll see who wins."

"What about you and Carter, Molly?"

She shrugged. "I don't care. We're really in no hurry for the baby thing."

Carter leaned over and nuzzled her neck, giving her a kiss. "Right now we're too busy practicing."

Molly laughed. "Carter."

Megan adored seeing her friends so in love.

She turned to Brady. "And how about you, Brady? Boys or girls for you?"

"I don't intend to have kids."

"Ever?"

"No."

"Care to elaborate?"

"Not really."

She could tell he wasn't in the mood for an in-depth discussion on children. "Well, you know, your opinion on that might change. Maybe you haven't found the right person yet. And when you do, you might want to have ten babies with her."

He shot her a look she couldn't define, then asked, "Is that how you'll feel when you find the right guy?"

"Absolutely. Once you find that right person, it's all about biology. Right now kids aren't on my radar, but I've seen it happen with quite a few of my friends who thought they'd never get married or they'd never have or want children. Then suddenly they're in love and they're getting married and they're having a baby. It's the love mind-set."

He cocked his head to the side. "The love mind-set."

She slanted a smile at him. "Yes. You fall in love, and you can see yourself with that person for the rest of your life, and suddenly you want something that's a part of both of you."

Brady took a bite of chicken, chewed, and swallowed. "My mind-set won't change. This world is hard, and I won't bring kids into it."

That sounded rather definite. Megan sighed. "Then I guess you and I can never be, because I want a whole lot of kids."

Again he gave her that look she couldn't define—a mix of curiosity and maybe a little sadness?

"I guess not," he said.

"Oh, come on, you two," Chelsea said. "I never in a million years thought Bash and I would end up together and have plans to get married in less than a year. Let alone talking about someday having babies."

"Someday very soon," Bash added.

Chelsea grinned, then smoothed her hand down his face. "Yes. Someday soon. It just goes to show you that what you think right this moment could change by tomorrow."

"This is true," Megan said.

But Brady shook his head. "Yeah, my mind won't change."

Okay. So there was a finality to that, which Megan found unsettling.

He got up from his spot. "Excuse me. I'm going to refill my plate."

Megan watched him walk toward the house.

Chelsea grasped her hand. "Men. Pay no attention to them. They're as fickle as our weather."

"Hey," Bash said.

Chelsea looked over at Bash and made a kissy face at him. "All men except you, babe."

"You're totally placating me right now, aren't you?" Bash asked.

"Totally," Chelsea said.

Megan laughed. "I don't know what to make of Brady. He's so enigmatic. And I just can't seem to break through that wall of utter . . . stoniness."

"Oh, but it's a sexy wall, Megan," Chelsea said. "Hang in there."

She breathed in a sigh, then dug into her coleslaw. "I will. For now."

Chapter 8

OKAY, SO MAYBE Brady was a total downer at this party. Which was why he didn't socialize much. He didn't bring much to the table.

But he had to admit, these cakes and cupcakes were damn good, and he sure wouldn't have wanted to miss them.

They had all gathered to celebrate and offer congratulations to Des and Emma, who, in his opinion, looked ready to give birth any second. Then again, what the hell did he know about pregnant women? Admittedly, nothing. But they were moving around just fine and seemed content and healthy. Both of them had taken the time to seek him out to tell him they were happy he'd come. They were all currently gathered in the dining room eating and laughing and talking baby names, since both were still trying to decide on names. Everyone was currently trying to suggest names.

"Beauregard," Carter said to Logan, who gave him a frown.

"Beauregard McCormack?" Logan said. "What? You wanna test my kid's spelling skills?"

Des laughed. "I kind of like it. We could shorten it to Beau."

Logan shot Des a look. "No."

"I like Felicia if it's a girl," Megan said.

Brady grimaced and leaned over to whisper to her, "Really? Felicia?"

She turned to him. "What's wrong with Felicia?"

He shrugged. "Nothing."

"It's a cute name," Emma said with a smile. "I like it."

"Good," Brady said. "You can have it."

Megan lifted her chin. "Well, since you and I are clearly never having babies together, then you don't have to worry about Felicia."

Brady laughed, and that earned him a glare from Megan.

"Ralph," Carter said.

"You do not ever get to name our future children, Carter," Molly said.

Carter looked over at Brady and winked. Brady tried not to grin, since Molly was shooting visual daggers at Carter.

Then it became a free-for-all of names.

"Steven."

"Lane."

"Kathleen."

"Martha."

"Awww," Des said, grasping Martha's hand after someone had shouted out her name. "Wouldn't that be sweet?"

"Don't you dare name one of your babies after me," Martha said, but Brady noticed her eyes looked a little misty.

Brady knew that after the McCormack brothers' mother up and left them when they were younger, Martha had taken over as pseudomother for all of them. He knew how much she meant to the entire McCormack family.

"Uh-oh," Emma said from her spot on her comfortable cushioned rocking chair. She followed that up by laying her hand across her stomach.

Luke looked over at her and frowned. "Uh-oh. What does 'uh-oh' mean?"

Emma looked over at Luke. "It means my water just broke."

Martha stood. "I need you all to excuse us for a minute. Can we clear the room?"

Megan got up and Brady followed her outside. Torches were lit and there was a fire pit to keep everyone warm by the picnic tables. Everyone piled out there, with the exception of the McCormack family, who'd stayed inside, along with Emma's sister, Molly.

"Is Emma going to be all right?" Brady asked.

Megan grinned. "She's going into labor, and this party is likely over."

"So, we should leave then?"

"Not just yet."

Sure enough, about ten minutes later Martha came outside.

"Sorry everyone, but as I'm sure you've guessed, Emma's labor is starting and they have a long drive to the hospital in Tulsa. I'm pleased to tell you the party's over, and I don't think I've ever felt that way before."

Megan laughed. Emma and Luke came down the stairs. Emma had changed clothes, and Logan carried her bag while Luke helped her into the car.

"Wish me luck, everyone," Emma said, a big grin on her face. "We're off to have a baby. And whoa, baby, my contractions have already started, so hopefully I won't be at this long."

"We'll take care of your dogs here, honey," Ben said. "Don't you worry about a thing."

"I'm so excited," Molly said to Megan. "I wish I could be there with her. We all do. But she doesn't need an entourage to give birth."

"No, she doesn't," Georgia Burnett said. "Even though she's my daughter and I'd give anything to be there with her, all she needs right now is her husband. And he'll call us when she has the baby."

"It's so exciting," Megan said. "Will someone call me after she delivers?"

"I've been officially put in charge of spreading the news, so you'll hear from me, Megan," Molly said.

The group trooped inside and helped Martha clean up and put stuff away. Megan doled out the rest of the cupcakes, because she certainly had enough sweets, between her place and the bakery. She turned to Brady.

"You want some cake and cupcakes, right?" she asked.

Brady shrugged, trying to look uninterested. "If you insist."

"Oh, please. Your tongue is practically hanging out. I'll put a few in a container for you."

Everyone ended up hanging out at the ranch after the cleanup was done. Des rubbed her stomach, as though she could stimulate contractions.

"Wouldn't it be great if Emma and I gave birth on the same day?" Des said. "The cousins could share birth dates."

Logan put his arms around her. "You just want that baby out of you and you're jealous Emma got to go first."

Des laughed. "Okay, that's true."

"Your time will come soon enough," Georgia said. "And those cousins will be so close in age that they'll be best friends for life."

Des grinned. "I can't wait. Especially if we both have boys—or two girls."

"I don't think it'll matter either way," Logan said. "They're going to be McCormacks."

After lingering for a couple of hours longer than they had intended, Megan and Brady said their good-byes, and Megan noticed that Brady made sure to thank Martha and Ben as well as Logan and Des for having him. Then he whistled for Roxie, who came running.

"Training her, huh?" Megan asked.

He shrugged. "That part, at least, is working."

They climbed into Megan's car and drove off the ranch property.

"All in all, that wasn't too bad," Brady said.

Megan gave him a glance. "And you were expecting what? Baby shower games?"

"Kind of."

She laughed. "I told you it wasn't that kind of party."

"Well, it was a good party. Thanks for asking me."

"You're welcome. I'm glad you came along. You should do it more often."

"What? Go to baby showers?"

"No. Come hang out with us."

He studied her, and she felt his gaze roaming over her. "Maybe."

When they reached the outskirts of town and she hit a red light, she turned to him. "Would you like to come to my place for some coffee?"

He looked at his phone. "I don't know."

"It's Friday night, Brady. And it's only eleven. Do you turn into a gargoyle at midnight or something?"

His lips curved. "No."

"Then come over. Have some coffee with me. Maybe I can entice you with something sweet."

He arched a brow. "Are you talking about another dessert?"

Her lips curved. "What else would I be talking about?"

His gaze bore down on her, intense and hot, making her quiver with sexual anticipation.

"Sure. I'll take some coffee and . . . dessert."

She pressed a little too hard on the gas pedal when the light turned green.

Okay, calm down, Megan. Just coffee and dessert.

"You should stop by my place so I can grab my bike," Brady said. "It's on the way, and then you won't have to drive me home."

"It's not a big deal for me to take you home."

"But it's already late and I'll feel better about you not having to go out again. Plus, I think Roxie is beat. I'm sure she wants to go to sleep."

She liked that he thought about things like that. "Sure."

She parked outside the auto shop, and he grabbed the box of desserts out of the backseat. "I'll just take these up with me now so I don't forget later."

"Yes, you wouldn't want to forget those."

He had Roxie on the leash and the desserts in his other hand. "I'll be right back."

He was only gone a few minutes, then she heard the rumble of a motorcycle, and Brady appeared behind her car on his bike. She had to admit, even in the dark, there was something dark, imposing, and utterly magnetic about the way he rode his bike. Plus, he looked sexy as hell wearing his leather jacket.

She had to remind herself to keep her eyes on the road ahead of her and not on her rearview mirror all the way home.

She pulled into her garage, and Brady parked in the driveway. He helped her carry the leftovers into the house.

"You can just set those on the island," she said, then went over to the coffeemaker. "Regular or decaf for you?" she asked.

"Regular."

She brewed him a cup from her Keurig, which was easier for her to make on the go in the early mornings. She then made decaf for herself. "I'd be up all night if I drank caffeine this late."

"I can take it. Not much keeps me up at night."

"Must be nice."

She pulled out a cheesecake she'd made earlier in the day and set it on the table.

He arched a brow. "You make that for me?"

"Would it make you feel special if I said yes?"

"Kind of."

"Then yes." She got out plates and forks and cut into the cheesecake, giving Brady a large slice and taking only a sliver for herself.

"That's not a very big piece," he said, eyeing her portion.

"I had more than enough dessert already today."

He took a seat at the island and dug in, his eyes closing as he chewed and swallowed. "Mmm. This is damn good, Megan."

"Thanks." She took a taste, satisfied it had turned out well.

He finished off the cheesecake, and she made him another cup of coffee.

"You're not going to eat that?" he asked, pointing to the sliver on her plate.

"No, I just wanted to taste it."

"Mind if I eat it?"

"Go right ahead."

So he ate hers as well while she sipped her coffee and watched him.

"This is a little weird, ya know," he said.

"What's weird?"

"You watching me eat."

"Oh, I like watching you eat. It gives me great pleasure seeing you enjoy something I've baked."

He finished and pushed his plate to the side, then took a sip of coffee. "So is this what you do? You spend all day baking at work, then you come home and bake some more?"

She laughed. "Pretty much, yes."

He looked around. "I mean it's a great kitchen and all, Megan, but shouldn't you be doing . . . other things?"

"Such as?"

"I don't know. Going out. Dating. Having a life beyond baking."

"Says the guy who spends all of his time holed up above the auto shop and does nothing but work on motorcycles on nights and weekends."

He frowned. "That's different."

"Really. And how is it different?"

"Because I love painting bikes. It's my passion."

"And baking is mine."

He stared at her for a few seconds, before nodding. "Okay, you got me."

"Thanks. And yes, I'd rather be out dating some hot guy than in the kitchen baking every night, but my love life lately has been stalled."

"What guy would be dumb enough to overlook you?"

She laid her palms on the counter and gave him a pointed look. "I don't know, Brady. What guy would?"

He arched a brow, and if smoldering eyes could give a woman a scorching-hot orgasm, her kitchen would be up in flames right now—and so would she.

He laid his cup down and slid off the kitchen barstool. He walked around to her side and pulled her against him.

He studied her face. "Yeah, pretty stupid of me, huh?"

She barely had time to catch her breath before his lips descended on hers.

Hot. Incendiary. His lips were demanding, taking what he wanted, what she needed. It was just what she expected from him after that first short kiss he'd given her. She responded by tangling her fingers in the soft thickness of his hair. When he groaned against her mouth, everything within her quivered in response.

She wanted this man. Naked. In her bed. Right now.

His hands roamed over her back, drifting ever lower to grip her butt and pull her against his very impressive erection.

Now it was her turn to let out a moan. He pulled his lips from hers and looked down at her. His eyes were half-lidded and loaded with passion.

"How do you feel about your bedroom?"

She licked her lips. "I feel very good about it, if you're in it with me."

Her phone buzzed. She thought about ignoring it. After all, Brady had uttered the word *bedroom*. He had an erection, and his hands were currently roaming over her butt. She was primed and ready to go, and if he got her naked and touched her, she would go off in seconds.

But her gaze drifted to her phone, and she saw Molly's name.

With a great amount of reluctance, she said, "I need to get that."

He took a step back and nodded.

She grabbed her phone. "Hey, Molly."

"It's a boy," Molly said in a very excited voice. "Eight pounds, three ounces, twenty-one inches long. He's perfect and pink and gorgeous. I've seen pics and I'm going to head up to the hospital now. Emma's doing great."

Megan took a deep breath, then looked over at Brady, who was raking his fingers through all that glorious hair of his.

"That's so awesome, Molly. Give Emma and Luke my love."

"I will. Gotta go and call a million other people. Love you."

"Love you, too. Bye."

She hung up. "It's a boy."

Brady's lips curved. "Good. Everyone's okay?"

"Yes."

"Are you going over to the hospital?"

She shook her head. "Not tonight. I will in the morning. I'm sure Emma is exhausted, and tonight is for family."

"Okay."

She could tell the atmosphere had changed. He didn't move back to pull her back into his arms. If anything, he was making sure to keep a certain amount of distance between them.

Well, damn.

"So, it's getting late," he said.

"So it is."

"I should go."

"Are you sure?"

"Yeah. I think that would be for the best."

She wasn't going to force him into her bed if that's not what he wanted. But she sure was disappointed in the abrupt turnaround. "Okay."

She walked him to her front door. "Thanks for coming with me tonight."

He turned to her and smiled. "I had a good time. I'll see you later, Megan."

"Sure. See you, Brady."

She closed the door and shook her head.

One minute he was hot and passionate and ready to take her to bed. The next it was like he couldn't get out of her house fast enough.

She did not understand Brady Conners at all.

* * *

BRADY LET THE cool April wind blow against his face. It wasn't a long ride back to his apartment, but he wanted some cruising time, so he chose back roads, taking an indirect route. It was quiet and peaceful this late at night, with few cars on the road.

Just the way he liked it. Alone on the road. Just him, the bike, and his thoughts.

He was glad Molly had called, breaking the spell Megan had weaved over him.

What the hell had he been thinking? If they hadn't been interrupted by that phone call, he'd have taken Megan to bed.

And then what? Entanglements, awkwardness, and likely she'd hate him in the morning when he told her there'd be no next time.

He enjoyed sex as much as the next guy, but Megan seemed like a relationship type of woman, not the one-night-stand kind. And he preferred sex to be uncompli-cated, so he generally chose women who wanted a good time with no strings and no promises of tomorrows.

He was going to have to be a lot more careful around Megan in the future, because not only was she smart and pretty, she was also sweet and kind, and the last damn thing he wanted to do was hurt her.

He pushed the throttle on his Harley as he hit a straight-away, enjoying the speed and freedom a quiet, dark road afforded him.

Maybe the cold air slashing along his face would cool down the heat within him. Because no matter how hard he tried to shut off the images in his head, he could still feel the way Megan's body moved against his, could still taste the lush softness of her mouth, could still remember the sweetness of her scent, and could still recall the wide-eyed surprise in her eyes when he'd kissed her.

When he'd kissed her, she'd fallen so eagerly into his embrace, had given as well as she'd received. He could already envision how it would go with her, how she'd be his match in bed. He could already imagine her sweet mouth wrapped around his—

Dammit. No amount of late-night, cold-air rides on his bike were gonna cool him down tonight.

Megan made him hot. He was going to think about her all night long.

Chapter 9

ON SATURDAYS, MEGAN opened the bakery an hour later than on weekdays and closed at noon. There were always crowds in the morning. Families with kids coming in to get baked goods, people buying donuts for sporting events, couples grabbing breakfast goods and coffee to start off their weekend. She was always happy to see everyone, and her shop was constantly full until closing. The atmosphere was fun and upbeat and a little chaotic. She loved the weekend energy.

But today she was anxious to get to the hospital to see Emma and Luke and the baby, so after she cleaned up and closed down the shop, she hustled home to take a quick shower and change clothes.

The first thing she did before heading over to the hospital was drop by Emma and Luke's house. Since she had the code to their garage, she ducked inside and left them a gift of confections on the counter. She'd also baked them a casserole early this morning, so she tucked that away in their freezer. She left a note on the counter letting them know the casserole was there, then headed out to the hospital in Tulsa.

She couldn't wait to see little baby McCormack, and when she got to the room, she heard laughing, so she knew Emma was awake. Still, she knocked softly on the partially open door.

"Come on in," Molly answered.

She pushed the door open and walked in. Emma was sitting up in bed, looking utterly beautiful for someone who had just given birth the night before. Her long blond hair was pulled up in a high ponytail, her cheeks were pink, and Luke sat on the edge of the bed next to her. Molly and Carter were there, along with Sam and Reid and Logan and Des.

Emma smiled when she saw her. "Hi, Megan."

"If it's too crowded in here I can come back another time."

"Don't be silly. There's plenty of space. I booked a private room, knowing that with all the McCormacks—as well as my friends—I'd likely need it."

As Megan got closer to Emma, her chest tightened at the sight of the newborn cradled in Emma's arms. Luke got up and Molly made space so she could give Emma a kiss on the cheek. "Congratulations to both of you."

"Thank you. We're over the moon about this little guy. And he came out pretty fast, so I'm grateful for that."

She looked down at the baby. He was beautiful, with his round face, pink cheeks, perfect cherub lips, and wisps of brown hair. He was asleep, making sucking motions with his lips.

"Oh, Emma, he's gorgeous."

Emma's gaze met hers. "He is, isn't he?"

Megan looked from Emma to Luke. "You both did a really great job."

Luke beamed a grin. "We did, didn't we?"

"Have you chosen a name?"

Emma nodded. "Michael John McCormack."

"John is my middle name," Luke said.

Megan smiled. "It's perfect. Michael suits him."

"We think so."

"Take a seat, Megan," Luke said, grabbing a chair for her and putting it next to Des's chair. "I think I need some fresh air."

"I'll go with you," Logan said.

"Me, too," Carter said.

"Time for the men to flee so we can talk childbirth and girl things," Emma said with a laugh.

"You know it." Luke leaned over and brushed his lips against hers. "You need anything?"

Emma laid her palm against Luke's cheek. "You've already given me everything I could ever want."

Luke lingered, staring at Emma.

"Come on, Luke," Logan said. "Before you get her pregnant again."

Emma laughed. "Uh, not yet, please. I need at least a little recovery time."

The guys walked out and closed the door. Des leaned back in the most comfortable cushioned chair in the room.

"How are you doing?" Megan asked Des.

"Unfortunately, still pregnant, as you can see." Des rested her hands on her rounded belly. "But now I have a gorgeous new nephew, so I'm going to suffer in relative silence."

Emma laughed. "Your time will come soon enough."

"How was labor for you?" Megan asked.

"Fast, once I got here. It seems like I was barely situated in my room before he was ready to make his appearance."

"Typical McCormack men," Sam said. "A decided lack of patience."

"This is true," Emma said.

"I'm glad it all worked out," Megan said, "and he's obviously gorgeous."

"Thank you. Would you like to hold him?" Emma asked her.

"I would love to."

She went and thoroughly washed and dried her hands, used hand sanitizer, and then scooped the adorable bundle from Emma's arms.

She looked down at Michael, who was still sound

asleep, and a sudden pang of something magical struck her. He was so small, and he smelled amazing. There was something about the scent of newborn babies that was so perfect—a combination of baby powder and heaven.

She wanted a baby. No, she wanted what her friends had. Someone who loved her unconditionally. And then a baby.

She sighed, then looked over at Emma, who was smiling at her.

"He's incredible."

Emma nodded. "I never knew I could love someone like this. But one look at him, and I was a goner."

Emma directed Megan to lay Michael in his bassinet, which was next to her bed. She did, then took a seat.

"The party last night was fun," Megan said.

"It was. And how did things go with you and Brady?" Emma asked.

"Oh, well. That was interesting."

"Define *interesting*," Sam said.

"He came back to my place with me and we had dessert. And then he kissed me and things got even more interesting."

"Do define this *interesting* thing in a lot more detail, honey," Des said.

"Well, it was about to get *bedroom* interesting, but then Molly called saying Emma had given birth, and for some reason that put a stop to things."

Emma frowned. "Leave it me to put a stop to sex by popping a baby out at the most inopportune time."

Megan laughed. "I don't think it was your fault, Emma. I think it's more Brady's reluctance to enter a relationship."

"I don't think having sex signifies a relationship, does it?" Molly asked.

"In his mind, I have a feeling he sees me as some kind of homespun bakery girl who's looking for a husband and a happily-ever-after."

"Well you're definitely not a homespun bakery girl," Des said. "But are you looking for a husband and a happily-ever-after?"

She had to answer that question honestly. "Eventually,

yes. But I wouldn't mind a little sex to start out with. I don't necessarily want to marry every guy I sleep with."

"Brady would be a fun guy to have sex with—that's for sure," Emma said. "Not that I'm at all thinking about sex at the moment."

Megan laughed. "No, I'm sure you're not. And I agree. He's definitely hot and sexy."

"I believe you mentioned to me sometime last year that you'd like to slather him up with butter and lick him all over," Sam said. "Or something along those lines."

Her lips curved. "Yes. I do believe I said something like that."

"So go get yourself some," Sam said. "And if he's nothing more than a hot spring fling, then that's a good starting point."

"True. But he has to be willing."

"I'd say, based upon what happened in your kitchen last night," Sam said, "he's more than willing to at least take you to bed."

Emma nodded. "I think you have all our votes that Brady is hot and sex-worthy. Go for it, Megan. Just don't get your heart involved if you think he's not ready for a relationship."

"Thanks, everyone. I'll keep that in mind."

She had a lot to think about. As if Brady wasn't already first and foremost on her mind.

And her friends were right. She had to keep her heart out of the equation where he was concerned, because someone like Brady could definitely break it.

Chapter 10

IT HAD BEEN a grueling day. Brady was sweaty and damn tired. He'd worked on a wreck all day, a particularly tough one. Why the owner's insurance company hadn't totaled this car was beyond his ability to comprehend, but then again, it wasn't his job to understand. It was his job to fix the damn car.

He'd smoothed out the dents in both the front and rear quarter panels and applied primer. He'd already done the front hood and put on the new bumper and doors. Tomorrow, he'd paint.

By the time he was finished, this baby would look brand-new. Or as brand-new as an almost-totaled car could look.

He closed his part of the shop and had Roxie on the leash. He was headed toward his apartment when he ran into Carter.

"How'd it go on that hot mess of a Dodge today?" Carter asked.

"It was rough, but it should be ready for paint tomorrow."

Carter nodded. "Knew you could fix it."

"They should have junked it."

"You know that and I know that, but when an insurance company won't total a vehicle, it's up to us to make it run again for the customer. We had to replace several engine parts. It'll end up costing them more in repairs than if they had replaced it. But we can only do what the insurance company wants. And in the end, the client will get back a well-running vehicle that will probably look better than it did before the accident."

"You've got that right."

"Hey, a bunch of us are meeting at Bash's bar. Care to join us?"

His first instinct was to say no. But he was beat after today, and he could really use a beer. "Sure. I need a shower first."

"Okay. Meet you there?"

"Yup."

He went upstairs and, after taking Roxie for a short walk, spent several minutes under the hot water, scrubbing off the dust and primer from the day. Then he changed into clean clothes and climbed on his bike for the short ride to Bash's bar.

It was crowded for a weeknight, but then again, it was Bash's bar, a hot-ticket item in a small town like Hope. Sports were always on the bar's TVs, and now that Bash was also serving food, people could stop in and grab something to eat, catch a game on TV, or play pool.

Brady spotted Carter and the guys at one of the larger tables in the corner. Carter waved him over and he grabbed a seat. Along with Carter were Reid McCormack, Deacon Fox, and Zach Powers, a high school teacher and the new football coach.

"Luke was going to join us, but the baby was fussy and he said Emma was having some kind of new-mother meltdown, so he thought it was more prudent to head home and help take care of Michael," Carter said.

"Probably a wise idea."

"Molly's going to be here as well. And I think Chelsea will, too."

"I have no problem with women," Deacon said. "Though your women are already taken."

"Damn straight they are," Carter said. "You'll have to find your own."

"Not really looking for one of my own. Just someone to pass the time with," Deacon said, lifting his beer to his lips.

"Haven't seen you out with anyone lately," Reid said.

"That's because I've been too busy on my off time building your damn house, McCormack."

"Suck it, Fox. And no one asked you to build my house."

"As I recall, you did."

"You guys whine as much as my football players," Zach said.

"Are you gonna make us do push-ups now, Coach?" Reid asked with a grin.

"I might if you don't stop bitching at each other."

Brady shook his head, smiled, and went to the bar to grab a beer from Bash.

Bash slid the beer across to him. "You're all freshly showered. Got a hot date tonight?"

"No. Just had a rough day. You wouldn't have wanted me shaking off dust in your bar, would you?"

Bash shrugged. "Wouldn't be the worst thing that's gotten dumped on my floor."

Bash's dog, Lou, came running over, so Brady picked her up and petted her.

"She likes you," Bash said, grinning. "And she's a pretty good judge of character, so you're okay in my book."

Brady laughed. "Thanks."

Bash looked around the bar. "Where's your dog? She's welcome to join you. We've set up a fenced-in play area out back for people who want to bring their dogs in to hang out with Lou."

"I rode my bike, so I didn't bring her along."

Bash leaned his hands on the bar. "I guess you need to

get her used to riding on your bike. Then you can bring her places with you."

He hadn't thought of that. He'd been on a lot of rides with other bikers who brought their little dogs with them. He could make that work. "I'll have to do that."

Bash's lips curved. "She'd look cute in dog goggles."

Brady laughed. "Yeah, she would."

They chatted about the baseball game for a few minutes, but then Bash had to tend to a customer, so Brady took his beer and headed back to the table, surprised to see that in the short time he'd been talking with Bash their group had expanded. Molly, Sam, and Megan had appeared, and Chelsea was walking past him on her way to the bar.

"Hey, Brady," Chelsea said, giving him a friendly smile.

"Hi, Chelsea."

He made his way over to the table.

"Saved you a seat," Molly said.

He noticed that the seat Molly had saved him was right next to Megan's.

Damn, she looked pretty. She wore tight, dark jeans, some kind of heels, and a white button-down shirt. Her hair was loose, and he wanted to sit down and run his fingers through it.

Hell, that's not all he wanted to do.

He smiled at her. "How's it going, Megan?"

She smiled back. "Pretty good, Brady. How was your day?"

"Busy. Yours?"

"Intense. Which is why I'm here tonight having a cocktail."

"And because it's her birthday," Sam said.

Brady's brows rose. "It's your birthday?"

She looked down at her lap, then back up at him. "It is."

"Happy birthday, Megan."

"Thank you."

He liked the blush of pink on her cheeks, as if she didn't want to make a fuss about her birthday.

He threw his arm over the back of her chair. "Did you make yourself a cake today?"

Her lips curved. "I did not."

"I can't believe that. You, the queen of everything sweet."

Her gaze snapped to his. "Are you making fun of me?"

He leaned back and gave her a look. "Why would you think that?"

"I . . . don't know. I'm sorry. I'm in a weird mood today." She tucked her hair behind her ear, and he could tell something was bothering her.

"That was meant as a compliment, Megan."

"I know it was. I'm sorry." She waved her hand back and forth. "I told you. Weird mood." She polished off whatever she was drinking in two strong swallows. "We should have more drinks."

He pulled her empty glass from the table. "I'll get that."

"You don't—"

But he was already off to the bar. He needed a minute to try to figure out what was going on with Megan.

He set the empty glass down.

"Let's do another round for the table," he said to Bash.

"Got it. I'll have the waitress bring those by," Bash said.

He nodded, then leaned against the bar top, ostensibly to catch one of the games on TV. But his gaze kept drifting to the table. Megan was in conversation with Sam, Chelsea, and Molly, though she was mostly listening while the rest of them talked.

So today was her birthday. Shouldn't she be animated and excited and feeling like the center of attention?

She *should* feel like the center of attention tonight. She gave so much to everyone around her. She should be made to feel special on her birthday.

He went back to the table and sat.

The waitress came by with the drinks for everyone.

"Compliments of Brady," she said as she handed them out.

Brady stood. "On her birthday, let's all drink to Megan, who does so much for everyone else."

They all held up their drinks. "To Megan," everyone said.

Megan blushed while they all toasted her and drank.

"Thank you all so much. This makes me feel very special."

"You should feel special, honey," Sam said. "We all love you."

Brady noticed the tears well up in her eyes. "I love you all, too."

She took several more swallows of her drink.

Yeah, something was up with her.

"Have you had dinner yet?" he asked.

She shook her head. "I had a muffin before I closed the shop."

He rolled his eyes. "That's not dinner. How about a nice juicy steak?"

She sighed. "That does sound nice."

"Wait right here. I'll be back shortly. I'm going to get my truck."

She reached out for his arm. "Brady, you don't have to—"

"I want to." He looked around the table. "I'm heading out to get my truck. Then I'm taking Megan out for a steak dinner. Anyone who cares to join us is welcome."

"I like steak," Reid said.

"You like food," Sam said.

Reid grinned. "This is true."

"You all decide. I'll be back in a few."

He leaned over and looked at Megan. "Don't move."

She smiled. "I'm not going anywhere."

He went over to the bar and signaled for Bash. When Bash came over, he said, "Can you get someone to cover the bar for you? We're taking Megan out for a steak dinner for her birthday. I have to go get my truck."

Bash grinned. "I think I can manage that."

Brady left and rode his bike back to the auto shop. Roxie

greeted him with a few barks and wiggles, so he ran her outside so she could stretch her legs and do her business, then he went back upstairs, grabbed his truck keys, and drove back over to the bar.

"Deacon had to leave, and so did Zach," Bash said. "But the rest of us are all about steak dinners."

"Good. Let's go eat."

"Got a place in mind, Brady?" Reid asked.

"Yeah. I thought we'd hit up Mahogany."

"Oh, I'm not dressed for that," Megan said, looking down at her outfit.

He cocked his head to the side. "First, you look hot. Second, you don't have to dress up."

"Yes, I do."

"No, you don't. Oil tycoons have been in there in jeans and cowboy hats."

"And you know this because . . ."

"Because I know. Trust me on this. Now come on. We're having steak at Mahogany."

She pursed her lips, finally nodding. "Okay."

They went outside to the parking lot. He held the passenger door for Megan while she slid into the truck, then he went around to the other side and got in, and they headed out of the parking lot.

"This is really nice of you, Brady, but totally unnecessary."

"You have to eat, don't you?"

"Well, yes."

"And it's your birthday, so you should be treated to something special."

"I don't need special."

He slid her a glance. "Why not?"

"Because it's just another day."

"Who told you that?"

Megan decided she should probably just shut up and appreciate the fact that Brady was being nice to her on her birthday. All her friends were, and that was sweet.

"Oh, no one. I just didn't want anyone to feel like they had to make a fuss over me."

"What if I want to make a fuss?"

She felt herself grow warm. "Well, thanks."

Her parents had never made a big deal over her on her birthday, even when she was a little girl. They had told her it was a day to evaluate the past year, and strive to do better the next, not to eat cake and expect to be coddled. One scientist and the other a doctor, her parents had bought her science books and microscopes for her birthday, not dolls and Dr. Seuss.

Her parents had put the *O* in *Overachiever*.

"You're awfully quiet over there."

"Oh, am I? Just, you know, thinking."

"Wanna tell me what you're thinking about?"

"My childhood birthdays."

His lips curved. "Reminiscing about the good old days of birthday cake and ice cream?"

"Hmm. Not exactly. My parents didn't believe in birthday cake and ice cream."

He frowned. "What? Why not?"

"They . . . I don't know. They're weird."

He pulled onto the highway. "Care to expand on that?"

"Not particularly." She never talked about her parents or her childhood. She'd grown up in Hope, and after her parents had left, she'd stayed.

When he pulled into the restaurant parking lot and turned off the engine, Brady picked up her hand. "I know all about not wanting to talk about things. But if you change your mind, I'll listen."

"Thanks."

He got out of the truck and went over to let Megan out. She took his outstretched hand.

"This is really nice of you. I'm sure all you wanted to do was grab some beers with the guys and hang out at the bar tonight, not take me to dinner."

He slid his arm around her waist. "I'm having steak

tonight. And celebrating your birthday. Trust me, Megan—this is right where I want to be."

It sure beat the heck out of her spending the night at home in her pajamas, eating something she'd baked for herself.

So she was all in on this birthday shindig.

Chapter 11

BRADY WASN'T SURE what had been bothering Megan earlier, but whatever it was, she'd either brushed it off or was hiding it well, because all through dinner she smiled and laughed and seemed to have a great time.

When the waiter brought her a slice of chocolate cake with a lit candle on top, her eyes widened in surprise.

"Cake? Really? For me?" she asked.

"Someone told me it was your birthday," the waiter said.

Megan slid her glance over at Sam.

"Don't look at me," Sam said, then eyed Brady.

Megan turned her attention to Brady. "You did this?"

He shrugged. "I might have mentioned it."

"Make a wish and blow out the candle before it melts wax all over that decadent-looking cake," Chelsea said.

"Thank you." Megan grasped his arm and he saw the warmth in her eyes, as if people didn't do this for her very often.

He knew these people at the table were her friends, and he'd wager they celebrated her birthday with her every year. So maybe it was guys who didn't treat her like she was special.

Which sucked. Because she looked happy as hell right now as she closed her eyes, took in a breath, then blew out her candle.

"You're all going to have to help me eat this, because I'm already stuffed from that magnificent steak, and this is the biggest slice of cake I've ever seen."

The waiter had brought several plates, so Megan cut off a few pieces.

Chelsea declined, but Reid said he'd have a piece, as did Carter, who was going to share his with Molly.

"You want some of mine?" Megan asked Brady.

"I wouldn't say no to a bite."

She handed him a fork. "You'd better eat more than a bite. I wasn't joking when I said I was full. You saw that steak I ate, right?"

He took the fork she gave him and slid it into the cake. "But you liked the steak?"

"It melted in my mouth. It was perfect."

He tasted it. "This is pretty good, too. Not as good as the stuff you make. Don't tell the waiter I said that."

She smiled and took a bite of the cake. "It's very good. And thank you for the compliment."

"So we got you something," Sam said, pulling a card out of her purse. "It's from all of us girls, including Des and Emma, and Jane, too, who are sorry they couldn't be here tonight. Jane's on vacation with Will right now, as you know, and Des and Emma's absences are for obvious reasons."

"You got me a gift?" Megan took the card, then grinned when she opened it. "A spa day? That's amazing."

"You need one," Chelsea said. "You never pamper yourself. So on one of your days off, you book the spa day and you get a massage and a mani-pedi and have your hair and makeup done."

Megan looked up from the card. "Wow. Thank you all—so much."

"You're welcome." Sam grinned. "Can I also say I'm a wee bit jealous, because a full spa day sounds like a real treat right now?"

Megan held the card against her chest. "I'm so going to enjoy this. It's just what I need. I love you all so much."

"We love you, too, honey," Molly said.

They all finished their desserts, then paid for dinner. Outside, Megan said her good-byes with hugs and thanks for everyone, and then she and Brady headed back to Hope.

"Would you like to come to my place for coffee?" she asked.

"Actually, I need to check on Roxie."

"Okay. Some other time then."

He could tell she was disappointed, but he had no intention of ending their night just yet. He stopped at the auto shop. "I was thinking you could come up to my place. Not as fancy as yours, but I know Roxie would like to see you."

"Oh. Sure. I'd like that."

He led her up the back stairs, where his apartment was located. As usual when Roxie heard him coming, she started barking.

"Is that your alarm system?"

He put the key in the door. "Yeah. She's very effective. No break-ins. I'm sure would-be burglars are terrified when they hear her tiny, little bark."

Her lips lifted as she listened to Roxie's puppy bark. "I know I would be."

He opened the door, and Roxie took several steps back, her tail wagging like crazy.

"Yes, you're such a good girl," Brady said. "And I'll bet you'd like to go outside, wouldn't you?"

He grabbed the leash off the hook on the wall by the door. "I'll just be a minute. There's water and beer in the refrigerator. Some soda, maybe. I could make some coffee."

"I'm fine right now. Thanks."

"I'll be right back."

He took Roxie for a quick walk outside, only tonight Roxie wanted to stop and sniff every damn blade of grass.

"Really?" he asked after he'd walked around the yard out back with her for the fifth time.

She looked up at him as if to say, "Look, dude. You left me in the house all night. So suck it up and let's go another round."

They went another round, and finally she did what needed to be done, so they went back upstairs.

Megan was on his beat-up, old brown sofa. She'd fixed herself a glass of ice water and kicked off her shoes.

After Brady detached Roxie's leash and pulled off her harness, Roxie went running over to her, so Megan leaned down and picked her up.

"How's Miss Roxie tonight?" Megan asked, cuddling her close to her chest. "You are just so adorable."

"And she knows it, too."

Megan looked up at him. "She should feel loved. Hey, did you ever get any response about her?"

He went to the refrigerator to grab a bottle of water, then came and sat down beside her on the sofa. "No. I put up some posters with a picture of her around the outside of the shop and down the street. The vet's office hasn't had a response either."

"I guess she's yours, then."

"So far. We'll see." He wouldn't admit this to anyone, but he'd have a really hard time giving her up. She'd even wrangled her way into sleeping in his bed once in a while.

"Like you'd give her up."

"Okay, maybe not."

"Now you have to make her a biker dog."

His lips curved. "Bash mentioned that, too. I'll have to get her some gear. Probably not in time for the event this weekend."

She cocked a brow. "You have an event this weekend?"

"A poker run for charity."

"What charity?"

"It's a domestic abuse charity. They run it every year and it always raises a lot of money."

"That sounds great. I haven't been on a bike since—"

He waited, but she didn't finish. He knew why.

"Since you dated my brother?"

She nodded.

"It's okay to talk about him."

"That didn't go so well the last time."

"I know. And I'm sorry about that. I didn't know the two of you had gone out, and I was surprised to hear it. To hear his name mentioned. I didn't handle it well. I apologize for how I reacted to it. But I'm okay with you talking about him."

She didn't look like she believed him. He couldn't blame her for that. His reactions since Kurt's death had been all over the place. Mostly from polite nods to sullen silences. He was going to have to make a concerted effort to get past it.

Plus, for some reason he wanted to know more about Megan's relationship with his brother. "So tell me about you and Kurt."

"We had fun together. He was nice to me. He took me on bike rides." She smiled. "He liked being outdoors."

"Yeah, he did. He always wanted to be on his bike. Got him in a lot of trouble when he was in school."

Roxie had fallen asleep in Megan's lap, so Megan leaned back against the sofa, propping her head in her hand. "He told me some stories about how he'd cut out of last period so he could meet friends for rides on his Harley."

"The funny thing was, I'd want to go with him and he'd bitch at me about staying in class. He wouldn't let me cut with him. Pissed me off."

She laughed. "Well, at least he wasn't dragging you into his truancy."

"He probably figured one of us getting in trouble with our parents was enough."

"I was always the good girl in school. I can't imagine the wrath my parents would have brought down on me if I'd ever gotten in trouble."

He wanted to know more about her childhood—and the lack of birthdays. "Tell me about your growing-up years. What the hell is it with your parents and birthdays?"

"Oh. My father is a scientist and my mother a physician. They groomed me to be intelligent and thoughtful and not fall prey to frivolous childhood things. It's not like they didn't celebrate my birthday, it was just always very . . . low-key. Gifts were typically textbooks that would further my intellectual education. I'd ask for a doll or a cookbook or an Easy-Bake Oven, and I'd get a microscope or a robot-building kit."

"Sounds like they weren't listening to your needs."

She shrugged. "My grandmother took care of that. She loved to bake, so I spent a lot of time with her. I live in her house, actually. She left it to me when she died, along with a decent inheritance. I redid the kitchen with the retro mint green oven because I love vintage things. And I had to have the oversized island so I'd have extra space for cooking prep. I bought the bakery with the money my grandmother left me after she passed away."

He laid his arm behind hers on the sofa and toyed with the ends of her hair. "Then I'm glad you had your grandmother to see to it that your dreams were fulfilled."

She smiled. "Me, too."

"And what about your parents? How do they feel about you owning the bakery?"

She shrugged. "We don't talk much anymore. They moved to California when I graduated high school. I didn't move with them. I loved Hope and decided to stay here with my grandmother."

"That must have been hard on all of you."

"We weren't close. I think they were disappointed in my lack of interest in their interests. And I was disappointed in their constant attempts to mold me into a version of themselves. So we were all better off without each other."

"I'm sorry about your parents."

"I'm over it."

He didn't think she was over it. How could anyone ever get over having parents who didn't love you, who couldn't appreciate your value? He saw the sadness in her eyes. "Are you?"

"Okay, maybe not. But I don't want to talk about my parents anymore."

He understood wanting to bury the painful parts of one's past. He was a master at it. "Then let's talk about your birthday today. You need a present."

"I got a present. I have a spa day to look forward to."

"Oh, but that's from your girlfriends. I didn't give you a gift."

"Yes, you did. You took me out for an amazing steak dinner. Have I mentioned to you how much I love steak?"

"You haven't, but now I know. Have I mentioned how much I appreciate a woman who can appreciate a good steak?"

"You haven't. But now I know."

He liked this woman. That knowledge sent warning bells clanging off in his head. But tonight he wasn't going to think about himself. Tonight was all about Megan. "Yeah, steak is fine and all, and so is that spa thing, but what you really need is a good shoulder rub. You seem a little tense."

He caught the slight raise of her brows. "Do I?"

"Yeah. Turn around."

She gently laid Roxie down on the sofa, then shifted. "Gladly. I'll never turn down a good shoulder massage."

He had to admit he liked putting his hands on her. Her muscles were soft and pliant, and she relaxed when he massaged her shoulders.

"Mmm. Keep doing that. It feels good."

The sound of her voice and the way she moaned when he pressed in on her muscles made him hard. And all he was doing was touching her shoulders.

He wanted more than that. He leaned in to whisper in her ear, breathing in her scent.

"Why is it that you always smell like powdered sugar and cookies?"

She half turned to look at him. "Is that bad?"

"Hell no, it isn't bad. It makes me want to lick every part of you."

He felt her body tremble. "Oh. That definitely isn't bad."

She turned around and laid her hand on his thigh, which didn't do much to tamp down the steely quaking of his dick.

He leaned in to kiss her.

And then her phone ringtone went off.

She frowned. "Kind of late for that."

"Do you need to get it?"

She shook her head. "Probably not. Well, maybe I should."

He leaned back. "Go ahead."

She fished in her bag for her phone, then pressed the button. "Hey, Sam, what's up?"

She listened, smiling. "Really. She must be over the moon. I know she didn't want to wait much longer."

Her gaze met Brady's as she listened further. "Keep me updated, okay? Thanks."

She hung up. "Des is having her baby."

"I kind of figured that out from your side of the conversation."

She looked down at her phone as if she was thinking, and he felt the shift in the atmosphere. All that warmth between them from earlier had gone away.

"Megan, do you want to go home?"

She looked around, hesitating before she nodded. "Uh, probably. I have to be at the bakery pretty early tomorrow."

He was surprised by how disappointed he was. "Sure. I'll drive you home."

When they got to her house, Brady walked her to the front door, where she turned around and faced him.

"Thank you for taking me to dinner tonight."

"You're welcome."

Then she grabbed the front of his shirt and tugged him close. "At some point, people will stop interrupting us by having babies and calling, and then maybe we'll be able to see what could happen between us."

She rose up to kiss him. He scooped his arm around her back and tugged her close, his mouth coming down on hers to take what he'd wanted earlier at his place.

Her kiss was hot and passionate, and when she moaned against his lips he wanted to open her front door, push her inside her house, and finish what they'd started.

But if she'd wanted that, she'd have stayed at his place instead of asking him to bring her home.

She wasn't ready yet. It wasn't the right time. He understood that. So he slowed down the kiss and pulled away.

"So about that poker run I mentioned."

"Yes?"

"Would you like to go with me this weekend?"

Her lips curved, and he could swear that whenever she smiled there was a sparkle in her eyes. "I'd love to."

"Great. I'll call you with details."

"You do that." She smoothed her hands over his chest, making his heart beat faster. "I'll see you later, Brady."

"Yeah. See you, Megan."

MEGAN WATCHED BRADY drive off, then closed her door.

As birthdays went, this had been one of her better ones.

Though she could have gone to bed with him. She knew it, but when her phone rang and Molly called, something had pulled her back.

It wasn't the right time. Not just yet. Maybe telling him about her parents and her childhood was like opening old wounds, and she didn't want him to use sex as a way to comfort her. Or maybe it seemed like he felt sorry for her, and she didn't want pity sex. She wanted him to want her because she was desirable.

Birthdays had always been a confusing mess for her, and it wasn't the right day or the right time to climb into bed with Brady.

She flipped the light on and headed into her kitchen, laying her purse on the counter.

Typical of her—she had to overanalyze everything.

He could have just wished her a happy birthday at the bar like the rest of the guys had. Instead, he'd taken her out for dinner. And he'd taken her back to his place. For someone who was all about wanting to be alone, he'd gone out of his way to be with her tonight.

So maybe it wasn't just pity, and was more about him being interested in her.

And he did ask her to the poker run this weekend, so she had that to look forward to.

She flipped off the light and headed into her bedroom, determined to be a lot less analytical this weekend.

It was time to just go for it and see what happened.

Chapter 12

DES HAD HAD her baby in record time, and before Megan had a chance to make it out to the hospital, she was already home.

Always an overachiever, that one.

So it was a few days after Des had the baby that Megan and Sam coordinated their schedules to make the trek to the ranch after work. Sam had to check on Grammy Claire before they left, so Megan decided to pack up a few baked goods, head home, and take a shower first. She'd made a mess of her shirt today with an unfortunate jelly roll incident, and a cleanup was definitely in order.

She stripped down and took a quick shower, dried and brushed her hair, then put on a pair of jeans and a long-sleeved shirt and slipped into her tennis shoes before tucking the baked goods in the trunk and heading out to pick up Sam.

Sam was already out the door when she pulled up. She had food, so Megan popped the trunk for Sam to slide it in.

"In a hurry to get out of the house?" Megan asked once Sam was situated in the car. "I was going to come to the door."

"Not necessary," she said. "Let's hit it."

Megan grinned. "Okay, then."

She backed out of the driveway.

"Where's Reid?"

"He was at the ranch earlier today to see the baby. He and Deacon are working on the house tonight."

"That's exciting. How's it going?"

"Progressing faster now, but still not fast enough."

On the way, they discussed their days at work. Megan told Sam about the jelly roll incident.

"Bet that was a bloody mess," Sam said.

Megan laughed. "It looked like a bloody mess. Red jelly all over the floor—and all over me. It looked like a crime scene. A sticky one."

"Yuck. I had no such disasters, so I'll consider my day a success."

"You do that. How's Grammy Claire doing?"

"Oh, you know, she has her good days, but those are growing more scarce each month."

Megan sighed. "I'm sorry, Sam."

"Me, too. But we at least know what we're facing, so we're all prepared for it. And I'm enjoying the days where she's fully aware of who she is and who we all are. I'll embrace those as long as I have them with her."

"It's really all you can do."

"I know. She and I sat down and spent a lot of time talking when she was first diagnosed with Alzheimer's. She told me she didn't want me to put my life on hold for her, and that she didn't want me to spend forever being sad about it. She was happy with the life she had lived, and she made me promise when the time comes that she doesn't remember anything or any of us anymore, I'll only focus on the happy times she and I have had together. I told her I would."

"It's a good thing. And you two have shared some wonderful memories."

Sam smiled. "We have. And since Reid and I got married last fall, Grammy Claire got to take part in that, while her memories were still intact. And we have wonderful pictures and videos from the wedding."

"Yeah, we did manage to pull off the fastest wedding on record—that's for sure."

Sam laughed. "Right? I'm so grateful to everyone who helped put it together. And especially to you for giving me such an amazing wedding cake."

"Oh, please. It was nothing. As if you wouldn't give me the best wedding flowers ever if I had a time crunch."

"I would. Now you just have to find the hot and sexy man of your dreams and make it happen."

Megan shrugged. "Not in any hurry here."

"Hmm. Speaking of hot and sexy men of your dreams, how's Brady?"

"Fine. We're going on a poker run on his motorcycle this weekend."

"Oh, fun. So you two are dating?"

Megan turned off the main highway and onto one of the county roads. "I don't know. I . . . guess? Maybe?"

Sam laughed. "Megan. That's not very definitive. Are you or aren't you dating Brady Conners?"

"I honestly don't know. We've seen each other a few times socially. We've kissed. Nothing more. We either keep getting interrupted or one of us has pulled back before anything more intimate can happen."

"Hmm."

"You keep saying that."

"I'm thinking."

Megan had been doing plenty of that as well. She pulled through the ranch gates, and they tabled their conversation about Brady, which was fine with her, since she didn't have answers to any of Sam's questions.

Martha came out and greeted them.

"Hey, Grandma," Sam said, giving her a hug.

Martha grinned. "I've been smiling for two weeks now. There are two new babies to fuss over."

"I'm sure you're in heaven," Megan said, hugging her

before handing her one of the boxes she'd pulled out of the trunk.

"This is so sweet of you, Megan."

"I'm sure you're busy enough running around helping Des, and then heading into town to see Emma and the baby. The least I can do is bring some desserts and a casserole."

"I brought one, too," Sam said. "Someone's got to feed your ranch hands and Des and Logan. One less thing to worry about, at least for a couple of days."

Martha hugged them both again. "I love you two. Thank you. Now come on inside."

Megan and Sam helped Martha put the food away.

Logan stepped into the kitchen.

"Hey," he said.

"Hey yourself," Megan said, giving him a hug. "And congratulations."

That might have been the biggest smile Megan had ever seen on Logan's face, except maybe for the day he'd married Des.

"Thanks. Des and the baby are in the living room. I'll see you both later."

"Go on. I'll fix you both some iced tea," Martha said.

They both washed their hands in the kitchen sink and spread on some hand sanitizer, as well, so they could hold the baby.

Des was in one of the comfy chairs next to the sofa, her feet propped up, a soft blue bundle in her arms. She wore cotton pants, and her raven hair was pulled up in a messy bun. And still, she looked gorgeous.

She always looked gorgeous. Her cheeks were pink, and she smiled when she saw them walk in.

"Oh, hi. I'm so glad you're here."

"We missed you at the hospital, considering you were in and out in a matter of hours."

Des sat up straighter. "Well, I wanted to avoid the paparazzi getting wind of me being there, and I had him pretty fast. Lucky for me, it was a fairly easy labor and delivery, so the doc said I would likely recover with a lot less stress at home."

"That's probably true." Megan leaned over and took a peek. "He's gorgeous, Des. With a photo-ready face. A future actor like his mama."

Des laughed. "Bite your tongue, woman. I wouldn't want anyone to go into this business, and definitely not my kid. He's going to be a rancher like his daddy."

Sam looked over Megan's shoulder. "He definitely is beautiful, though."

Des was grinning as wide as Logan. "Thank you. We named him Benjamin Dale McCormack, after Ben and after Logan's dad."

Megan's eyes filled with tears. "That's so sweet. I'll bet Martha and Ben are beside themselves."

"Martha cried, of course. Ben teared up as well. And then I sobbed. Hormones and all."

"Aww," Sam said, blinking back tears of her own. "Now you're going to make me cry."

Des gave Sam a stern look. "Don't even. You'll make me start up again. Here, hold a baby instead."

Sam scooped up Benjamin in her arms. "Oh right, like holding this bundle of sweet baby won't make me cry?"

Des gave a little chuckle. "I hope not."

Megan got closer to Sam as she held the baby. "He's so adorable. Look at all that dark hair."

Benjamin was awake, and his eyes were a dark blue.

"And those long eyelashes," Sam said. "He's going to be a lady-killer, Des."

Des gave a smug smile. "I know. He's also quite the crier. And very loud, especially in the middle of the night."

Sam passed him over to Megan, who breathed in that sweet baby scent as she held him close and took a seat on the sofa. "And what does Logan think of his middle-of-the-night cries?"

"He's actually surprised me so far. He's up with him in the night, changes his diaper, holds him for a few minutes and rocks him while I wake up and get ready to feed him. He's been . . . amazing."

Megan looked over at Des. "That's awesome."

"I think so. And if he doesn't need to eat, Logan's right there to hold him and walk with him or rock him."

"Which gives you time to rest," Sam said.

"Yes."

"I'm so happy for you both," Megan said.

Des pulled her sweater tighter around her. "Thank you. I couldn't have asked for a better life. Or a better man to spend forever with."

Megan had never heard anything sweeter. She and Sam ended up staying for dinner at Martha's insistence, and she enjoyed seeing Logan hover over Des, fetch her plate for her, and take the baby so Des could eat.

They really were a lovely family, and she couldn't be happier for her friends.

After they helped Martha with the dishes, they hung out for only a little while longer, since it was obvious Des was tired. They said their good-byes, and Megan made the drive back to town with Sam in tow.

"So what's the timeline for completion of the house?" she asked Sam.

"Uh, not nearly soon enough?"

Megan laughed. "I know you're really anxious to get moved in there."

"I am. But I understand delays due to weather. They barely got things started before winter hit, and recently we've had all the spring rain, so it's been a lot of frustrated waiting. Plus, now that Reid and Deacon have gone into business together, that has to take priority, and the house becomes a side project. We're very fortunate that Deacon is willing to work on it with Reid—and that we still have my old house to live in in the interim."

"That's true. And before you know it your awesome new home will be ready, and you and Reid and Not My Dog will move in."

Sam's lips lifted. "I know. I just need to be patient."

Megan pulled up in front of Sam's house.

"Would you like to come in?"

She didn't see Reid's truck, so she nodded. "Sure."

Sam opened the door, and the house was quiet.

"Where's Not My Dog?"

"On the job site with Reid, like always. He goes to the office with him, too. The tenants at the mercantile are so used to seeing him there that they would think it was odd if he didn't accompany Reid—everywhere."

Megan laughed. "He does love Reid, doesn't he?"

"It's a mutual thing." Sam went to the refrigerator and pulled out a bottle of white wine, uncorked it, and poured two glasses. "I figured after today you could use a glass."

"I'll definitely have one."

She brought the two glasses into the living room. Megan followed her, and they kicked off their shoes and pulled their feet up on the sofa.

"Now, let's talk about Brady. You should definitely have sex with him."

That had come out of nowhere. "You think so?"

Sam nodded. "Absolutely. He's so hot in a smoldering, quietly intense kind of way. Obviously the two of you have chemistry, right?"

"Like off the charts."

"That's fantastic. So why haven't the two of you done it yet?"

Having a best friend like Sam meant they could talk about anything, even something as intimate as sex. "I have no idea. Timing, and maybe a little reluctance on both our parts?"

Sam took a sip of wine and studied her over the rim of her wineglass, then set the glass down on the end table. "I'm not sure what either of you has to be reluctant about. He isn't seeing anyone else, is he?"

"Not that I'm aware of."

"I get that he's kind of reserved, but can you imagine what it might be like once he lets go?"

Megan sighed and took a swallow of wine. "Believe me, I've imagined it over and over again."

Sam laughed. "Then you should definitely go for it. And quit being so reluctant about it. And if he's reluctant, then . . . talk him out of it."

Sam made a good point. She and Brady were both consenting adults, and the time for hesitation was over. If nothing came from it other than a great time and some physical release, there was nothing wrong with that.

She could use a little fun—and a little sex.

She'd see what happened when they got together this weekend.

Chapter 13

MEGAN HAD BEEN up very early that Saturday morning. She'd arranged for her assistant, Stacy, to run the bakery for the day, but Megan had gone there before dawn to do all the baking and make sure everything was set out and ready to go. All Stacy had to do was run the register, clean up after, and lock up. Satisfied that everything was in order, Megan headed home to clean up and get ready.

They were taking off early, and the mornings were still a little cool, so Megan had dressed in jeans, boots, and a long-sleeved shirt. She pulled her leather jacket out of her closet, and when she heard the rumble of Brady's motorcycle pulling into her driveway, she went outside to greet him.

She was shocked to see Roxie tucked into a basket affixed to the luggage rack on the back of the bike. And she had her chicken in her mouth as well.

Hilarious. And adorable.

And damn, did the man look sexy. He leaned against the bike, his long legs encased in dark jeans, his boots peeking out from under the hem of his jeans. He wore a black leather jacket and dark sunglasses and oh, did everything female in her react to him as she made her way to the bike.

"Hi, cutie," she said, leaning over to ruffle her fingers over Roxie's fur. "And you found goggles for her."

"Yeah. We've been on the bike a few times. She loves it."

"Of course she does."

He pushed off the bike and reached into the saddlebag to pull out a helmet. "You ready for today?"

"I'm excited."

"Good. The poker run starts at one of the motorcycle dealerships in Tulsa. We'll pick up our cards and instructions there."

She put on her helmet and glasses.

Brady took a moment to check the tightness of her helmet and finish zipping up her jacket, his fingers lingering on her zipper. She was caught in his gaze, his mirrored sunglasses revealing nothing. But his body was close and his knuckles rested on her breasts.

"You look hot today, Megan."

Her heart started to thump in a fast rhythm.

"So do you, Brady."

He brushed his lips across hers, the briefest of kisses, but enough to fire her up and make her wish they could just go inside, strip off their leather jackets, and . . .

Well, more than just their leather jackets, actually.

"Guess we should go," he said.

"I guess we should."

Brady climbed on the bike, and she got on the seat behind him. She leaned into him, inhaling the delicious combination of leather and man. Tingles of awareness skittered down her spine as he fired up the bike, the vibrations hitting her most sensitive spots.

Oh, yes. She was more than ready for today.

He took off down the road, and she enjoyed the cool spring air blowing on her face. She peered around Brady and caught sight of Roxie, her face turned toward the front of the bike, her little ears blowing in the breeze, her chicken covered in puppy drool.

She looked comfortable, at ease, like she was having the time of her life being on the bike.

Megan agreed. It had been years since she'd been on a motorcycle, and she'd forgotten how freeing it was. Riding on a motorcycle was nothing like being in a car. She was exposed to the air, felt the thundering power and rumble of the bike as it moved down the road. She felt at one with nature, and she was so thankful that Brady took the back roads into the city instead of the highway. In this way she could take in every sight and sound, could breathe in the smells of nature, could enjoy the sights of deer and cattle instead of concrete.

It took them a little longer, but at one of the stop signs Brady told her they had plenty of time before the start of the poker run. She told him she was in no hurry, that she was his for the day. He responded by reaching back and running his hand up and down her leg.

She shuddered, her anticipation growing by every second.

They finally reached the dealership, and Megan was surprised by the turnout. It was a sea of motorcycles. Brady parked and they climbed off the bikes, shedding their helmets and sunglasses. He got Roxie off the bike and tethered her leash to her harness.

"This charity event is always a big one," he explained. "Which not only means a big win for the charity in terms of how much they take in—the potential pot for winners is larger."

"Explain to me how it works," she said as they made their way inside, Roxie wandering between them.

"We'll get instructions and a map to five locations. Each entrant gets five poker cards—you pull one at each location. The idea is to make a poker hand. You can also buy more hands if you like. Obviously, the more hands you play, the better chance you have to put together a winning hand."

"I see."

"I've entered both of us, so at each location, each of us will pull a card."

She smiled at him. "Thank you. I'm excited now."

"At the end of the run we turn in our hands, and by a certain time period today the poker run ends and they tally up who wins. There's a cash jackpot, usually with a certain number of winners determined by the value of the hands. Plus there are sponsors involved who donate prizes as well."

"Sounds exciting. We're going to win, right?"

His lips curved. "Hell yeah."

He led her inside and they went to the registration desk. Brady gave his name and pulled out his wallet.

"I can pay for mine," she said.

Brady slanted her a look. "I invited you. I'm paying."

"Okay."

"I thought we'd each get an extra hand. Double our chances of winning."

She smiled at him. "If you say so. I'm game for anything today."

"That's what I wanna hear."

After registration, they headed over to a table where there was coffee and donuts. Megan fixed a cup of coffee, then couldn't resist a sprinkled donut. Brady grabbed coffee and a donut as well. They mingled with the other participants, and several people waved at Brady, so he wandered over to talk.

They ended up in a group of about six people—four guys and two girls. Brady introduced her to all of them, though she wasn't sure she'd remember all their names. She knew the women were Penny and Donna. Penny was a tall, slender blonde, and Donna was shorter and curvier and had the most beautiful long red hair pulled into a braid.

So while the guys talked about bikes and paint schemes and engine things that made no sense to Megan, she engaged the women in conversation.

"Do you do events like this often?" she asked.

Donna nodded. "Several times a year. Anything to be on the bikes."

"Is this your first time?" Penny asked her.

"For a poker run? Yes. I'm very excited."

Donna grinned. "And you're with Brady?"

She wasn't sure how to answer that. "For today I am."

Donna seemed to accept that without asking any more questions. "You're gonna have a blast. These things are a party and a half, honey."

"Hey, Tony," Donna said to her guy. "Brady and Megan are gonna ride with us today, right?"

Tony, a big burly guy with a pretty lengthy dark beard, looked over at Brady. "Wanna run with us today?"

Brady nodded. "Sure."

Donna grinned as she met Megan's gaze. "It is on, honey."

"We're going to have so much fun," Penny said.

Megan was already stoked. She was ready to ride. And win her poker hand.

They headed outside, and Megan took Roxie over to a grassy area for her to walk around before they climbed on their bikes and headed out.

It was incredibly noisy with all the bikes firing up at the same time. Megan felt a thrilling chill as they rode out of the parking lot together. She and Brady stayed with their group, since not everyone would travel to the same spot first. He had told her before they left that the event coordinators did this to avoid bike traffic and congestion.

Their first stop was thirty minutes away at one of the local casinos. They went inside and pulled their first cards. She got a queen and a ten, then compared hers to Brady's, who had a nine and an ace.

He grinned at her. "Good start."

They chatted a bit with the others before Megan put Roxie back in her basket and they rode on.

Their next stop was farther south, this time at a sporting goods store.

She pulled another queen and a four. Brady got another ace and an eight.

Donna leaned over to look at their cards. "It looks like you two are both pulling winning hands."

Megan smiled. "I hope so."

But on their next stop, she pulled a two and a six, while Brady pulled another ace and a seven.

"I'm doomed," she said. "You're looking really good, though."

He had grabbed a water bowl out of his saddlebag and poured some bottled water into it for Roxie. "Maybe. It all depends on how it plays out through five cards."

"I don't know, Brady," Tony said. "You've got three aces already. Plus you're working on a straight. Might be your lucky day."

Brady looked over at Megan when he answered, tilting his sunglasses down and giving her a very pointed look. "I hope so."

She suddenly felt overly warm in her leather jacket. And how much longer was this poker run going to last, anyway?

The sporting goods store provided drinks, so they grabbed a cold one, then got back on the bike.

Their next stop was north, toward one of the bigger lakes about forty miles north of Hope. That ride that took a bit longer and gave her a chance to really enjoy the scenery. By now the sun was shining and it had grown warmer, but she was having a great time riding with all the other bikers. Having never done this before, she'd had no idea what it was like to ride with other motorcycles in front, beside, and behind her. There was a pack mentality, but everyone was courteous at keeping their distance. And she felt like she was part of the group. Occasionally Tony and Donna would pull up beside them and Donna would wave at her. Penny and her husband, Lance, would do the same.

Megan was having a great time just feeling the freedom of the bike.

They arrived at a biker bar. There were countless bikes in the parking lot, and extremely loud music poured out through the open doors. When she attached the leash to Roxie's harness, the puppy was obviously reluctant to move in the direction of the bar entrance.

"Too loud for her, I think," Megan said. "I'll wait outside while you go in."

Brady nodded. "I'll come take over after I get my cards."

He disappeared inside with the group, and Megan waited outside in the parking lot. She walked Roxie to the grassy area at the end of the lot to let her wander.

"Cute dog."

She lifted her head and found a very nice-looking guy dressed all in leathers. He was tall and lean, with long, dark hair and a silver earring in his left ear.

"Thanks."

"Yours?"

She shook her head. "No, she belongs to my . . ."

She had no idea how to describe her relationship with Brady.

The guy cocked his head to the side. "Your . . ."

"Friend."

The guy smiled, then squatted down to pet Roxie, who came over to him, tail wagging. "Ah. I'm Navar."

"Megan."

"Nice to meet you, Megan. Good day for riding."

"Yes, it is."

"Do you ride often?"

"No, I haven't ridden in years."

"So, a novice. Do you have your own bike?"

She laughed. "No, I'm a backseat rider only."

"I see. For some reason when I spotted you, I thought you were someone who was a veteran rider. A woman with her own bike."

"Really?" That made her smile. She liked feeling as if she belonged. "That's good to know."

He lingered, so he was obviously interested in conversation. He was friendly enough, so she was game. "Are you here by yourself, Navar?"

He stood. "Nah. I have a group. Just came over here because I thought you might be riding alone today. If you were, I was going to ask you to join me."

"She's not alone."

Brady had come up beside Megan. Like . . . very close to her.

Navar slanted a smile toward Brady. "Oh, hey. I'm Navar."

"Brady."

"Nice to meet you. So you must be the friend Megan told me about who owns this dog."

"I am."

"Cute pup."

"Thanks."

Megan could tell Brady was not happy, though she had no idea why. And anyone with half a brain could feel the negative signals he was throwing out.

Apparently Navar did, because he said, "Well, I'll see you later. Nice meeting you."

"You, too, Navar."

After he walked away, she turned to Brady. "What's wrong?"

"He was hitting on you."

She frowned. "No he wasn't. He came over to pet Roxie."

"Babe. He zeroed in on you like you were the fresh meat of the day. Trust me. I know guys like him at events like this. He saw you alone and thought he could make a move on you."

She looked over at Navar, who was currently talking to some other woman. "Huh. That's interesting."

"What the hell does that mean?"

She tilted her gaze up to meet his. "It means that I wasn't the least bit interested in him. I'm with you. I intend to go home with you today. Can I make it any clearer?"

He tipped his fingers under her chin and brushed his lips across hers, then wrapped an arm around her and brought her closer, deepening the kiss. It was the kind of kiss that stole her breath, the kind of kiss that made her forget they were in a public place, surrounded by hundreds of people.

When he pulled away, she lost herself in the depths of his passion-filled eyes.

"Just so we're clear about who you're with today."

She laid her palms on his chest. "I never had any doubt."

His lips curved and he stepped back, taking the leash from her. "You can go on inside and get your poker cards. I'll walk Roxie."

"Sure."

She was a little dizzy from his kiss, and she couldn't help the smile on her face as she walked inside the bar.

Who knew the man had such a possessive streak? She had to admit, she didn't mind that one bit.

She grabbed her cards and looked at them as she headed back outside.

She had a six and a jack.

Whatever. As far as she was concerned, she had nothing. She was more interested in what Brady had pulled on his cards, which she had forgotten to ask because of that confrontation—and that amazing kiss he'd laid on her.

"What did you get?" he asked when she got back to the bike. He was surrounded by their group. Penny and Donna were walking Roxie nearby.

She showed him her cards.

"Eh. Not much going on for you there."

"True. How about you?"

"I've got a queen and a six."

She smiled up at him. "Wow. Still going strong."

"It's all down to the last stop."

She looked at their map. "Which is where?"

"At the park in Tulsa. Everyone meets up there."

"Fun."

They rode toward the city and were joined by all of the bikers for the event. It was like a parade of motorcycles as they hit the main road leading to the park. They pulled in, and Megan got off the bike. After hours of riding, she knew she was going to be sore tomorrow.

"I'll bet you're happy to be out of your basket, aren't you, Roxie?" she asked, pulling Roxie's goggles off and tucking them into the side bag. She attached the leash to Roxie's harness, and they headed toward the tables where they'd pick up their final cards.

She pulled a two and an ace. She did end up with two pair—queens and twos—but she was pretty sure that wouldn't get her anywhere. She'd seen other people's hands throughout the day, and she knew many people had better hands than her two pair.

It was all up to Brady now. She waited, her heart actually pounding when he pulled his final two cards.

He had a straight going in one hand. On that he pulled a four, which totally blew his potential straight.

On his final card he pulled a queen.

"Full house, ace high," Brady said, one corner of his mouth lifting into a satisfied smile.

"It's looking pretty good for you," the event coordinator said as he turned his card in. "We'll see how it goes."

He turned to her. "I guess we'll have to hang out to see if I win anything."

She looped her arm in his. "I guess so. I'd say you have a pretty good chance."

"Maybe."

"What are the prizes?"

"Top prize is a motorcycle. There are also some cash prizes, and some gift cards from the sponsors."

"Sweet."

"In the meantime, let's go grab some food and listen to music. It'll be a while before they announce the winners."

They went with their group to the food stands. Megan got a hot dog, while Brady opted for a burger. They decided to share a large order of fries, then grabbed an oversized table under a tree. Brady tied the end of Roxie's leash to the leg of the table. He put her water dish under the table, along with a bowl of dog food. Roxie nibbled on her food, drank some water, then settled next to Megan's feet for a nap while they ate.

"How did you do on your hands?" Megan asked the rest of them.

"Mine was crap," Penny said.

"Ditto," Donna said. "So was Tony's, though we had some hope for the first three stops. After that, nothing."

"Yeah, same with us," Penny said. "You're our only hope now, Brady."

Brady shrugged as he bit into his burger, then swallowed. "We'll see. You just never know with these things. Sometimes you think you have an awesome hand, and then five people come in with a royal flush and kick your ass."

Tony nodded. "This is true."

After they ate they all got up to wander. There was a band playing, and there were vendor booths set up. Brady untied Roxie's leash so they could investigate the vendors, who offered everything from clothes to biker gear to seats to just about anything you could want for your motorcycle.

They bought beers along the way and sipped those while they strolled.

"Did you have a good time riding today?" Brady asked her.

She looked up at him and smiled. "I had a great time today, though I think my butt might be sore tomorrow. It's been a while since I've spent the day on a bike, and I never spent that much time riding."

He frowned. "You didn't say anything. You could have asked for a break."

"I was fine."

"You're not much of a complainer, are you?"

"Not really. Unless I have something major to complain about. Besides, I wasn't uncomfortable. I was too busy gawking at the scenery."

He put his arm around her as they walked. "You're a good riding buddy."

"I hope so. The last thing you need is to be distracted."

"If your butt is sore, I volunteer to massage it for you later."

She was glad she'd shed her leather jacket when they got off the bikes, because that comment made her entire body heat up. She looked up at him, and she'd love to know what was going on behind his sunglasses. "I'll keep that in mind."

His lips curved, that sexy smile of his devastating to her senses. "It's definitely on my mind."

She tried to focus on the items in the vendor booths, but her thoughts were on Brady, on the way he played with her hair or absently stroked his hand down her back, making her wonder what it would feel like to have his strong, callused hands rubbing all over her naked body.

Goose bumps broke out on her skin and her nipples hardened, and she was thinking decidedly dirty thoughts.

Did the man have any idea what he was doing to her? Obviously not, because he stroked her arm in a very sensual fashion while he was talking carburetors with a vendor, completely oblivious to the fact that if he continued to touch her this way she might have to throw him to the ground and have her way with him.

That wayward thought wasn't helping her current condition at all.

"I'm going to—take a stroll with Roxie," she murmured to Brady, pulling away from temptation.

He nodded, and she wandered off to take a few deep breaths and get her unhinged libido under control.

"Come on, Roxie. Let's go find some grass and a shady tree."

Where, hopefully, she could also find her self-control as well.

Chapter 14

BRADY KEPT AN eye on Megan as she wandered nearby with Roxie. He didn't want another random guy to come over and make any moves on her, so while he was talking with one of the vendors, he made sure part of his focus stayed on Megan.

Not that he didn't think she could take care of herself. He knew she could, but he also figured it was his responsibility to look out for her. And while the majority of the biker community consisted of stand-up people, there were always a handful that were suspect. It was that handful he wanted to keep far away from Megan.

Fortunately, Donna and Penny soon joined her, so he could breathe a sigh of relief. No one was getting near Megan while those two were with her. He'd known Donna and Penny and their husbands for years. He'd ridden with them before, and they were die-hard bikers, as tough as they came. No one would dare step into their midst to try to hit on Megan. So now he could finish transacting his business with the parts vendor without keeping one eye on her.

When he finished, he saw Tony and Lance had joined the women, so he walked over to them.

"Finally get those parts ordered?" Lance asked.

"Yeah."

"We thought we might head over to where the music was playing and grab a seat until they announce the winners," Donna said.

Brady nodded. "Sounds like a good idea. I also picked these up," he said, showing Megan the small set of headphones. "For Roxie, in case the music is too loud."

"Awww. Aren't you sweet? Do you think she'll keep them on?"

He shrugged. "We'll find out."

When they got to the band area, they grabbed some chairs, and he put Roxie on his lap. The headphones were very soft, so he slid them over Roxie's ears and waited for her reaction. Since the band had started up, she cocked her head to the side, but didn't try to dislodge the headphones. Instead, she nuzzled her stuffed chicken as if she couldn't hear a thing.

"Looks like she's okay with them," Megan said.

"For now, at least. I'll watch her."

It appeared he didn't have to, because she curled up on his lap and went to sleep while they listened to the band play. So he draped his arm over Megan's shoulders and relaxed.

The band played for about an hour, then the event emcee came on to announce the winners of the poker run.

"Fingers crossed," Megan said.

Brady didn't hold out much hope. He'd been to plenty of these events, and occasionally had ended up with a pretty decent hand, only to come away with nothing.

So as the emcee started to call names, he was surprised when Megan's name was called.

Her eyes widened as she got up and went to the stage to take the envelope from the coordinators. She came back to her seat and opened the envelope, grinning.

"I won a hundred dollars. All I had was two pair."

"That's awesome," Donna said. "You're in the money, honey."

Brady rubbed her back. "Good job."

"That means you'll definitely win something," Tony said to him.

"I guess so."

Megan grabbed his arm. "Now I'm really excited for you. I'm even excited for me. I had no idea I'd win anything."

"A hundred bucks is nothing to sneeze at."

"Not at all. I'm going to buy shoes."

He laughed. "Shoes? Really?"

"Yes. This is play money. Maybe a new purse."

They called several more names, and Brady started to get nervous.

"And for our fifth place winner of fifteen hundred dollars, Brady Conners."

His heart leaped against his chest.

Megan had already taken Roxie, so he went up to the stage.

"Congratulations," the event coordinator said. "Good hand."

"Thanks." He took the envelope back to his seat.

"Wow," Megan said. "That's a lot of money."

"Sure is," Lance said. "You get to buy the next round of drinks."

Brady grinned. "I'll pass on the beer since we'll be getting on the bikes soon, but I'll be happy to buy a round."

They got up, and he went and bought drinks for everyone. Penny and Donna had beers, but Lance and Tony had sodas. So did he and Megan.

"You about ready to head back?" he asked.

She nodded, and she hugged both Donna and Penny.

"I had a great time today," Megan said. "I hope I have the chance to see both of you again."

"You need to make sure Brady brings you along for some rides," Donna said, giving Brady a pointed look.

Brady smiled. "I'll do that."

Brady shook hands with Tony and Lance, then he and Megan headed toward his bike.

"I'd say that was an eventful day," Megan said as she waited while Brady put Roxie's goggles on and got her fastened into her basket.

"It was a good day. And we both made money."

"I know, right? That was unexpected. I was looking forward to riding today. I sure didn't think I'd win anything."

"Neither did I. But I'll take it."

She laughed. "Me, too."

She put on her helmet and her jacket, then waited while he got on the bike before she climbed on. Since it was dark now, he provided clear goggles for her and put a pair of his own on as well.

They started heading home, and it was cool outside, so she nestled her body against Brady's back, wrapping her arms around him. At a stoplight, she asked, "Does this bother you?"

"Having your body pressed up against mine? Hell no."

She smiled and thoroughly enjoyed the ride back to Hope. He pulled up in her driveway and she climbed off the bike, handing him her goggles and helmet. He tucked those into the saddlebag.

"You're coming in, right?" she asked.

"If you want me to."

"I definitely want you to."

He leveled a very hot smile at her. "Okay."

He scooped the dog out of her basket and took her for a quick walk on the front lawn so she could relieve herself. After that, they all went inside. Megan put a dish of water on the floor for Roxie, who sniffed at it, took a couple of sips, then looked around.

Megan knew what she needed, so she went to the hall closet, pulled out an old blanket, and set it down on the floor in the living room. Roxie walked over to it, ruffled it up a bit to her liking, then settled in with her chicken and went right to sleep.

"She's had a long day," Brady said.

Megan looked over at Brady, who was leaning against her kitchen island. "Apparently."

"She'll be out for the night now. And thanks for getting a blanket for her."

"Not a problem. She needed a soft place to sleep."

He pushed off the island and came over to her.

"Wait," she said.

Brady frowned and she knew why. He thought she was going to put the brakes on—again. But not this time.

"I'll need your phone, Brady."

"My—what?"

She held out her hand. "Your phone, please."

He dug his phone out of his jeans pocket an handed it to her. She turned it off, then picked hers up and turned it off, too.

"No interruptions anymore. Not tonight."

The smile he leveled at her was devastating. She held her breath as he approached. And when he put his hands on her upper arms, her heart started beating faster.

"So, the dog's out cold. What about you, Megan? Are you ready to sleep?"

She laid her palms on his chest, craving the feel of his heartbeat to see if it was pumping a fast rhythm like hers. It was. She tilted her head back to look at him. "No, what I need right now is you."

He drew her against him.

"I've been waiting all damn day for this, Megan."

So had she. And when his mouth came down on hers, it was everything she'd been waiting for—and more.

Chapter 15

MEGAN TRIED TO hold back the moan as Brady's hands roamed over her back and lifted her shirt. When his hands found her skin, she let that moan escape.

His kiss was hot, his tongue sliding inside to lick against hers. Her knees weakened, and she grasped his arms to hold on as he roamed her bare back with his hands. And the entire time she kept thinking that this was the best damn thing that had ever happened in her kitchen. Actually, she couldn't believe this was actually finally happening. After Brady's reluctance at first, and then all the interruptions, she half expected someone to knock at the door. Or maybe an alien invasion or the zombie apocalypse.

And as he kissed her, part of her waited for that doorbell or the end of times. Because it sure seemed as if the universe had been trying to keep them apart.

When there was nothing except the sound of the two of them breathing, she went lax against him, feeling like this was definitely the right time. Their time.

He backed her against the counter and pressed into her, all his glorious hard muscle aligned with her body. She forgot all about possible interruptions and let herself be swept up in the passion, for the first time letting herself truly fall into the way he expertly moved his mouth over hers, the way he moved his hands over her body as if he was trying to touch every inch of her. She especially enjoyed that part. Who knew that being manhandled while being kissed would be such a turn-on?

Here was a man who knew exactly what he wanted and went after it. He raised her shirt and bent down to press kisses to her stomach, and she realized that she was panting so hard it felt like she'd just run a mile.

And they were still fully clothed. Though Brady was working on that—he began to undo the button of her jeans.

Okay, so it had been a while since she'd last had sex, but she didn't remember it being so . . . breathtaking.

"Brady," she finally said.

He looked up at her, and the sheer hot passion in his eyes made her heart beat even faster.

"Yeah."

"Let's move this into the bedroom."

His lips curved. "Oh, so you're the more traditional type, huh?"

She frowned at him. "Was that an insult?"

"Nope." He stood and took her by the hand. "I'm good with wherever you want it."

Something in his tone irked her. "Hey. I'm adventurous."

"Sure you are."

She tugged on his hand. "I'll prove it. We can do it right here in the hallway."

He laughed. "Ooh, right in the hallway? The dog might see us."

"Now you're just being a jerk."

He pushed her against the wall, his hands coming around to cup her butt. "Are you mad?"

"A little."

He snaked his hand up her hip and along her rib cage. He'd grabbed a handful of her shirt, taking it up as well. "I'll make it up to you."

His lips met hers, hard this time. Her irritation forgotten, passion took over, and she moaned against his mouth.

His hand slid over her breasts, his thumb drawing circles over her bra. Her breath escaped in short pants, and she was lost in the sensation his fingers evoked. When he pulled the cup of her bra down and teased her nipple with his fingers, she gasped against his mouth.

He pulled his lips from hers and looked at her. "I like the way you tell me without words how I make you feel."

He bent and licked her nipple, then captured it between his lips before pulling it into his mouth.

She banged her head against the wall, so lost in the deliciously hot sensations she didn't even care that her head hurt. Brady's mouth was magic, heated soft suction against her nipple, hot lightning shooting straight to her sex.

He popped her nipple out of his mouth and kissed his way across her breasts.

She heard a whimper, then realized she'd made that needy sound when he drew her other nipple into his mouth and sweetly tormented it in the same way he'd done the first one.

He slid her nipple from his lips and raised up, searching her face.

"I'm going to make you come, Megan."

She believed him, because she was halfway there already. She was damp and quivering and he hadn't even made his way to her southern hemisphere yet.

And when he drew the zipper down on her jeans and tugged the pants over her hips, she felt exposed, and yet she didn't care. He slid his hand inside to cup her sex, and she was afraid this was going to be over all too soon.

His fingers were rough as they rubbed against her. A rush of hot sensation enveloped her, and she arched her hips against him.

"That's it," he said, his voice harsh and yet sweetly coaxing as he tucked a finger inside of her and used his thumb to find the crest of her clit.

She gasped, and he lifted his gaze to hers.

"Good?"

All she could do was nod, and dig her nails into his shoulders, because it really was good. So good that she couldn't form words. She was incoherent and lost in mad, crazy, delicious sensation.

And then he kissed her again with that same force and passion that drove her wild.

It was perfect. She came with a shuddering cry, her nails raking down his arms as she shuddered through one amazing orgasm that seemed to light her up from the inside out. His fingers continued to gently stroke her through the pulses that continued even after her climax had abated.

He brushed his lips softly against hers then pulled back. "Yeah, that felt good to me, too."

She shuddered as she took in a breath. "I don't even know what to say. Other than thank you, of course."

He surprised her then by lifting her into his arms. "Which way to your bedroom?"

She directed him, and he carried her down the hall and pushed open the door, then settled her on the bed. She removed her boots and socks, then pushed off her jeans, her actions absentminded, as she was more interested in watching Brady pull off his shirt.

Oh, my. The man was sculpted well, with killer shoulders, a wide chest, muscled arms, and a tapered waist. She had to pause for a moment to admire his tattoos. She skimmed her hand down his right arm, where most of them were located.

But before she had a chance to closely inspect them, he had grasped her shirt and was pulling it over her head.

"Time to get you naked."

Now that she couldn't complain about, especially if Brady planned to do the same.

And he did, undoing his pants and dropping them to the floor. When he shrugged out of his boxer briefs, she breathed in a sigh of pure appreciation for his amazing body.

She leaned back on her elbows and ogled him.

He grinned, then climbed onto the bed, scooped one

arm around her back, and undid the clasp of her bra. He drew the straps down and pulled the bra off, discarding it onto the floor.

"Hey, that's my best bra."

He frowned. "Is it?"

She laughed. "No. I'm fine with it on the floor."

He arched his brow. "Messing with me, huh?"

"Maybe a little."

He bent and nuzzled her stomach, then licked her rib cage. She took in a deep breath as their skin touched when he arched up to take her nipple in his mouth.

Wow. She really liked his mouth on her. Anywhere would be great, but she could already imagine what would happen when he—

She lost her train of thought when his lips closed over her nipple, his tongue flicking across the bud. He grasped her breast in his hand to fit more of it into his mouth, as if he couldn't get enough of her.

She couldn't get enough of his touch. She threaded her fingers into his hair to hold him there, because she wanted more. The sensations from his mouth shot straight south, and she moaned as he worshipped at her breasts, giving more attention to them than any man ever had.

She throbbed and quivered all over, and when he kissed his way down her ribs and stomach, she gripped the sheets in her hand and held tight, anxiously awaiting where his amazing mouth would go next.

He shouldered his way in between her thighs, pressing a kiss to each one before lifting his head to look at her.

"Unbelievable."

She looked down at him. "What?"

"How do you always smell like sugar and cookies? Even here. I've wanted to lick you all over from the first time I met you."

She shuddered, and when he took a long, slow swipe of her sex, she wanted to die the most blissful death ever. His tongue was hot and wet, and as he pressed it against her, she quivered in delight.

"That's . . . perfect," she murmured, letting herself fall into the rhythm he set as he made his way slowly, languorously over her flesh.

He used his mouth and his hands to take her ever higher, a slow, steady rush that made her body hot and shivery at the same time. Oh, he had a talented tongue, and it was much, much more than she expected. And when she came, she surged against him and arched her hips and she was sure she cried out something utterly unintelligible, but it might have been his name.

He held on to her, cupping her butt and letting her sail through the magnificent orgasm. It was like floating on a cloud of sweet pulses. He kissed her hip bone and made his way up her body, nestling beside her while she caught her breath.

He nipped at her shoulder while he splayed his hands over her lower stomach, letting his fingertips rest just above her sex.

"You taste like cookies, too."

Her lips curved. He was excellent with the compliments. She turned to face him. "Thank you. For the compliment, and for the orgasms. How about we give you one now?"

He toyed with the ends of her hair. "I wouldn't complain about that."

She'd been dying to explore his body, and now she had the opportunity. She rolled over on top of him and sat on his thighs.

He gripped her hips and stared up at her. "Now there's a vision."

She couldn't help the smile that lifted her lips. "I beg to differ. You're the vision." She leaned forward and splayed her hands across his chest. Everything about him was hard muscle, from his shoulders to his chest to that amazing six-pack of a stomach. She traced his tattoos, so many of them that she could spend hours trying to decipher them all. But she sensed now wasn't the time to ask questions about their origins. Not when his incredible erection bumped against her sex.

She slid down his legs and spread them, letting her hair sift across his thighs as she picked up his cock in her hands, smoothing her hand down the veiny surface of his shaft.

She heard him hiss and met his gaze with a knowing smile.

She was going to blow his mind in the same way he'd done for her.

She lifted to her knees, swept her hair out of the way, then let her tongue slide over the crested head.

"Damn," he said, his voice lowered to a whisper.

She took the head of his shaft between her lips and pulled it into her mouth, loving the different textures as she drew him inside. She delighted in the sound of his groans as she began to lick his cockhead, then gave him a rhythm she thought he might enjoy.

When he grasped her hair in his hand and tugged, she moaned against his cock.

"Sonofabitch," he said, which led her to believe he enjoyed what she was doing. And when he began to lift his hips, pumping into her mouth, she knew she was on the right track. His body moved like a caged animal under hers, as if he was poised to explode but fought the urge. She loved feeling Brady's barely leashed passion, knowing what that restraint cost him. She breathed in his musky scent, pulling away only to tease him by licking his cockhead and giving him a look that told him she was going to go beyond the bounds of what he could endure.

He reared up and swept his thumb over her cheek. "You sure about this?"

She responded by engulfing him, and he let out a series of moans that only increased her own need.

There was something so primal and sensual about giving him this pleasure, knowing she could take him right to the edge—then over. She knew what it felt like to have your body in the hands of someone who could give you this kind of intimacy, since Brady had just taken her there. She so wanted to give him that same pleasure.

And when he let out a barely leashed groan and burst into her mouth, she held tight to his cock and pumped him farther into the recesses of her mouth, taking in all he had to give until he went lax against her.

She rested her head against his thigh, but Brady withdrew and pulled her up against him, rolling her onto her back to kiss her, a deep, passionate kiss that heightened her desire to unbearable levels.

She pressed her hands to his chest, and when he pulled back she said, "Now I'm thirsty. How about you?"

His lips curved. "Yeah. Water sounds good."

She slipped off the bed and fixed them two glasses of water. While she was in the kitchen, she checked on Roxie, who hadn't budged from her spot on the blanket, so she shut off the light and made her way back to the bedroom.

Brady had propped himself up on a pillow and was leaning against the headboard, looking all too sexily like some naked Greek god in her bed.

She might kidnap him, tie him to her bed, and have her way with him night after night until one or both of them died happy.

She grinned as she handed him a glass and climbed into bed next to him.

"What was that smile about?" he asked after he'd downed half the water in his glass.

"I was thinking of holding you naked and captive in my bedroom for the rest of your natural life."

He set the glass on the coaster on the nightstand. "I see. Like some kind of sex slave?"

After taking several sips, she set her glass down. "Something along those lines."

He grabbed her legs and pulled her down flat on the bed. "I live to serve, you know."

He reached for the condom on the nightstand, tore the package open and put it on, then positioned himself between her legs.

She figured this was the time, and she was more than

ready for it. But he surprised her when he kissed her, one of those all-consuming, last-a-long-time kind of kisses that made her lose all focus—except for his mouth.

Oh, could Brady kiss. It was as if he used kissing as artistry, as if he'd spent his entire adult life studying how to move his lips and in what different ways he could tease her with his tongue. She was hopelessly lost in the softness of his lips, the way his day's growth of beard brushed against her, and the way he constantly moved his hands over her body as he kissed her. All of these things were like the best form of sensory overload, making her body throb with the need to have him inside of her.

And when he did enter her, she quivered, wrapped her legs around his hips, and pulled him in.

He stilled and she felt every inch of him, her sex a shuddering mass of nerve endings enveloping him. She raked her nails down his arms and immersed herself in the sensations.

"Do you feel that?" Brady asked, obviously as caught up as she was.

"Yes. I feel it. I want more."

"Yeah." He drove in deeper, giving her everything she asked for, taking her to soaring heights as she lifted against him and he rocked against her over and over again until all she felt was him.

When she splintered, she cried out, and he cupped her butt, drawing her closer, murmuring dark words to her as she came. She held tight to him as her world spun out of control.

She was still catching her breath when she felt him tighten, and now it was her turn to offer words of encouragement as he shuddered against her. She dug her heels into him and held him close as he climaxed, a sensation that made her tremble as much as her own orgasm had.

They were stuck together, their bodies merged in sweat, and it was glorious.

It had been a while for her, and she'd forgotten how utterly wonderful and messy and fun sex was.

She wanted to do this all night long.

When he withdrew, he disappeared into the bathroom for a few seconds, then came back and grabbed his glass of water, emptying it with a few deep swallows while Megan simply enjoyed the view of him standing naked next to her bed.

"Refill?" he asked.

She responded by offering up a very satisfied grin.

He smiled down at her. "I meant your water glass."

"Oh. Sure, I'll take water, too." She reached over to grab her glass from the nightstand, then found him ogling her in the same manner she had been watching him.

It actually made her blush. She handed the glass to him.

"I'll be right back."

She leaned against the headboard, uncertain whether to slide under the sheets.

Well, that would be ridiculous. Brady had already seen everything she had. He'd had his hands on her. His mouth on her.

Everywhere.

Her body heated. She'd remember this night for a very long time.

He came back in and handed her the glass of ice water.

"Thanks." She took a couple of sips, then a couple more, before setting the glass on the nightstand.

Brady climbed in bed next to her and pulled her against him. "That was fun."

"Yes, it was."

"We should do it again."

She definitely liked his way of thinking. She laid her head on his shoulder, then twirled her fingers over his tattoos. "So I noticed you mostly have them on your right arm, and some on your back."

"Yeah. I'm a work in progress."

Her lips curved. "Most of us are. So you're going to get more?"

"Yeah. I'll eventually get some on the other arm."

She sat up and grasped his arm. The first one she

noticed was his brother's name on his biceps. "You have Kurt's name. And the date he died."

He nodded. "I had that one done right after he died. I guess it's a way to always have him with me."

She traced the outline of Kurt's name with her fingertips. "It's nice."

She moved his arm around and looked at the others. "I love this one."

"The mermaid?"

"Yes." She pulled her gaze from his arm to his face. "But none of these have color. The mermaid would have been pretty in color."

"Nah. I don't want color on me. I save the paint for the bikes."

"I see." She went back to the tattoos. "And what's this one? Poetry?"

He shrugged. "Just some words."

She read them. "'No matter how long gone, you'll always be here. A heartbeat close. A whisper's near.'"

She took in a deep breath at the power of those words. "That's beautiful. What's it from?"

"I wrote it."

Her gaze snapped to his. "You did?"

"Yeah."

"Wow, Brady. It's amazing."

"It's nothing."

He'd looked away from her, but she tipped his chin and made him look at her. "It's not nothing. Those words have meaning. That when someone goes away, they're always in our hearts. And no matter how much time passes, they will never pass from our memories. That with every beat of our hearts, every breath we take, we remember those we loved and lost."

"That was the point, yeah."

She settled against him. "So, you really are an artist."

He laughed. "I don't think so."

"You don't give yourself enough credit."

He smoothed his hand along her back. "Thanks."

She could tell her praise made him uncomfortable, but she really was impressed.

"It's been a good day," she said.

"I'll say. Won money and got laid."

She shook her head. "I can see how those two would be meaningful for a guy."

He looked down at her. "Oh, and not for you?"

"I liked winning money." He cocked a brow, and she laughed. "Yes, Brady, the other part was pretty good, too."

"Pretty good?"

"Yes. And I'm really happy that you won a big jackpot in the poker run. What will you do with the money?"

"Pay for some equipment for the bike painting I do. The rest I'll tuck away in my savings account."

"And you're saving up for?"

"To open my own custom bike painting shop."

She sat up to face him. "I never knew you wanted to do that."

"No reason for you to know. But that's why I've stayed in Hope. I have the job at Carter's shop, and it pays me well enough to save money. Plus the rent at the apartment over the shop is cheap, and I can work on some nights and weekends taking bike paint jobs."

"Oh, I see. What's your timeline to open your paint shop?"

He shrugged. "Whenever I have the money."

"Do you have a location in Hope where you intend to open your shop?"

"I never said I was going to open the shop in Hope."

She hadn't expected to hear that. "Really. So you might consider moving out of town?"

"Maybe. I don't know. I haven't given the where of it a lot of thought."

"Huh. Interesting." She swung her legs over the bed. "I need to go to the bathroom. Excuse me for a minute."

Megan closed the door behind her and stared into the

mirror. She knew she'd abruptly fled the conversation with
Brady. She didn't really have to use the bathroom, but she
did anyway since she was already in there, and staring at
herself in the mirror wasn't providing any answers. Plus,
she needed the time to get her head on straight.

She'd imagined this entire day—and possibly her entire
relationship with Brady—as something blissfully romantic. When in reality it was nothing more than physical
chemistry between them. She needed to remind herself
that there was nothing going on besides that.

Brady had long-term plans for his future, and those
plans didn't include her.

When she came out, he smiled at her.

"Ready for round two?"

"Actually, I'm kind of tired."

"Oh. Sure." He climbed out of bed and, much to her
regret, he got dressed. She did, too, and he went into the
living room and gathered up Roxie.

All the while, she mentally berated herself for kicking
this gorgeous man out of her house—and her bed.

He turned to her. "I had fun today. Thanks for coming
along."

"Thanks for asking me."

He scooped his arm around her waist and tugged her
against him, brushing his lips across hers. "See you later."

She couldn't resist laying her hands on him just one
more time. "Sure. See you, Brady."

When she closed the door behind him, she laid her head
against it.

Dumb, Megan. You are so dumb.

They could be having round two right now. Followed
by round three.

He wasn't a forever kind of guy. She'd known that going
in. So what did it matter that maybe he wasn't going to
stay in Hope long-term? That didn't mean she couldn't
enjoy some fun, hot sex with him in the meantime.

Sometimes the nontraditional "Whee, let's have fun,
anything goes" side of her clashed with the traditional "I

want the house and the kids and the dog and the happily-ever-after" side. And tonight she'd let the traditional side of herself win. Which was too bad, because she sure had been having fun with Brady.

She pushed off the door and turned off the light, heading to her bed.

Alone. Because she was an utter dumbass.

Chapter 16

EMMA HAD TEXTED Megan Tuesday morning and told her Des would be coming over to her house with her baby that afternoon. She also said Jane and Chelsea were visiting after school. So Megan texted Sam to see if she'd be done with work in time to go with her. Fortunately, Sam had a light day, and her deliveries would all be taken care of in the morning, so they made plans to meet over at Emma's around four, which should coincide with Chelsea and Jane showing up as well.

Megan couldn't wait to see the babies. She hadn't seen them since right after their births, and she was sure they'd changed a ton already.

And they would give her something to occupy her mind, since she hadn't spoken to Brady in a few days.

They'd had such a great time together, and could have probably continued to do that if she hadn't had a major freak-out and all but thrown him out of her house for no good reason at all.

She sighed and focused on her customers, deciding less thinking about men and more concentration on business was much better for her emotional state. By the time she closed up for the day, she was more than ready to spend the afternoon with her friends.

Sam came by and picked her up a little after three thirty. "I don't know about you," Sam said after Megan climbed into the car, "but I am so ready to have a glass of wine with the girls."

Megan laughed. "Rough day?"

"You have no idea. First, I delivered a half dozen centerpieces for a business meeting that the coordinator insisted were not what she ordered. I have it written down. It's exactly how she ordered it, and she was a total pain in the butt about it. So of course I had to dash back to the shop and redo the centerpieces according to the client's 'new' specs, which weren't what she asked for originally. I was a giant sweat-ball by the time I got them back to her, just before their event began."

"That sounds like a nightmare."

"It was. But in the end she was happy, even though she was the one who couldn't remember what she ordered in the first place."

"That's always tough, since you have to go with the 'customer is always right' philosophy, even when you know they're not."

"Exactly. So now I'm grumpy and I need some wine."

Megan laughed. "You drink all the wine you need. I'll drive home."

"You're a good friend, Megan."

When they got to the driveway, Sam parked while Megan pulled out the box she'd brought with her.

"You brought muffins, didn't you?"

"Actually, they're molten chocolate cakes. It's a new recipe, and I thought I'd test them out on all of you to see if you like them."

"I'm sure my thighs will love them just fine. Thanks. Do they go with wine?"

Megan followed Sam up the stairs. "Doesn't everything?"

Sam slung her arm around Megan. "I love you."

Megan laughed, and they went to the door and rang the bell.

"Door's open," someone inside hollered.

Sam opened and held the door for her, so Megan slid inside and Sam followed.

Emma was on the sofa, and Jane was sitting next to her, holding Michael.

"Hey," Megan said. "I'm going to put this box in the kitchen."

"There's wine and coffee and tea and whatever you might want," Emma said. "Make yourselves at home."

"We'll definitely do that," Sam said, heading straight for one of the bottles of wine.

Megan opted for a glass of iced tea, since she'd offered to be the designated driver.

They headed into the living room, where Chelsea, Jane, and Emma were already situated on the sofa, so Megan took a seat in one of the side chairs and Sam took another.

"Where's Des?" Megan asked.

"She texted that she's running a little late," Emma said. "Benjamin was fussy, and then it was feeding time, so she decided to feed him before she came over. She should be here any minute."

As soon as she said that, the door opened and Des came in. Chelsea jumped up to take the baby in his car seat carrier.

"Thanks, Chelsea," Des said. "Hey, everyone."

"Hi, Des," Megan said. "You should take a seat. What would you like to drink?"

"I'll have some water. Thanks, Megan."

"Coming right up. You take my chair. I'll grab another."

Megan went into the kitchen and poured water from the pitcher she knew Emma kept in her fridge, then brought it out and set it on the table. Since it didn't look like she was going to get a chance to hold the babies anytime soon, she took a peek at Michael, who Jane was holding, and at Ben, who was asleep in his carrier.

"They've both gotten so much bigger already."

"They do grow fast," Des said.

"He's doing well?" Megan asked, dragging one of the chairs over to sit next to Des.

"He's doing so well. I don't want to say perfect, because that would be arrogant of me."

"Oh, go ahead."

Des laughed. "Fine. He's perfect."

"Of course he is." She looked over at Emma. "And how's Michael?"

Jane looked down at the sleeping baby in her arms, then up at Megan. "He's perfect, too."

Emma laughed. "That he is."

"Makes me want another one," Jane said.

"Bite your tongue," Chelsea said. "Ryan and Tabitha are the perfect ages now, at ten and seven."

Jane nodded. "Exactly. The ideal ages to add a new little one to the mix."

"Will would enjoy having a baby in the house, wouldn't he?" Sam asked, then took a long swallow of wine.

"He would love one. We've talked about it. He loves my kids, but I have to admit I wouldn't mind adding to the family with another baby. And if I'm ever going to do that, it needs to be sooner rather than later."

"How do the kids feel about that?" Emma asked.

"Tabby bugs me all the time about having a baby. She'd love a little sister or brother. As you can imagine, Ryan is completely uninterested and cares more about football and baseball than having a sibling." Jane looked down at Michael. "And now, holding this one, I feel the urge."

"And who will shop with me if you're off having babies?" Chelsea asked.

Jane rolled her eyes. "Oh, please. You and Bash will be popping out babies of your own soon enough. And wouldn't it be fun if we were pregnant together?"

"Please. We have to get married first."

"And when exactly is that event going to occur?" Des asked.

Chelsea shrugged. "We're working on setting a date. First we had to get moved into the new house. Now that that's done, the wedding is next."

"You're not getting any younger, you know," Jane said.

Chelsea slanted a look at Jane. "And neither are you, since you and I are the same age."

"Exactly my point. Which is why I'm thinking of having a baby now rather than later."

"And Bash and I will get around to that. After the wedding." Then she added in a whisper, "Hopefully after the wedding."

"What does that mean?" Emma asked.

"Oh . . . nothing." Chelsea picked up her glass of water.

"You're not drinking wine, Chelsea," Megan said, just now noticing that. Chelsea always had a glass of wine at these get-togethers. "Are you . . . ?"

Chelsea shrugged. "I might be. Which would be extremely bad timing, since we haven't even set a date for our wedding yet."

Jane handed the baby back over to Emma, then turned and took Chelsea's hand. "Are you serious?"

"Yeah. As someone who has taken her birth control conscientiously her entire adult life, I find the possibility of being pregnant utterly ridiculous. But I had to go off the pill for a while because of medical reasons, and I thought we were being super careful. But . . . maybe not."

Megan looked over at Sam, who had by now emptied her glass of wine and was sitting there smiling. "You're being quiet."

"I find the idea of Chelsea being knocked up supremely amusing."

Chelsea shot a glare at Sam. "I am not amused."

"Oh, come on, Chelse. You are the great planner. You even made a list of all the traits of the perfect guy before you fell in love with Bash and that ridiculous notion was tossed out the window. And then you had to have the perfect house before you could plan your perfect wedding.

Everything in order, ya know? It would be a great irony for you to end up pregnant before you could have the biggest wedding the town has ever seen."

Chelsea stared at Sam, and for a second Megan was certain that Chelsea was going to burst into tears. But she ended up laughing.

"You know what? You're right. Irony is a bitch sometimes."

"And how do you think Bash would react?" Emma asked.

"Are you kidding? Bash is so damn eager to have a baby he'd be thrilled. And frankly, the whole ordeal with finding the right house and having the renovations done has been exhausting. At first I thought planning this huge wedding would be the greatest thing ever. But now? Honestly? I just want to be married and start our lives together."

"The first thing you should probably do is find out if you're pregnant," Des said.

"I have an extra pregnancy test or two still hanging around here," Emma said. "You know, if you want to find out today. While we're all here."

"You keep pregnancy tests just lying around?" Chelsea asked.

"No. They're from when I thought I was pregnant with Michael. I took a test but I was too early. Then I bought a lot more tests so I took another. Then when that was positive I took another."

Des laughed. "I did the same thing."

Emma looked over at Des and grinned. "I'm so glad I'm not the only weird one."

"You should definitely take the test, Chelsea," Jane said. "First, you need to know, and second, we need to know."

Chelsea took several swallows of water. "I'm not sure I want to know."

"You want to know," Megan said. "I think. Or at least, if it was me, I'd want to know."

"Fine." Chelsea stood. "I'll go pee on the damn stick."

"Awesome." Emma got up and handed the baby to Megan. "I'll go with you. You'll want someone to hold your hand."

"This day isn't turning out at all like I expected," Sam said. "It's so much better. Anyone want wine?"

"I'm good with water," Des said.

"I'm perfect now that I'm holding a baby," Megan said.

"Fine. More wine for me." Sam stood and left the room. Just as she did, the doorbell rang.

"I'll get it," Sam said.

"It's probably Molly," Jane said. "She said she'd be late."

Megan looked down at Michael, who, despite being handed around, had stayed asleep. He was so sweet with his pink chubby cheeks and the way his mouth made sucking motions even in sleep. He looked like a tiny cherub with hair. She breathed in that baby powder scent and, if possible, her uterus did a tumble.

Okay, maybe not, but there was something about holding a baby that made her hormones go haywire.

"He's awfully cute," Sam said as she walked by with her glass of wine in her hand and Molly behind her, also with a glass of wine.

"He is," Megan said. "So is Benjamin. I can already see the two of them getting into all kinds of trouble when they get older."

Des grinned. "So can I. Logan and I have talked about that. I think the two of them are going to be thick as thieves."

"And judging by the looks of them already—very dangerous to girls' hearts."

"Yes," Jane said. "I feel bad for all those female Hope babies. They'll all be vying for the new generation of McCormacks."

"Oh my God."

Megan looked up at the high-pitched sound of Chelsea's voice emanating from Emma's master bedroom. She looked from Jane to Des to Sam to Molly, and they all grinned at each other.

"I was filled in by Sam in the kitchen," Molly said.

"I'm going to assume that meant a positive on the pregnancy test," Des said.

Emma came out a few seconds later, sporting the same grin everyone else was wearing.

"Chelsea's going to need a few minutes," Emma said.

"So that's a yes?" Megan asked.

Emma nodded, then whispered, "I'll let her tell you, though. And it's possible she's taking a second test, because I'm not sure she believed the first one."

Megan handed the baby back to Emma, who laid him in the nearby cradle. Des put a sleeping Benjamin in the Pack 'n Play Emma had provided.

And now they all waited for Chelsea.

Sure enough, it took Chelsea about ten minutes to surface from the bathroom. And when she did, she had a very stunned look on her face.

"Okay, so I peed on the stick—two of them. And they were both positive."

"Congratulations, Chelsea," Jane said, coming over to give her a hug.

There were tears in Chelsea's eyes as everyone went over to hug and congratulate her.

But she was laughing through the tears. "I think I might need to sit down."

She sat on the sofa and took several sips of water.

"How do you feel?" Emma asked.

"Stunned, mostly. I mean, I knew it was a possibility. I was late. But we were careful, you know? I've always been careful. And this isn't part of the plan." She looked at all of them. "Oh my God, I have to talk to Bash. I can't believe you all knew before Bash."

"I think he'll be fine with it," Megan said. "All things considered, this was kind of a fluke."

Chelsea let out a short laugh. "I'll say. But I really have to talk to Bash. And I'm going to need to plan a very quick wedding. A very quick, elaborate wedding, because no way am I skimping on the . . . everything."

"Hey, I can help there," Des said. "I have Hollywood in my corner. I know people who can give you elaborate at a moment's notice."

"So maybe . . . a short-notice, but incredibly elaborate, wedding?" Sam asked. "I can guarantee you that I'm an expert at that kind of thing, since Reid and I did that recently."

"That's true," Megan said. "And it was a lovely wedding. And don't forget you have me for your cake and Sam for your flowers."

"That's right," Sam said. "We're all here for you."

Chelsea nodded. "I love all of you. So we can do this, right?"

"We absolutely can," Des said.

"Okay," Chelsea said. "I have to go tell Bash. And then we wedding plan—like really soon. Like tomorrow or something. Oh my God, I'm pregnant."

She laughed again, got up and grabbed her purse, then turned around and looked at all of them. "I can't believe this. I'm pregnant."

"We can't believe it either, Chelse," Jane said with a wide grin. "But you're going to make an amazing mother."

Chelsea practically wriggled with excitement. "Now that I know it's true, I can't wait. Okay, I'm off. I'll be talking to all of you very soon."

She hugged all of them individually again, then dashed out the door.

"Well," Emma said. "And here I thought we'd all be staring at a couple of sleeping babies. This was much more exciting."

Megan laughed. "It was. Though never discount the sleeping-baby factor. They're both awfully cute, Emma."

Emma smiled. "Okay, they are."

"And now our group is having another baby," Jane said.

"Which is really pushing your baby meter, isn't it, Jane?" Sam asked.

Jane's lips curved. "Maybe a little. Or a lot."

"Time to order pizza and discuss that in depth," Emma said, grabbing her phone.

It was turning out to be a much more eventful night than Megan had anticipated.

And it looked like she had more wedding and baby cakes coming up.

Awesome.

Chapter 17

BRADY HAD AN early paint job that morning, so he was in the shop before anyone else. He'd left Roxie to run the halls of the offices, figuring Molly would grab her and take her out as soon as she came in.

By the time he finished, the office staff had come in and all the engine bays were filled. He slid out of his coveralls and brushed his fingers through his hair, checking in with Molly, who informed him she and Roxie were fine.

What he wanted was a good cup of coffee and maybe a cinnamon roll.

Or maybe he just wanted to see Megan, who he hadn't talked to since that night she'd made it clear she wanted him to leave.

He'd given her space, figuring whatever sudden mood she'd fallen into would dissipate and she'd call or text him.

She hadn't. She hadn't brought him coffee or anything from the bakery all week. In fact, since the night they'd had sex, he hadn't seen or heard from her.

What the hell?

He scrubbed his hands and washed the sweat from his face, then stared at his reflection in the mirror.

Maybe he'd failed to satisfy her.

Nah. That was utter bullshit. She'd responded. Hell, she'd more than responded. As he thought back to that night, his dick twitched.

Bad time to think about sex with Megan. But it couldn't be that she thought the sex was awful. He was great in the sack. That couldn't be the reason she'd avoided him.

She was probably busy, just like him. He decided he'd head over to the bakery and get a coffee and say hi.

He told the receptionist he was going to take a break, then headed up the street to Cups and Cupcakes.

When he pushed through the door of the bakery, he was surprised at how crowded it was. He got in line and waited his turn, inhaling the scent of fresh-brewed coffee.

He'd gotten to work so early this morning that even Megan's bakery hadn't been open yet. Not that he'd been going in there for coffee, though he didn't know why. Instead, he'd been brewing that awful sludge in his apartment and drinking the stuff at the garage. Megan's coffee was so much better.

As he walked into her shop it smelled like he was standing at the gates of heaven. Between the coffee and the buttery scent of pastry, his stomach was growling. It looked like Megan and her assistant were staying busy, too. He picked up his phone to check the time.

Seven fifteen. Yeah, everyone wanted their brew and breakfast treats as they headed off to work.

When he got to the counter, Megan looked up, her brows raising as she saw him. "Hey, Brady."

"Mornin', Megan."

"What can I do for you?"

"I'll take an extralarge coffee and . . ." He perused the inventory. "How about a cinnamon roll?"

"Sure. I'll have those at the end of the counter for you shortly."

She was all business, but he supposed that, considering the crunch of people in here, she didn't have time for personal talk.

He walked to the end of the counter, where he got out his wallet. She had bagged his cinnamon roll and put a lid on the coffee.

"Anything else?"

He smiled at her. "Well, yeah, but I guess you don't have time to talk right now."

She looked at the line of customers behind him. "Not really."

"Okay." He paid her and she gave him change.

"Have a good day, Brady."

"You, too, Megan."

He walked out, feeling decidedly unsatisfied. At least until he made his way back to the shop and to the break room. Roxie ran in, and he scooped her up and put her on his lap. She sniffed the bag on the edge of the table.

"Sorry, Rox. Not for you."

He pulled the lid off the coffee and unpacked the cinnamon roll from the bag, taking a giant bite. It melted in his mouth, and he couldn't resist a groan.

"That good, huh?" Carter asked as he came in the room to pour himself a refill of coffee.

Brady swallowed before answering. "That good." He followed it up with a sip of the perfect coffee.

"How's Megan this morning?" Carter asked.

"Busy."

"Like always around this time. I usually wait until after the morning rush before I go in. That way I can stare at all the baked goods without being hustled out of there by the starving hordes."

Brady was busy stuffing the cinnamon roll in his mouth, so he nodded. "Good advice. I'll remember that for the future."

Carter leaned against the doorway. "What's on tap for you today?"

"I did a final coat on Wendell Wood's Dodge early this

morning. I'm sanding Larry Hohman's Jeep next. Then I'll start on prepping Cathy Patterson's Mustang this afternoon."

Carter nodded. "Sounds good. I'm really happy you're staying busy."

"I'm pretty surprised to be this busy. But I'm not complaining. Happy to have the work."

"And I'm happy to have someone of your caliber here."

"Thanks, man. And thanks for letting me stay above the shop."

Carter shrugged. "The apartment's there for as long as you want."

"Appreciate it. It helps keep my monthly costs down so I can save money."

Carter arched a brow. "That's right. You want to open your own custom paint shop. Maybe I should raise your rent so you stay here longer."

Brady laughed. "You wouldn't do that."

"No, I wouldn't. But I don't think I'll be able to find someone who does bodywork like you do, so letting you stay above the shop might be like shooting myself in the foot. You'll end up as my competition."

Brady polished off the last of his cinnamon roll, then took a big gulp of his coffee. "Only if I stay in Hope."

Carter frowned. "I didn't know you were thinking of leaving town."

"Haven't decided yet. And anyway, that's not gonna happen anytime soon."

"Well, if I get a vote, which I know I don't, I'd like you to stay. Even if you do end up as competition for the shop."

It wasn't often he heard from someone who cared whether he left or stayed. "Hey, thanks. That means a lot."

Carter's lips lifted. "Yeah well, before you want a hug or something, get your ass back to work."

Brady laughed. "Okay, boss."

He tossed the empty bag in the trash and went back into the painting bay, holding his coffee cup in his hand as he walked around the Dodge he'd painted earlier. He surveyed every inch of the vehicle, looking for pits, flaws or imperfections, making sure the paint looked perfect.

It was, so he moved the vehicle out and brought the next one in to begin sanding.

Before he got started, though, he pulled out his phone and sent a text message to Megan.

Cinnamon roll and coffee hit the spot this morning. Thanks. How about dinner tonight?

He knew she was busy and wouldn't have time to answer right away, so he tucked his phone back into his pocket and got back to work. It was hours later before he had a chance to check his phone for messages.

There was one from Megan.

Dinner sounds good.

He texted her that he'd pick her up after he got off work.

He cracked a smile as he slid his phone back in his pocket.

Yeah, he was looking forward to seeing Megan later.

Chapter 18

MEGAN HAD HAD an extremely busy day, so she had to spend a lot of time cleaning up the bakery, working on the next morning's inventory list and doing some advance baking before she headed home.

She felt like she was covered in flour, sugar, and icing. Which then reminded her of what Brady had said to her the night they'd had sex, about how she smelled and tasted sweet.

She wondered if he wanted to come over right now and lick some of this icing off of her?

She shivered as she recalled exactly where his mouth had been on her body, and was ever so grateful they had a date tonight.

She went home and took a shower, which felt magnificent and very rejuvenating. She dried her hair and put on makeup.

Before she got dressed, she sent Brady a text message.

Are we going out on your bike tonight? I'm trying to decide what to wear.

He texted back within a few minutes.

Yeah. The bike. Is that okay?

She texted him back, It's perfect. See you soon.

She chose a pair of jeans and a short-sleeved cotton T-shirt, then put on her boots and headed into the kitchen to tidy up in there and see what she had in the way of sweets just in case Brady wanted to come in after.

When the doorbell rang, she hung up the dish towel and went to the door.

As was typical for Brady, he looked delectable in dark jeans, a navy blue T-shirt, and his boots.

She smiled at him. "Hey."

"Hey yourself. You look gorgeous."

"Really? Thanks." She was surprised at how much his compliments pleased her.

"Are you ready to go? I have Roxie on the bike already."

She loved that he'd made Roxie a part of his life and that the dog went everywhere with him. It showed how much he cared about animals. You had to like a guy who cared about little furry creatures. "Let me just grab my jacket."

He nodded. "Okay. I'll be outside."

She grabbed her jacket and her purse and went out to the driveway.

Roxie was all set in her basket with her goggles and her stuffed chicken. Megan ruffled her fur and bent down to give her a kiss.

"Well, hello there, cutie," she said to Roxie.

Brady took her purse and handed her a helmet.

"I'll stash this for you," he said, tucking her purse into the saddlebag while she put her helmet on.

He got on, and she climbed on behind him, inhaling the scent of his worn leather jacket as he fired up the bike.

It was always a thrill to hear the engine roar.

He backed down the driveway, and they were off. She'd forgotten to ask him where they were going. Not that it mattered to her. It was warm out since the sun hadn't gone down yet. The weather was warming, though the nights were still a little cool.

She intended to enjoy every minute of their ride as Brady headed them out of Hope.

They rode for about an hour, and she had fun looking at all the scenery. He took a lot of back roads, so she sat back and enjoyed not only the view of the houses and trees and ranches they rode past, but also the extremely attractive eye candy in front of her. Once in a while he'd look over his shoulder at a stop sign and ask her if she was okay.

Oh, she was most definitely okay.

He finally backtracked toward Hope, stopping just outside of town at one of the parks. Woodsy, yet utterly beautiful, with thick trees and a lovely lake. He'd parked at one of the picnic benches.

Megan stretched her legs when she got off, then laid her jacket over one of the handlebars and retrieved Roxie from her basket. Brady handed her Roxie's leash, which she attached to the dog's harness. Roxie sniffed around on the grass, her little stuffed chicken a seemingly permanent fixture in her mouth.

When Brady pulled a cooler out of the saddlebag, she was surprised, and even more pleasantly surprised when he pulled out a blanket.

"Thought we might have a picnic for dinner."

She arched a brow. "You made dinner?"

His lips curved. "Don't get too excited. I picked up turkey sandwiches from Louie's sandwich shop."

"That works for me. Did you get their homemade salt and vinegar chips, too?"

"Do I look stupid? Of course I did."

"See? I knew I liked you for a good reason, Brady."

He walked over to a grassy area by the lake, one that was bathed in sunshine. "And it's for my awesome chip selection?"

"Of course."

He grinned, then set the bag down. She helped him spread out the blanket, and they sat.

Brady poured water into a bowl for Roxie, who went over, took a sip, wandering as far as her leash would allow.

Then she laid down in the sun and nuzzled her chicken, obviously content with her chosen spot.

Brady handed Megan her sandwich, and they split the oversized order of chips. He'd brought bottled water for them, so they sipped on that as they ate and enjoyed the view of the water.

"It's beautiful here," Megan said. "I can imagine with all the trees it's a great spot to hit when it gets really hot in the summer."

"Yeah, a nice spot for a picnic. I ride my bike here in the summer. You see a lot of families out here doing birthday parties and things. And if you get here early in the morning, there's good fishing."

She wrinkled her nose. "Fishing is not exactly my thing."

He took a bite of his sandwich, then followed it up with a drink from the water bottle. "Don't knock fishing unless you've tried it."

"Okay, I admit I haven't tried it. It doesn't sound like it's my thing. Icky worm things on the end of a hook and then slimy fish things that you have to clean? No, thanks."

"Describing it that way makes it sound awful. It's actually peaceful. Gives you time to think. It's quiet out here early in the morning before the sun comes up. Just you and nature and your own thoughts."

She listened to him while she was eating, and she wondered what thoughts occupied his mind.

"So you come out and fish often?"

"Sometimes. Not as often as I used to. Kurt and I used to ride out here all the time and fish when we were younger. We'd bring our bikes out around four a.m. and just sit and fish and drink coffee and talk nonstop about stuff."

She could envision that. "I'll bet that was fun."

His lips curved as he stared out over the water. "It was. Though we'd argue, too. Kurt had a loud voice, and then I'd jump all over him about scaring the fish away, which would make him yell even louder."

She laughed. "I can picture that."

"It probably makes you want to take up fishing now."

"No, it really doesn't."

"Damn. And here I thought we could make it a regular thing."

"Sorry. You're going to have to paint a better picture for me. Something that doesn't involve worms and fish guts."

They finished their sandwiches and then got up to take Roxie for a walk around the lake.

"So, you've been busy this past week?" he asked as Roxie dropped her chicken to attack a random stick.

She tilted her head. "About normal for me. How about you?"

"Pretty busy. Which is why I didn't call you. Sorry."

"No need to apologize. Though I need to apologize for kind of rushing you out of my house the other night. It was rude."

"I didn't notice. I just figured you didn't want me to stay the night."

"It wasn't that at all. I would have loved for you to stay. I was just in a weird mood."

His lips curved. "Which means you didn't want me to stay the night."

"No, it's not like that. I was actually sorry as soon as you left. I wanted you to stay." She shook her head. "Don't ask me to explain it. I couldn't even if I wanted to."

He laughed. "It's okay, Megan. I wasn't offended."

"I'm glad."

They made the circle back to the blanket. Roxie had obviously worked up a thirst, because she attacked her water bowl with a vengeance, then plopped down on the edge of the blanket, laid her head on her chicken and promptly went to sleep.

Megan and Brady sat as well. She took a long swallow of her water.

"But I do have a question about the other night," Brady said.

"Oh. Okay, sure." She was fiddling with the paper on her bottle of water as she listened to him.

"Was the sex bad?"

Megan's eyes widened and she snapped her head up to look at Brady. "What?"

"Sex. The other night. You and me. Was it bad?"

He looked so concerned she bit back the urge to laugh. "Brady. No. Sex with you was . . . amazing." She screwed the top on her bottle of water, then climbed onto his lap. "Like, the best sex I've had in a really long time."

His response was immediate. He grasped her hips and drew her closer.

"Okay."

"Why would you even ask me that question?"

He shrugged. "I don't know. I guess because you threw me out of your house right after."

"Oh my God. I did not. I knew you were offended."

He laughed. "No I wasn't. But I was a little concerned that maybe you thought the sex was awful, and that's why you threw me out."

She rolled her eyes. "I did not throw you out. Okay, it might have seemed like I did. But I really didn't. Or at least I didn't mean to. And it certainly had nothing to do with your sexual prowess, which, I'll be happy to repeat, was exceptional."

His lips curved. "Good to know."

She laid her hands on his shoulders, letting her nails dig into him. Her physical response to being this close to him was fairly immediate as well. A rush of desire heated her, making her breasts feel heavy and swollen, and all the parts south took notice.

"In fact, if you'd like to come back to my place tonight, I'd be happy to show my appreciation for your amazing skills in the sack."

He arched a brow. "Is that right?"

"Indeed." Unable to resist, she slid her fingers into the soft thickness of his hair, tilting his head back so she could lean in and kiss him.

He cupped her butt, making her moan against his lips.

In an instant her world tilted and she was on her back on the blanket with Brady's hard body covering hers. She wrapped a leg around his, drawing him closer. His erection brushed the most sensitive part of her, and if it wasn't for the fact they were in a very public place, she'd beg him to shed some clothes so he could be inside of her in a matter of seconds.

He lifted his head, and she was more than happy to see him breathing as hard as she was.

"Dammit," he whispered, before taking a nibble of her lower lip. "Now I'm going to have to ride all the way back to your place with a hard-on."

She brushed his hair away from his forehead. "You won't be the only one suffering."

He let out a short groan, surging against her one last time, which made her moan.

"That's not helping," he said.

"You started it."

His lips curved, and if a smile could make a woman come, he should have that wickedly sexy half grin bottled and sold on the open market. He could make millions.

He hopped up, then held out his hand and hauled her up as well.

Brady folded the blanket while Megan scooped up Roxie and got her situated with her goggles and her chicken into the basket on the bike. Then she put on her helmet and glasses and she climbed onto the bike behind Brady.

She wouldn't say he exactly broke speed records, but she knew for a fact he wasn't going the speed limit as they made their way back to her house.

She had no complaints about that, since she was in as much of a hurry as Brady was to get back home. So when he pulled into the driveway, she hopped off, removed her helmet and grabbed Roxie, while Brady pulled her purse from the saddlebag. Since she had the dog in her arms, she handed over the keys to her house to Brady, who unlocked the door.

She put Roxie on the floor and went to the kitchen and put water in a bowl for the dog. She set it down, but Roxie obviously wasn't thirsty, so she got out Roxie's blanket and the dog settled in.

Megan looked over at Brady. "Do you want something to drink?"

He came over and slipped his arms around her waist. "No, the only thing I want is you."

She tilted her head back. "I'm all yours for tonight. I promise I won't even kick you out of my house."

His lips curved as he leaned down, his lips brushing across hers. "Or your bed?"

"Definitely not my bed. Or anywhere else you decide to have me."

He groaned against her mouth. "Let's start with the couch, and see where we go from there."

He lifted her shirt off as he backed her into the living room, his lips blazing a scorching trail along her throat. Her pulse instantly reacted, thrumming up a frantic rhythm that went along with the wildly out-of-control beating of her heart when Brady pulled off his shirt.

Her legs were draped over the sofa, so he jerked off her boots, then went to work on unbuttoning and unzipping her jeans. He drew the denim over her hips and down her legs, appreciating her skin with his mouth by kissing her hip bone, her thighs, and her knees as he removed her jeans.

She swallowed past the dry lump in her throat when he stood in front of her and toed off his boots, pulled off his socks, then made seriously sexy eye contact with her while he unzipped his jeans and dropped them—along with his boxer briefs—to the floor.

Nothing like a gloriously hot naked man to raise the temperature in the room about forty degrees. Her skin felt raw and tingly as he climbed over the edge of the sofa and pressed on top of her.

He threaded his fingers in her hair, his mouth coming

down on hers in a kiss raging with raw animal passion. She wrapped her legs around his hips and lifted against him, a feeling of needy desperation tunneling through her nerve endings.

He surged forward, rubbing his cock against her panty-clad sex.

Her eyes opened and she let out a gasp.

"You feel damp against me," he said. "Think I could make you come this way?"

"Yes." She could think of about a hundred ways he could get her there, all without leaving the couch.

"I can think of a better way." He lifted off of her and slid onto the floor, then flipped her legs to the floor, drawing her underwear off.

Her legs trembled as he draped them over his shoulders, kissed her inner thighs, then put his mouth on her sex.

She moaned and lifted against him, needing the release he promised with his tongue and lips. He was relentless in his pursuit of her orgasm, and she gladly let him control the reins as he took her on a gliding hot quest that left her whimpering and quaking as she crested, then cried out with a blistering-hot climax.

Shaking and spent, she let herself fall lax on the sofa. Brady released her legs and then climbed between them, crawling up her body as she caught her breath.

He brushed his lips against hers, then met her gaze with a teasing smile. "That was a good beginning."

"It was. Now let's go for round two."

This time, it was Megan who got up.

"Sit," she said.

He did, and she grabbed one of the pillows from the sofa and settled it on the floor, then kneeled.

Brady sucked in a breath as he watched Megan shoulder between his thighs. Her hair tickled his legs and all he wanted to do was lean forward, grab a handful of it and kiss her.

He loved her mouth, but he got the idea that she had

other plans for her mouth right now, and he didn't want to derail those plans.

His cock was tight and hard and as she took his shaft in her hands, it was all he could do not to explode right then.

Hell, he'd been hot and hard since she'd straddled him and kissed him in the park. All he'd wanted to do then and there was kiss her, undress her, closing out every thought but getting her naked and losing himself within her.

And now she was exceeding his every thought as she lifted up and put her mouth over the crest of his cock, flicking her tongue over the head.

He hissed out a breath and held on to the sofa as she expertly pleasured him. He wasn't sure if watching it or experiencing it was better. All he knew was he had to hold on tight as she took him for one hell of a hot ride with her lips and tongue. And when she took him deep, he let out a groan.

She was beautiful, with her hair spread out over his thighs, her mouth hot, wet, and unraveling him with every swipe of her tongue. His balls tightened and he knew he wasn't going to be able to hold out much longer.

"Megan," he said, his voice croaking out her name. "You need to stop now or I'm gonna come."

She didn't, instead stroking the base of his shaft, feeding his cock deeper into the recesses of her mouth.

And when she made a sound, the vibration was his undoing. He couldn't hold back the rush of his orgasm. She held on to him as he rocketed through his climax, jerking into her mouth with unyielding pleasure bursts until he was left spent and shuddering and barely able to form a coherent thought.

Megan rested her head on his thigh and looked up at him with a smile while he caught his breath.

"Not bad for round two, either," she finally said.

What she'd done to him. Damn. Megan was a constant surprise.

He looked down at her and grinned. "Yeah, and round three is about to rock your world."

"Bring it," she said.

He pulled her to her feet and kissed her, a deeper, hotter one this time, and his passion fired to life again. She threaded her fingers in his hair, holding him in place. He felt that need and fed off of it.

He maneuvered her down the hall, undoing her bra as they moved in unison. Her bra ended up somewhere between the guest room and the master bedroom.

"Condoms are in the nightstand's top drawer," she murmured against his mouth.

He reached into the drawer and pulled one out, tossing it to the side as his fingers dove into her hair.

He could get so lost in her, in the feel of her foot rubbing along his calf, in the way she arched her back to rub her nipples along his chest. She made him ache to be inside of her.

And when he put on the condom and spread her legs, she looked up at him. He read wild passion in her eyes. He felt the same out-of-control beating in his heart, the mad rushing of his blood, that need to be inside of her right now.

And when he eased inside of her, her breath caught.

He paused.

"Okay?" he whispered against her lips.

"Mmm, more than okay."

The passion-fueled tone of her voice spurred him on, made him eager to get her off again, to make her feel the same way she made him feel. He moved within her, loving how her body tightened around him. And when he kissed her, he soaked in her whimpers, the way she clasped him closer as if she couldn't get enough.

Yeah, he knew that feeling.

"You make me feel so good, Brady," she murmured. Her eyes were open and the naked honesty in her eyes tore him up. "I love when we're connected, when you're moving inside of me like this."

He shuddered at her words. He'd never had a woman tell him that before. But damn if he didn't feel the same way. It was damn good to be inside of her, to be close to her like this. He'd never thought much about sex other than a means to get off, to lose himself for a few minutes and not have to think. To be completely focused on sexual release.

But here he was, staring at those beautiful brown eyes of Megan's and actually feeling something.

It was damned uncomfortable, but also damned amazing at the same time.

A connection. He hadn't felt a connection to someone in a really long time.

He slid his hand in hers and lifted her arm over her head, entwining his fingers with hers. Then he kissed her, and it was like an instantaneous explosion of sensation and feelings, as if lightning had struck him.

And when she moved under him, when she made those sexy whimpering noises that never failed to make his balls tighten up, he wanted to take her there, to make her feel as good as she made him feel.

He plumped her breast with his other hand and brushed his thumb across her nipple.

She gasped, and his body responded. He knew she was going to go off.

So was he. He couldn't help but react to her every sound, her every movement. But he waited for her, and he pulled up, watching her as she released. She let him watch her reaction, as if she wanted to give that to him, to let him know what he did to her.

Damn if it wasn't the most beautiful thing he'd ever seen, watching her climax.

He went after her, shuddering out his own release, burying his face in her neck as he came.

After, he kissed her neck and lifted, smiling down at her.

"So how was round three?"

Her lips lifted. "It was good."

"Just good?"

"Exceptionally good. You don't get report cards for sex. You know it was stupendous." She pushed at his chest and he rolled off.

"I can live with stupendous." He disappeared into the bathroom to dispose of the condom, then came back in to climb on the bed next to her.

She rolled over to face him, nestling her shoulder under his arm.

"Ready for round four?" he asked.

She laughed. "Not quite yet. I need a few rounds of oxygen first."

That made him grin. "Okay."

"So tell me about your brother and fishing. Or any of the other things the two of you used to do together."

His brows knit together. "Why?"

She shrugged. "I want to know more about you. About you and Kurt."

"I don't really like to talk about it."

"I know." She laid her hand on his chest. "But maybe it's good to talk about it."

He stared straight ahead and went quiet for a few minutes, and Megan was afraid she'd once again broken the spell, that Brady would hop up and leave just when things had settled between them.

"I left town when things got bad with him," he finally said. "He'd gone from pot to crack to heroin, and I tried to get him into rehab. Shit, I tried more than once. He wouldn't go."

She lifted her gaze to his. "Not much you could do about that. An addict has to want to get clean."

He shifted and sat up. So did she.

"I know. But it was tearing my parents apart, because they thought they could help him. They tried everything. Hell, I tried everything. Kurt and I had a big blowout of a fight right before I left. I told him if he was going to kill himself with that shit, I wasn't going to stay around and watch it. That's when I left."

Her heart ached for him. "And you somehow feel responsible for him overdosing and dying."

He didn't answer.

She laid her hand on his arm, felt the tension there. "We

all tried to get him to seek help, Brady. I ran into him at Bert's diner one day and he and I sat down at one of the booths. For some reason I thought the short past he and I had together would mean something. We stayed friends even after we decided to stop dating, so I thought talking to him might help. I told him I cared about him and I wanted him to get help."

Brady slanted a look at her. "I'll bet that went over well."

"He told me there was nothing wrong with him and he was fine. And then he thanked me for my concern. That was about it. We ate together and went our separate ways."

"Yeah. He wasn't interested in hearing anyone's concerns."

She nodded. "I wasn't the only one who tried. In the end, Kurt was the one who owned his addiction. And no one could help him if he didn't want to help himself."

"You know, logically, I understand that. But I was family. I was closer to him than anyone else. And I was the one who walked out on him. Maybe there was something I could have done. At some point maybe I could have reached him."

She cocked her head to the side. "You know that's not true. You would have just been here to see Kurt destroy his life."

He was still staring at her bedroom wall as if it held all the answers he was looking for. "Maybe. I know my parents partially blame me for Kurt's death."

Her breath caught. "What? How could they possibly blame you?"

"Because I wasn't here."

She shook her head. "That's not how it works. You couldn't have helped him. No one could."

"Yeah. You're right about that."

He finally dragged his gaze away from the wall and laid his hand on her thigh, giving her a smile, but there was no joy in his eyes.

"Come here," he said. "You can rest against me and then we can work on round four."

"Sounds good to me."

She shifted and rolled over to lie against him, but the relaxed state Brady had been in after they'd made love was gone. Now it was like lying down next to a stone pillar.

She wished she hadn't brought up his brother. She had thought maybe talking with Brady about Kurt might help.

It had only made things worse.

Stupid, stupid mistake.

Chapter 19

IT HAD BEEN a hot damn day, and Brady had spent the majority of it sanding, which meant he was drenched in sweat. He finally finished up around five thirty, figuring he'd be the last one left in the shop.

He went in search of Roxie, surprised to find her sleeping next to Carter in his office.

Brady leaned his forearm against the doorway. "Where's Molly?"

"She dashed out of here early, mumbling something about shopping and showering and book club and . . . I don't think it was in that order, or maybe it was. I was only half paying attention. So I got the pup. How did the sanding go?"

"It was a piece of work, but I got the dents smoothed out in the passenger-side door and the rear quarter panel. All that's left is the trunk hood and I'll be ready to paint."

"Great. I've got two more coming in for you next week."

Brady nodded. "Guess it's good to be busy."

Carter cracked a satisfied smile. "It makes me damn happy."

"I'm sure it does. If there's nothing else, I'm outta here."

"Actually there is. You got plans tonight?"

"No."

"Good. Come play basketball with us."

Brady arched a brow. "Not really my thing."

"Really. You afraid of a little healthy competition?"

"No."

"Good. Then you could use the exercise."

"I just spent the better part of the day sweating my ass off. I don't think I need more exercise."

"I'll give you that. Then come along to help me kick the other guys' asses. And there's beer and burgers after."

This wasn't the first time Carter had asked him to join in on the group basketball game. He figured he should maybe say yes at least once.

"All right."

"Great. Meet you at the gym in a half hour."

That gave Brady time to get Roxie fed and take her on a short walk. He changed into his sweats and grabbed clean clothes to take along, then headed over to the gym, where he found Carter and a bunch of the other guys already warming up.

He was surprised to see so many of them there. Besides Carter, there was Luke, Will, Bash, Reid, Deacon, and Zach.

Carter waved him over.

"Hey," Deacon said as he made his way to the group. "Glad you made it tonight."

"Thanks. Figured spending eight hours sweating my ass off over a car wasn't enough exercise."

"Aww, you poor baby," Reid said. "The rest of us spent our workdays getting pampered at the spa. After that we all took naps. So we'll try to go easy on you."

Brady smirked. "Yeah, you do that."

They warmed up by taking a few jump shots with the ball, then broke up into two teams of four. Brady was on a team with Carter, Deacon, and Reid.

Okay so maybe playing basketball was a lot different from sanding a car. He used other muscles, for sure, and he got slammed by Will as he went for a lay-up, ending up on his ass on the floor.

Will grinned down at him and held out his hand. "You didn't really think we were going to go easy on you, did you?"

Brady grinned back. "I was hoping you wouldn't."

It was an hour of grueling running, shoving, and trash talking. Brady had to admit it was a hell of a lot of fun. When they stopped for a water break, he took several very thirsty swallows.

"I don't know about the rest of you," Zach said, "but I'm getting hungry."

"I could eat," Will said.

"You can always eat," Reid said. "Then again, I'm hungry, too."

Bash nodded. "I'm with you guys. Let's grab a shower and some food."

They hit the showers, cleaned up, and got dressed, then assembled in the parking lot.

"Where to?" Luke asked.

"Anyplace but my bar," Bash said. "It's my night off."

"Bert's?" Will asked.

Deacon shook his head. "Let's go get a steak."

"Lonestar in Tulsa?" Will asked.

"Works for me," Brady said. He was hungry. Anyplace sounded good to him right now.

They all agreed, so they piled into their cars and headed into Tulsa. Since it was a weeknight, it wasn't crowded. They were seated right away.

"Beers?" Luke asked.

Everyone nodded, so they ordered a couple of pitchers.

"How's work, Luke?" Will asked.

"Busy. I had to pick up an extra shift this week to cover for vacations, and thank God for Allison, the nanny Emma hired, because she's helping Emma with the baby so Emma can get some sleep while I'm working my ass off. All I do is come home, kiss Emma and cuddle Michael for five seconds, then pass out."

"Rough," Deacon said, pouring himself a beer.

Bash looked pained. "So that's what it's like having a baby?"

Luke laughed. "No. That's what it's like working double shifts. Having a baby around has been awesome. Michael is just the best thing ever."

"Look at him grinning," Will said. "It's like someone sprinkled magic freakin' fairy dust on him or something."

Deacon studied Luke. "I think it's the lack of sleep talking."

"Naw, that's the new baby glow," Zach said. "My older brother had that same look when he had his son last year. He didn't sleep well and the baby was up most nights, but he didn't even care. Just wore that same stupid grin on his face for months."

Brady checked Luke's face. Zach was right. Luke was definitely smiling.

"Good to know the whole baby thing isn't a total disaster," Bash said.

"I don't think you have anything to worry about just yet," Brady said.

"Well, actually . . ."

"Wait. You and Chelsea?" Zach asked.

Bash nodded. "Happened a bit before we were ready. Which ended up accelerating the wedding timeline. Like a lot."

"No shit," Zach said.

"Yeah. But we're really damned excited about it."

"Congratulations, man. I didn't know." Zach shook his hand and patted him on the back.

"I didn't know, either." Brady shook his hand as well.

"Thanks, guys. We haven't told everyone yet. We're still getting used to the idea, and now Chelsea is in wedding mode. Which is in two weeks. You'll get invites if you haven't already. So there's a lot going on."

"Two weeks?" Zach asked. "Wow, that's fast."

"Like, really fast," Bash said. "Good thing Chelsea has great friends who can put this all together in a hurry. And with Des being an actress, she said she has connections in Hollywood who will drop everything to help her. So I think we've got it all together."

Brady leaned back and took a long swallow of his beer. "So a wedding and a baby, huh?"

"Yeah. Actually, we're both kind of glad to get the wedding over with. It wasn't a big deal to either of us anyway. Finding the house? Now that was important. And once we did, getting it renovated was the next big thing, which, thanks to Reid and Deacon, has been done."

Reid raised his mug. "You're welcome."

"Ditto," Deacon said. "We were happy to help with that project, and it didn't take that long anyway."

Bash grinned. "So now we've moved into the new house and we're just ready to start our new lives. And we both really want kids and didn't want to wait on that, so this is kind of a blessing in disguise."

Will held up his mug. "To Bash and Chelsea and the bun in the oven."

Brady laughed and toasted.

Hell of a lot going on with his new friends. After celebrating and talking about Bash's good news, they drank and ate. Brady enjoyed a great steak. After a while, most of the guys headed home, leaving just him and Deacon at the table.

"Hell of a thing, huh?" Deacon asked.

"What's that?"

"Bash getting married and having a baby."

"Oh. Yeah."

"Life can surprise you sometimes. You never know what's just around the corner."

"Isn't that the truth?"

Deacon finished up his beer and his lips lifted. "Better him than me. I'm just damn glad I'm not in a relationship."

"Really? Why?"

"Too complicated. You think a woman wants one thing, then they end up wanting something completely different and you're left out in the cold."

Brady could tell Deacon had had a few drinks, but he

didn't appear drunk. Maybe he had a few things on his mind.

"Break up with someone recently?"

Deacon lifted his gaze to Brady's. "Recently? No. The last time I let a woman break my heart was a long time ago. I only let it happen once."

"Well, at least you got smart after that time."

Deacon laughed. "That's true. Problem is she's back in Hope now, so I keep running into her."

"Really. Who's that?"

"Loretta Black. Well, she's Loretta Simmons now, since she married that rich guy after high school."

Brady got the gist of what was going on. "Ah. So you and Loretta were a high school thing, huh?"

"Yeah." He waved his hand in dismissal. "But it was over a long time ago. It doesn't mean anything to me anymore."

That's why Deacon was bringing her up now. "Are you sure about that?"

"Definitely. Though I wish she'd have stayed in Texas with the rich guy."

"Is it hard to see her?"

Deacon shrugged. "Sort of. Dredges up the past, and I'm not much for that." Deacon poured another beer. "Anyway, I'm glad you came out with us tonight."

He could tell Deacon wanted to drop the subject. "Me, too. I had a good time."

"You should come play with us every week, Brady. You did great."

"I don't know how good I did, but I could try it again."

"Good. You need to get out more."

"So people keep telling me."

"Look, I know how it is to lose someone. I knew your brother. We weren't close in school, but we hung out some after high school. I'm really sorry, man."

"Thanks."

"I kept to myself a lot after my dad died. People didn't know what to say to offer comfort, or even worse, they'd tell me they knew how I felt. Until you lose someone you love, how the hell can you have any inkling of what it's like? It was my dad. He and I were close. I'll never have another father, no one who knows me like that."

Deacon stared at his mug of beer, no doubt lost in memories.

Brady knew exactly what that was like, being lost in the past, in all those what-ifs, like if you could have one more conversation with the person you loved, then maybe things would be different. Though Deacon's situation wasn't like his, he understood that feeling of loss.

"Anyway," Deacon said, "I didn't want to hear any of it. So I closed up and shut myself out of everyday life. And I still felt like shit. In the end, it didn't help. Couldn't bring my dad back, so I figured I might as well go on living."

Brady understood. "Well, I do know how you feel."

Deacon laughed. "I know you do. It hurts like hell. And it's going to hurt like hell until it doesn't hurt like hell anymore. And I'm not about to tell you how to feel. But the one thing I will tell you is that isolating yourself doesn't help. So come play basketball with us and come have beers with us. It won't cure the ache, but it'll take your mind off of life for an hour or two."

"Thanks. I'm working my way out of it, little by little. Even dating."

Deacon reared back. "God forbid."

Brady laughed. "Yeah."

"Who are you going out with?"

"Megan Lee."

Deacon nodded. "Really good-looking woman. And she makes the best damn croissants I've ever had. You could do a hell of a lot worse than a woman who bakes."

"This is true." Though he hadn't seen Megan in a few days. He should call her and see what was going on. Maybe take her out again.

He gave Deacon a ride home, which fortunately Deacon agreed to without argument.

He pulled into Deacon's driveway and put the car in park. Deacon climbed out, then leaned his head in.

"Had fun tonight."

Brady shot him a grin. "Yeah, me, too."

"You're in for next week's game, right?"

"You bet."

"See ya, Brady."

Brady waited for Deacon to make his way inside his house before he pulled out of his driveway.

Okay, so hanging out with the guys wasn't so bad. It gave him something to do besides work at the shop all the time, or hang out alone in his apartment.

He headed back to his place, took Roxie outside, then came in. He wasn't at all tired, so he paced the confines of his extremely small apartment.

He got out his phone and checked the time. It was only ten p.m., but then again, he knew Megan got up early in the morning to go to the bakery. So probably not a good idea to call or text.

He'd go the bakery tomorrow and see her. For tonight, he needed to go to bed.

But still, that restless feeling.

He went into the kitchen and filled a glass with ice water, then wandered into the living room.

He grabbed the remote and sat on the sofa. Roxie came over and looked up at him, so he scooped her up and she dropped her chicken on his lap, then climbed on and found a comfortable spot to sleep.

He propped his feet on the coffee table, surfed to a sports channel and found a West Coast baseball game.

Good enough. He laid his hand over Roxie and settled in for a sleepless night.

Chapter 20

MEGAN HAD HER hands full with a pan of burned cinnamon rolls. Something must be off with the oven, because she never burned anything. And she didn't have time to figure it out, because she had a bakery filled with eager customers. Fortunately, Stacy had handled orders out front this morning while she baked.

She'd opened the back door to clear out the smoke, then glared at her oven.

"Problems?"

She jerked her head up to see Brady standing at the doorway leading from the front of the shop.

"Oh. Hey. And yes. I burned the cinnamon rolls."

He frowned as he stepped in. "That sounds kind of tragic."

"Tell me about it. How are you doing?"

"Good. Took a break and came over to see you. Stacy said you were back here wrestling with an oven issue and that I could come on back. Is there something I can do to help?"

"I don't know. What do you know about ovens?"

"Not much. What's wrong with it?"

"I don't know. The temperature has always been predictable. And suddenly in the past day I've burned cookies, scones, and now the cinnamon rolls. That never happens."

"So there might be something wrong with your thermostat."

She pursed her lips and glared at the oven as if had grown horns. "This is not good. I have the owner's manual."

"Okay if I take a look?"

"I'm sure you have your own work to do."

"Actually, I have some free time. Unless you'd rather call someone more qualified."

"No, I'd be happy to have you look at it." She reached into the nearby drawer and shuffled through the manuals, pulling out the one for the oven. "Here."

"Okay."

He paged through the manual, rolled up his sleeves, and started to work. She backed away, salvaging what she could of the baked goods that had come out decently enough. Fortunately, she didn't need to bake anymore today, so maybe if Brady couldn't fix the oven she could get someone out here this afternoon who could.

"I'm going to run to the store for parts," Brady said, wiping his hands on a paper towel. "I'll be right back."

"Um, okay. But Brady?"

He stalled and turned around. "Yeah?"

"Do you think you can fix the oven?"

He held up hands. "Magic hands, Megan. Magic hands."

She arched a brow. "But does that mean yes?"

He shot her an incredulous look. "You doubt me and my magic hands?"

"Well, not exactly. It's just that I kind of need the oven to stay in business."

He walked over to her and slid his arm around her waist, then tugged her close. He smelled a lot like motor oil with a mix of oven grease. Not a bad combination, actually. She waited for him to kiss her, and when he didn't, she was disappointed.

"Never doubt my abilities, woman."

She laughed. "Duly noted. Go to the store. I'll run and get us sandwiches and fix us some iced tea for when you get back."

"Sounds like a plan."

So he hadn't kissed her. That wasn't a big deal, right? It was way more important for him to repair her oven than to cater to her emotions and her libido right now anyway.

She checked on Stacy, who had the bakery counter and cash register under control. This time of day people were more interested in lunch than baked goods, so traffic was light. She ran up the street and grabbed sandwiches, then came back and made a pot of iced tea. Brady showed up about twenty minutes later and started to work on her oven.

"You want to break for sandwiches?" she asked.

"Nah. Let me finish this first so you can try it out."

Since she didn't want to hover over him, she busied herself with cleaning up the kitchen. Though she couldn't help but skirt furtive glances his way as she did. First, because she was worried about the state of her oven, and second, how could she not? Brady wore relaxed jeans and a dark gray T-shirt that, despite being both stained and dirty, made him look sexier than ever. And there was something about watching a man work that was simply hot. Or maybe it was watching Brady work that made *her* hot.

Forty-five minutes later, he put her oven back in place. "Okay, give it a try."

She took a pan of cinnamon rolls she'd prepped earlier from the refrigerator, set the oven temperature and waited for it to preheat. While it did, she poured Brady a glass of iced tea and handed it to him.

"Thanks," he said, swiping the sweat from his forehead.

They both stared at the oven, watching the temperature rise to the appropriate setting. When it did, she slid the pan of cinnamon rolls in and set the timer.

"Now we wait," Megan said. "So we might as well eat. I'm sure you're hungry. You were probably hungry when you got here."

"Actually, I came by to see if you wanted to have lunch with me."

They took a seat at the small table in the back of the kitchen.

"Did you? I'm really sorry about this."

He unwrapped the sub sandwich from the paper and bit into it, then swallowed. "Why? Not your fault your oven broke. And you're not eating your sandwich."

She stared down at the food in front of her, her stomach a twisted knot of nerves. "I'm . . . not hungry right now."

"You're nervous because you're afraid your oven is broken and you don't know what you'll do if it is. Trust me—it'll work. Eat your sandwich."

She looked up at him. "So confident in your abilities, are you?"

"Yeah. Plus, your thermostat was shot and I replaced it. That was your problem. Eat your sandwich."

Keeping one eye on the oven, or rather keeping her nose on the oven, trying to breathe in any signs of her cinnamon rolls going up in flames, she took a bite of the sandwich and followed it up with a sip of the iced tea, mentally counting down the minutes until the rolls were finished.

So far, so good. Nothing was burning, except her desire to pull out beautifully baked cinnamon rolls.

"Sorry I haven't called you this week," Brady said, stealing her attention away from the oven. "I had back-to-back rush jobs and I've been working late. Then Carter pulled me into a basketball game last night with the guys."

"Really? That sounds fun."

"It was. I was going to text or call you after I got home, but I figured it was too late and you might have already gone to sleep."

"You could have called me anyway. I'd always pick up if it's you."

His lips lifted, and that smile he leveled on her was devastating. "Is that right? Anytime of the day or night?"

"Okay, maybe not here at seven a.m. when the shop is filled with customers. But if you want to give me a call at midnight, I'll answer. Unless you're already in my bed, in which case you don't have to call me."

He leaned forward. "Is that an invitation, Ms. Lee?"

His seductive voice was hypnotic. She leaned forward as well. "Maybe."

The timer dinged, dissolving the spell he'd woven over her. So far, no smoke from the oven, but she was still nervous. She stood and grabbed the potholders. "Nothing's burning."

Brady followed her over to the oven. "Of course nothing's burning. Because I fixed your oven."

She opened the door and pulled out the rack, revealing perfectly baked cinnamon rolls. She took them out and set them on the counter to cool, set the pot holders down, and threw her arms around Brady. "You fixed my oven."

He sported a cocky grin, then held his hands out. "I told you, Megan. Magic hands."

"So you did. Why don't you put those magic hands on me right now and I'll show you how much I appreciate what you did for me?"

He tugged her toward him and kissed her, a blazing kiss that enveloped her in its heat. For a minute she forgot where she was, until she heard Stacy clear her throat.

"Excuse me, Megan, but I've closed up the front of the shop."

Megan pulled back, staring at Brady's gorgeous, desire-laden green eyes for just a second before she turned around to face Stacy. "Oh, sure. Thanks, Stacy. I'll see you tomorrow."

Stacy gave her a knowing smile before she left the room.

Megan turned back to Brady, who wore a very satisfied smirk on his face. "Is that smile for the kiss, or the oven?"

"Maybe both?"

"Thank you."

"You're welcome. Now I need to go finish up at work."

"How about you come to my place tonight, where I can give you a proper, more thorough thank-you?"

He cocked his head to the side. "Is that a sexual invitation?"

"Well, I actually meant dinner and a decadent dessert, but . . ."

His lips curved. He gave her a quick kiss. "I'll assume it's an open-ended invitation, then. See you later, Megan."

"Thank you again, Brady."

He stepped out the back way and she closed the door.

She let out a very satisfied sigh.

All in all, a day that had started out terribly was ending on a really good note.

Now all she had to do was finish up these cinnamon rolls, clean up the shop, then figure out what she was going to fix for dinner tonight.

Because she had a hot date coming over.

Chapter 21

IT REALLY SUCKED that Brady was over an hour late. But he'd had a crisis. An epic damn crisis, and there was nothing he could do about it. Hopefully, the bottle of wine he'd stopped and bought might help to make up for being so late.

He rang the doorbell and Megan answered right away, a concerned look on her face.

"Is everything all right?" she asked as he walked inside with Roxie.

"It is now. It wasn't earlier."

"All you said in your text message was that you had a crisis and you'd be late. I was worried."

He looked down at Roxie. "I took Roxie for a walk and as we were crossing the street, she dropped her chicken down the storm drain."

"Oh. Oh, no. That is bad."

"Tell me about it. She loves that damn chicken. When I tried to get her to move along, she parked her butt at the curb and refused to move, then tried to scramble into the sewer drain to go after her chicken. Then she whimpered when I scooped her up and carried her upstairs to the apartment."

Megan cast a sympathetic look at Roxie, and swept her hand over the puppy's head. "Poor baby. I see she has a chicken now."

"Yeah. I had to take a quick shower and drive to the pet store to buy her a new one."

Megan's lips curved. "I assume you were smart about it and bought a backup?"

"I bought four."

She laughed. "Good call."

He held up the bottle. "And a bottle of wine for you as an apology."

Megan waved her hand and led him into the kitchen. "No apologies necessary. I totally understand the chicken emergency."

He unhooked the leash from Roxie's harness. She dashed off to the living room rug with her new chicken and settled in.

"Obviously she's a happy camper now," Megan said.

"Yeah, well, she should be. And we're never going for a walk with the chicken again. She's going to have to learn to deal with a little separation."

"Poor little thing."

"Her? How about poor me?"

She leaned up and wrapped her hand around the base of his neck to pull him down for a kiss. "Poor you. You've been in rescue mode all day today, haven't you? First me and my oven, and then Roxie and her chicken."

"Just call me Superman."

"I might just do that. We'll see what happens later."

He gave her a look. "Oh, now the pressure's on."

"I'm sure you can handle it." She grabbed two wine-glasses out of the cabinet. "Glass of wine?"

"Sure. I'll open the bottle."

She pulled an opener from the drawer and handed it off to him. He opened the bottle and poured the wine into the glasses.

"Something smells good in here."

"Thanks. I'm making stuffed pork chops."

"I love pork chops. With apple sauce?"

She nodded. "And mashed potatoes and green beans."

"I'm starving." He took a sip of wine. "Hey, this is pretty good."

She took a sip as well. "It is good. And you're surprised?"

"I don't know jack about wine. But the lady at the liquor store said it was a good brand."

"It is a good brand. You did well. Let's go take a seat in the living room. When you texted I hadn't put the pork chops in yet, so I waited. They'll be a little while."

"Okay."

While they drank wine, he asked her how her oven was. She told him she'd made a batch of cookies just to be sure before she cleaned up for the day, and the oven was working perfectly now. And then she thanked him again for fixing it for her.

"It really wasn't a big deal."

"It was to me. Who knows if I'd have been able to get someone over to fix it for me? You saved my life today."

"I'll let you pay me back later."

She smiled at him over the rim of her wineglass. "I look forward to that."

"Me, too."

The timer rang, so she got up to take the pork chops out. He followed her.

"Anything I can do?"

She handed plates and utensils to him. "You can take these into the dining room."

"Okay."

He set the table, and Megan brought out the food. By now his stomach was grumbling, so he grabbed the wine bottle and brought that into the dining room, and they sat to eat.

The pork chops were awesome, and so were the side dishes.

"Is there anything you can't do?" he asked in between mouthfuls of food.

She looked up at him. "I can't play piano. Or sing."

He laughed. "Well, neither can I."

"Then I guess we'll have to cross Christmas caroling or giving concerts off our list, won't we?"

"Yup. But you sure as hell can cook."

"Thank you. It's always been a stress reliever for me."

"Sex is a good stress reliever."

She coughed and put down her wineglass. "Yes, it is. But that's not always an available option. Cooking is."

"It's available now."

"True. But I enjoy cooking."

He frowned. "Wait. So you don't enjoy sex?"

She shook her head. "That's not at all what I meant. I meant that cooking is something I enjoy all the time and always have. Sex is obviously something I enjoy all the time as well, but I haven't always had a man in my life. Not that I need a man to enjoy sex—or at least an orgasm. Though it's way more fun to have a man give me an orgasm than to give myself one."

She paused, then stared at him.

"What?" he asked.

"I cannot believe I'm having this conversation with you at the dinner table."

"Would you rather discuss world events? Or sports? Because I have to tell you, I don't think I'd find them as stimulating as talking about sex with you. Especially if you want to describe in more detail how you give yourself orgasms."

Her gaze was heated. "Maybe we'll delve more deeply into that over dessert."

He reached for her hand, his thumb brushing over hers. "How about that dessert right now?"

"You haven't finished your pork chops."

"Yeah, but you're talking about sex. And sex trumps pork chops any day of the week."

"But I made an actual dessert."

He refused to be deterred. "Again . . . sex."

Her lips curved. "I don't know, Brady. I made cheesecake."

He opened his mouth, then closed it. Then sighed. "Damn. I really like cheesecake."

"I know you do."

"Then again, I really like you naked, too. Tough call."

She laughed, then picked up her wineglass and took a very long drink. He watched the way her lips clasped over the rim of the glass and his cock tightened.

Okay, so maybe he was thinking ahead toward the after-dessert portion of the night. And maybe the teasing they'd been doing had gotten to him. And maybe he'd missed her this past week.

Damn busy jobs.

"Fine," he said. "Pork chops. Then dessert. Then . . . *dessert*."

Her lips curved. "Have I mentioned I really like the way you say *dessert*?"

He was watching her mouth when she smiled. He really liked her mouth. "No. But I'll make sure to say the word more often if it turns you on."

"Pretty much everything about you turns me on, Brady."

"Keep talking to me that way and I'll never finish my pork chops."

She just gave him a devilish smile, then turned her attention to her food.

So he did the same. They finished their dinner, and he followed her into the kitchen to help with cleanup.

"I'll load these," he said, scraping food off the dishes while she ran water into the sink.

And who knew sliding their hands into soapy water together could be so sexy? They ended up touching fingers in the water, bumping hips at the counter as they dried pots and pans, and stopping to kiss every now and then.

He'd never thought of washing dishes as foreplay. Then again, he'd never done dishes with Megan before.

She put a pan into the sink and added soap. Since he'd filled the dishwasher with the dishes and utensils, he came up behind her and slid his hands down her arms and into the water.

"What are you doing?" she asked.

"I'm helping." He tangled his fingers with hers, grabbing the pot scrubber.

"Hmm. Can't say I've ever scrubbed a pan this way."

"Me neither." He washed the pan, her fingers teasing over his the entire time.

The pan forgotten, she turned to face him, her hands covered with bubbly soap. She ran her fingers up his arms.

"Slippery," she said.

"Hard."

She cocked her head to the side. "Hard?"

"You. Touching me. Makes me hard."

"Then we definitely need to do more of it." She reached behind her and grabbed a handful of suds, smoothing her hands along his forearms and up his biceps.

In turn, he grabbed her butt and drew her against his erection. There was something about the feel of her, the hot steam rising from the water behind them, that felt tropical and heated and, damn, he was getting worked up. "You're getting me all wet."

She raked her nails down his wet arms. "The feeling is mutual. Now how about that dessert I mentioned earlier?"

His gaze was direct. "Which one?"

"The one that doesn't have anything to do with food."

She wound her hand around his neck and pulled him toward her. His lips met hers in a fiery kiss filled with passion and need.

He backed her up against the sink, letting her feel the need he'd been holding in all day. She moaned against his mouth, and all he could think of right now was getting her naked and sinking inside of her.

But apparently Megan had other ideas. She broke the kiss and gave him a wicked smile, then slithered down his body.

"What are you doing, Megan?"

She tilted her head back and looked up at him. "Dessert."

"That's not cheesecake."

Her lips tilted. "Cheesecake will have to wait."

His heart rate ratcheted somewhere in the upper strato-
sphere as she undid the button on his jeans and drew the
zipper down, then tugged his jeans over his hips, along
with his boxer briefs.

When she put her warm, still wet hands on him, he
shuddered.

"That feels damn good."

And then he went into total meltdown when she put her
mouth over his cock. He stood still as stone to watch—and
feel—as she flicked her tongue over the head, then drew
his shaft into the warm, wet recesses of her mouth.

It was like dying, in the best way possible. There was
nothing like being blown apart by a sexy woman on her
knees. She had all the power, and he'd gladly give her
anything she wanted if she'd only keep performing that
magic with her lips and tongue that was slowly consuming
every working brain cell he had.

He was going to lose it, and he wanted to do that inside
of her. It had been all he'd thought about for days—and
nights. He reached for her, pulling her to stand, at the same
time kicking off his shoes and shrugging out of his jeans
and briefs.

"I wasn't finished," she said, giving him a wicked smile.
"And neither were you."

"I've got a better idea." He pulled off his shirt and cast
it aside.

She swept her finger across his bottom lip. "I'm not sure
what could be considered a better idea than giving you an
orgasm."

"Point taken, but work with me here." Now it was his
turn to kneel in front of her. He tugged at her capris.

"Okay, I'm not one to complain about the direction
you're headed," she said, "but shouldn't we finish you off
first?"

He tilted his head up to smile at her. "We'll get there.
Hang on to the counter while I get your sandals off."

She held on to the counter and he slipped off her shoes,
then her pants and underwear.

He stood, and pulled her against him and kissed her, breathing in the taste and scent that was uniquely Megan. Something about her always drew him in, made him want and need her in ways that he couldn't explain. All he knew was whenever he was around her, he wanted her. He wanted to touch her and taste her and get lost inside of her.

He'd never wanted to be this close to a woman before, never had those kinds of cravings and needs with one woman. That set off alarm bells, but right now he was running his tongue along her throat and inching his fingers under her T-shirt to tease her breasts through her bra, so he ignored the warning bells. This was way too much fun to be worried about emotion and entanglement. He'd think about all that serious shit later.

He lifted her top and tossed it somewhere across the room, then undid her bra so he could put his mouth on her nipples.

"Even here you taste sweet," he murmured, capturing a nipple between his lips.

He was rewarded with something that sounded like a sigh and whimper, which made his cock go even harder. He popped the nipple out of his mouth and went to work on the other, teasing and flicking his tongue around the soft bud until Megan's moans got louder. Then he drifted south, kneeling down to spread her legs and put his mouth on her sweet sex.

"Brady."

His name escaped her lips like a tortured whisper, and he had to admit he really liked the way she said it. He wanted to give her an epic orgasm, the kind that would make her scream his name instead of whisper it out.

He moved his tongue and lips over her, trying to find the right spot that would give her what she needed. When she moaned and thrust against him, he gave her more. And when she cried out, he held on to her hips and let her ride it out until she grew lax against him.

He stood and she tangled her fingers in his hair, drawing him down for a passionate kiss that fired him up hotter and faster than a supercharged Harley. He turned her around and grabbed the condom he'd shoved in the pocket of his discarded jeans. He kicked her legs apart and slid into her, her sex still quaking from her orgasm.

He leaned over and kissed the back of her neck. "I've been thinking about being inside of you every damn night. It keeps me awake at night. Hot, sweating, and hard all damn night long."

"Yes," she said. "I've wanted you, too. Every night."

He reached for her hands, twining his fingers with hers. He plunged them into the dishwater in the sink, the two of them tangled together as he drove into her with hard, fast thrusts, spurred on by the sounds she made as he moved against her.

"I can't stop thinking about you." He shifted, easing out, only to slide back in and still.

"Brady."

"Yeah."

"Move."

His lips lifted. "Where to?"

She squeezed his fingers. "You know where to."

He removed one hand and slipped it across her sex, finding her clit. "Here?"

She laid her head against his chest. "Oh, yes. Definitely there."

He moved then, using his slippery wet hand along with his cock to take her right to the edge. And when she tightened around him, he went faster, giving her the friction she needed to come.

And then he went with her, unable to hold back as she cried out with her orgasm, rocking back against him as she lost control.

It was the best damn orgasm he'd ever had. Hell, he felt light-headed.

He withdrew and they went into her bathroom to clean up.

She leaned against the bathroom counter. "You know, I'm never going to be able to stand at my sink and do the dishes ever again without thinking of sex."

He laughed. "That's not a bad thing, is it?"

"No. Not a bad thing at all."

He pulled her against him. "As long as it's me you're thinking about having sex with, I'd say it's a very good thing."

She hooked her leg around his hip. "Oh, trust me, it's all you."

That's all he needed to hear. He kissed her, intending for a light, easy, after-sex kiss. But it turned more passionate, and suddenly they were on the bed getting hot and tangled together all over again.

It was an hour later before they had cheesecake.

Chapter 22

IF THERE WAS one thing Megan knew about Chelsea, it was that she loved being the center of attention. So when they held her wedding shower that Saturday afternoon at the McCormack ranch, Chelsea ate it all up.

She didn't even seem to mind that the wedding prep was being handled with such a rush. In fact, she seemed happy about it.

As she sat and drank juice in the dining room with the girls, she seemed more relaxed than Megan had seen her in a while. Megan had actually expected Chelsea to be panicked—and have one of her typical lists. But that wasn't the case. She almost seemed serene, which was definitely not the usual Chelsea.

"I've turned over a new leaf," Chelsea said as they sat with Emma, Jane, Des, Sam, and Molly. "Now that I'm pregnant and we've decided to get the wedding over with, I'm actually kind of . . . relieved. Is that bad?"

Emma laughed. "It's not bad at all. Wedding planning

can be stressful. Getting the wedding out of the way means you can enjoy planning for the baby."

Chelsea nodded. "It probably helps that Bash didn't mind at all that we weren't going to have a huge blowout of a wedding. Just immediate family and friends, and then it's on to normal life." When everyone looked at her, she added, "Okay, fine, as normal as Bash and I get, anyway. Plus we were lucky to find an available church and a venue for the reception on such short notice."

"Don't forget to tell them about the dress," Jane said.

"Oh, that's right. I found a dress."

Sam's eyes widened. "You did?"

"I did. Also, it fits me perfectly. I'm not showing yet, so I don't have the baby belly issue to worry about. Jane went with me to the store since she's my matron of honor, and we found a dress for her as well."

Jane beamed a smile. "It's like fate has smiled down on you. Everything is as it should be. And in a week, you'll have your wedding and you can settle in and wait for your awesome baby to arrive."

"This is true."

"You've been to the doctor?" Des asked.

Chelsea nodded. "Got the pregnancy confirmed by the OB, all official-like. He gave me an exam and told me I was ridiculously healthy and everything should be fine. "

"When are you due?" Emma asked.

Chelsea gave them all a serene smile. "Mid-December."

"Aww," Molly said. "If you're late, you could have a Christmas baby."

"Or, if you're early," Jane said, "a Thanksgiving baby."

Chelsea laughed. "Either way, I'm happy. Like, obscenely happy. So is Bash. We're kind of disgusting right now."

"You are not disgusting," Jane said. "You're happy."

"And what about you, Jane?" Des asked. "Still having baby yearnings now that Chelsea is all pregnant and confirmed?"

Jane beamed a smile. "I've talked to Will. He's totally on board the baby-making train."

Emma's eyes widened and she placed her glass of iced tea on the table. "So you're going to try to get pregnant?"

"As we speak. I mean, not at this very moment or anything, but yes, we'd like to have a baby, so we're having sex all the time. Which, I have to tell you, is a lot of fun. And not easy to do when you have a husband who works strange hours and two kids who want a lot of attention when he's home."

Molly laughed. "Try showering together. Or make a rule about the kids not interrupting you when you're in the bedroom together with the door closed."

"We already have that rule. Unless someone is throwing up or bleeding, no one is allowed to come into the bedroom."

Des's lips curved. "I'm going to have to remember that rule for when Benjamin is older."

"But nightmares can totally usurp that rule, right?" Emma asked. "I can't imagine little ones having nightmares wouldn't trump the closed-door rule."

"And thunderstorms," Molly added. "I always hated those and would crawl into my parents' bed."

"Or mine," Emma said.

Molly laughed. "That's true."

Jane nodded. "Of course. Frightened children can always come into the bedroom."

"I should have brought my notebook," Chelsea said. "I'm going to have to start making lists."

Megan laughed. "You and your lists. Your little one is still cooking in your belly and you need lists already?"

Chelsea gave Megan a look of surprise. "It's like you don't even know me."

Megan laughed. "Okay, fine. List away. But you're not stressed right now, are you? I mean about the wedding?"

"Shockingly, not at all. With all of you helping out, and the incredible help that Des's Hollywood crew has provided, it's been amazingly stress-free. Thank you all so much. I couldn't have done this all so quickly without you."

Megan smiled at her. "Hey, that's what friends are for. And I'm going to make you a killer cake."

"And I'll give you the most beautiful flowers you could ever imagine," Sam said.

"Which is why I'm not stressed at all."

They ate wonderful food that Martha cooked, and Megan had made a sheet cake, along with a triple-decker chocolate and caramel cake that everyone pronounced delicious.

"How am I supposed to fit into my wedding dress if I keep eating stuff like this?" Chelsea asked as she slipped her fork into another slice. "I'm lucky that I haven't suffered any nausea with this pregnancy so far. All I want to do is eat."

Megan laughed. "Enjoy the cake, Chelsea."

"I intend to. But only one skinny slice. I mentioned my wedding dress fit perfectly, didn't I?"

"You did."

"I have to make sure it stays that way."

"I don't think one small slice of cake will make a difference."

She slid a bite between her lips, then moaned. "You never know. This baby could decide to make my belly pop out at any moment."

Megan laughed.

Chelsea had insisted on no gifts, since she and Bash already had their house and it was fully stocked, but all the girls got together and bought her a gift certificate for one of the spas in Tulsa so she could have a nice relaxing day before the wedding.

She teared up when she opened the envelope. "Oh, this is perfect. Thank you all so much. I'm really going to enjoy it. I'm going to have a massage and a facial and a mani-pedi and I'm going to knock Bash on his ass when he sees me."

Megan laughed. "I think you already do that every day."

"This is true. But I'll be even more alluring on my wedding day."

"You know we're all just as excited about the wedding as you are," Des said, cuddling baby Ben to her chest. "And I've got a babysitter, so Logan and I will get a night out."

"Same here," Emma said, looking over at the vibrating rocker where baby Michael lay sleeping. "It'll be a fun night."

"Of course it will," Chelsea said. "We're going to party that night. I won't be drinking, but we're all going to party."

Megan went into the kitchen to refresh her glass of sangria. Sam followed.

"Will you and Brady be going to the wedding together?" Sam asked.

Megan turned and leaned against the counter. "I actually hadn't given it much thought."

"In other words, you haven't talked to him about the wedding."

She took a sip of her sangria, which was delicious. "No, I haven't."

"So ask him. The two of you have been spending a lot of time together, right?"

"We have." She smiled just thinking about the other night.

"I'm sure he'd love to come to the wedding."

"I don't know about that. Big parties aren't really his thing."

Sam shot her a look. "And you know this how?"

Megan shrugged. "Okay, I don't know that it's not his thing. I'm totally guessing."

"Even if that's true, *you* are his thing. So ask him to be your date for the wedding."

"You're a very pushy friend, you know."

Sam laughed. "That's why you love me."

"True. Fine, I'll ask him."

It was Saturday, so she had no idea where Brady was. After the party she texted him but got no answer, so she took care of some housecleaning business that usually got left undone because she was typically busy doing other things—like baking.

It was an hour later by the time she realized Brady had texted her back and told her he was at the shop painting, but she should stop by.

She took a chance and decided to drive by the auto shop. When she saw the front was locked up tight, she drove around to the back of the shop. The garage door was open, so she figured Brady must still be working. She parked alongside the back wall and got out.

Brady was inside, painting a bike. Fascinated, she stayed quiet as she approached since she'd never watched him paint before. This wasn't like body paint. He was working a design on the tank of a beautiful cherry red bike. It looked like he was painting barbed wire onto the fender. He was leaning close, and the design was meticulous and oh-so-detailed.

She didn't want to disturb him and cause him to make a mistake.

"I know you're back there."

Obviously he was more aware than she knew. "I'm sorry. I didn't want to cause you to flinch."

"Roxie gave you away."

She hadn't even noticed Roxie on her pile of blankets in the corner of the shop. She was standing and wagging her tail.

"Oh, I see her now. Hey, Roxie."

He stopped, leaned back, and set down the paint he was using. He stood and stretched his back, then grabbed a rag to wipe his hands. "It's okay. I needed a break anyway."

When he stepped away, she got a full look at the work he'd been doing. It was more than barbed wire. It had a purple demon encased within it, and the details were breathtaking.

"Wow," she said. "You painted that?"

He looked down at it. "Yeah."

"That's . . ." She dragged her gaze away from the bike's tank and onto Brady. "It's amazing."

"Thanks."

"How do you do it? I mean, I don't see a stencil. You freehand that?"

He nodded.

She shook her head. "It's incredible, Brady. I don't know how people aren't lined up down the block to have you paint their bikes."

He laughed. "Well, thanks for that compliment. Maybe you should do my PR for me."

"I'm serious. This is kind of mind-blowing."

"It's okay. It's not done yet."

She couldn't believe he was being so matter-of-fact about it. "It's more than okay. It's a work of art."

He gave her a short laugh. "Hardly. It's just paint, Megan."

"How can you downplay something like this? I think it's magnificent. The level of detail, even down to the eyes." She leaned over to get a closer look, and suddenly Brady was behind her, his hand scooping up her hair.

"I don't think you want your hair in the wet paint."

She straightened immediately. "Oh. I'm so sorry. The last thing I want is to mess up that awesome paint job."

"I was more worried about you getting paint in your hair."

He *would* be more concerned about her. "Well, thank you for that. I'm sure whoever is getting this bike is going to love it. I would, if I rode one."

"You could, you know."

"Ride a bike? I don't think so."

He cocked his head to the side. "Why not?"

"I . . . I don't know. I guess it's never something I considered."

"Anyone can ride a bike, Megan. All it takes is desire."

"I suppose you're right. Maybe if I had a gorgeously

painted bike like that, I'd want to take it out and show it off."

He laughed. "There you go. If you ever decide you want a bike, I'll paint it for you."

She pulled her gaze away from the bike and onto him. "You will, huh? What if I want cakes and muffins on it?"

"If that's what you want, I'll do it."

"Really? I can't see you painting cakes and muffins on a Harley."

He shrugged. "You'd be surprised what I've painted on motorcycles before."

He headed to the back of the garage to release Roxie's leash from where he had her tethered.

"She needs a break, too. Wanna walk with us?"

"Sure."

He shut the garage door, and she followed him as he led the dog.

As they walked, she thought about what he'd said. "Okay, now I'm curious. What kinds of things have you painted on bikes?"

"One guy wanted a casket on the gas tank, flowers inside of it. Another asked me to do pink flowers all over the tank and fenders. One woman wanted all makeup thingies on hers—like lipstick and makeup cases. A guy wanted a picture of his mom. Oh yeah, and there was the one I did with worms."

She grimaced. "Worms?"

He laughed. "Yeah. Bloody worms. Some cut up, some whole. It was pretty gruesome, but it actually turned out awesome. I have photos of all the bikes I've done. Some are on my phone, but others are in photo books."

"I definitely want to see."

After they walked Roxie to the park and back, he took her upstairs, where Roxie got a drink of water and settled in on her dog bed with her chicken.

"You want something to drink?" Brady asked.

"I'd take a glass of water."

He filled two glasses with ice water and brought them

over to the sofa, where Megan had kicked off her shoes and pulled her legs under her.

Brady sat and handed Megan a glass.

"Thanks." She took a sip, then set the glass on the coffee table.

"What did you do today?" he asked.

"I went to Chelsea's wedding shower out at the McCormack ranch."

He nodded. "I heard about the shotgun wedding."

She laughed and nudged him. "It is not a shotgun wedding."

"Okay, so it's a she's-knocked-up-and-they're-doing-it-in-a-hurry kind of wedding."

"No, it's more like they want to get the wedding part over with since they found out she's pregnant. But it's not like Bash is in any way reluctant."

"That's true. He's pretty happy about becoming a dad."

"He told you that?"

"Yeah. The other night after basketball, when we all went out to eat. He seems pretty excited."

"They're both happy. It wasn't the way they planned it, but, you know, sometimes things happen that you don't expect."

He took a long swallow of water and set it down on the table. "Yup."

"Speaking of the wedding, that's actually why I came over."

He arched a brow. "You're not planning to propose or anything, are you?"

"Hardly."

"Oh, now I'm offended."

She snickered and grabbed his forearm, loving the solid warmth of his skin. "No, I wanted to ask if you'd be my date for Chelsea and Bash's wedding next Saturday night."

"Oh. Sure."

Well, that was easy. "Great."

"You know, you didn't have to come all the way over here to ask me that. You could have texted or called me."

"I could have, but then I wouldn't have seen that amazing bike you painted. And speaking of, how about some pictures?"

"Oh, right." He dug into his pocket, pulled out his phone, and scrolled through it. "Here are a few I've done recently."

She looked in awe at all the photos, including the ones he'd described to her when they were on a walk earlier. But there were more, incredibly beautiful photos of other bikes he'd done. They were all magnificent, exceptionally striking, and detailed paint jobs he'd performed.

She looked up at him. "You are very good at this. You must really love what you do."

His lips ticked up. "Thanks. It's something I've enjoyed doing for a long time. I'd like to think I've gotten better at it over the years."

"I'd say you have. Truly, Brady, you're an artist."

"Nah." He shoved his phone in his pocket. "Kurt was the artist. If you think what I do is good, you should see some of the work he used to do. I actually kept some of his drawings."

"Show me."

He tilted his head. "You don't really want to see those, do you?"

"Of course I do."

"Okay." He got up and disappeared downstairs. She sipped her water and looked over at Roxie, who was sound asleep on her bed.

Brady came up a short time later with a box.

"Just a few things," he said. "My parents have more of his stuff, but there were a few of his things I wanted to keep for myself."

He took the lid off the box and pulled out a sketchbook. "Kurt was always drawing things. Before he fell into drugs, when he was clearheaded, he was great at it."

He flipped through the sketchbook and passed it to her.

"He had a vivid imagination for fantasy. Like this dragon here. He did this in high school, and ended up painting it on someone's bike years later."

Megan studied the sketch. "Wow. The level of detail here is amazing for someone so young." She flipped through the pages. "These are all really good."

"There's more." He handed her book after book. "These are some he did later, when he and I started talking about painting bikes."

She could see the vision on the pages. "They're so striking. I love the skulls and the demons. Kind of scary beautiful."

"Right? You should have seen the rendering of that dragon on the bike. The scales were a deep green with gray undertones. He had such an eye for detail."

She lifted her gaze to his. "So do you."

He shook his head. "I could never be as good as Kurt was."

"I beg to differ." She handed the pages back to him. "You're just as talented as your brother was. It's clear you were both artists. You have a very special talent, Brady. Have you ever thought of doing a painting that isn't on a bike?"

He laid the sketch pad on top of the others, then put the lid on the box. "You mean like on canvas? No. I'm not that kind of artist."

"But you could be. What you do is art, just in a different form. You could experiment with different mediums."

"Expressing myself on motorcycles is where I do my best work."

She laid her hand on his thigh. "I understand that. I just thought maybe you might want to consider painting on canvas. Or even sketching, like Kurt did."

He frowned. "That was Kurt's thing, not mine. My imagination doesn't work that way."

"Okay." She could tell she'd touched a nerve, and the last thing she wanted to do was upset him. Brady was so sensitive and raw whenever the topic of his brother came up. She knew to tread lightly, even though at some point she'd love to be able to have a real, honest conversation with him about his brother.

She knew the pain inside of him was still a living, breathing thing that continued to hover around him. She wanted so badly to help him eradicate it. But until he was ready to face it and let it go, there wasn't much she could do.

But when he *was* ready, she intended to be the one who was going to hold his hand and help him exorcise those painful ghosts.

As if he wanted more than anything to erase that tense moment, he smiled at her. "I don't know about you, but I'm hungry. You wanna to grab something to eat and then hang out and watch a movie?"

She was more than grateful to let the moment go as well. So she smiled and nodded. "Sounds like a good plan to me. If you want to come over to my place, I baked some salted caramel muffins we could have for dessert."

"How's a guy supposed to say no to an invitation like that?"

"You're not. That's the idea."

When she stood, he slipped an arm around her waist and tugged her close.

"I'm glad you stopped by."

"I'm afraid I interrupted your painting momentum."

He grinned, then brushed his lips across hers, making her forget all about ghosts to exorcise and her worry about his anxious state.

"I'll get back to painting the bike tomorrow. You're a good distraction, and now my mind is on other things. Like cheeseburgers, a good movie, and sex. Followed by muffins."

Her lips curved. "All good ideas, Brady Conners. Except maybe substitute the cheeseburgers with Chinese food."

"Uh-huh. Obviously we'll discuss it on the way to get the cheeseburgers."

She laughed as she went to grab Roxie's leash. "Don't forget who wields the muffins."

He stood at the door. "I'm not going to win this one, am I?"

She picked up Roxie and scratched her behind the ear. "Not this time."

"Damn. Chinese food it is."

Chapter 23

BRADY FINISHED PUTTING the bike together just in time for his client to pick it up Saturday afternoon.

It had turned out pretty damn good, with a bright orange base, screaming yellow demons, and red flames.

"It's just like I described it to you," Randy said, walking around the bike. "It's perfect. More than perfect. You exceeded my expectations, Brady."

"Glad you like it."

Randy paid him, exclaimed about the bike for another twenty minutes, and told him he had at least three guys to refer to him, which made Brady happy, since referral business was important.

He should really think about having business cards made, but Randy had his number, so that worked as well. At some point, once he had his own shop and could launch his business, he'd have all that fancy shit. For now, this would do. He had more than enough work to keep him busy doing the bodywork during the week and the extra custom paint jobs on the nights and weekends. He was banking more money than he had thought he would, getting him closer and closer to his goal of being able to open his own shop.

Actually, he had enough money now, but he wanted to bank extra for those just-in-case situations that would crop up once he opened his shop.

He was patient. He could wait a while longer. Besides, he wasn't yet sure where he wanted to put his shop. Did he want to settle in Hope, or maybe some other town in another state? He didn't have answers to those questions yet, and until he did, he was fine staying right here.

Next on his agenda was taking Roxie out for a nice long walk and a play in the park. Once he had her suitably exhausted, they went upstairs and he took a shower to get ready for the wedding.

He'd had a lot of evening work this past week, and that had kept him away from Megan, but they'd managed to eke out a couple of hours here and there together. She'd brought over dinner one night and they'd camped out in the office with sandwiches. She'd also brought him a cinnamon roll on a couple of mornings, along with coffee.

But they hadn't carved out nearly enough alone time. He intended to rectify that tonight.

He got dressed. Oh, man, he hated wearing a suit, but it was a necessary evil for the wedding.

He packed up all of Roxie's things, because Megan had suggested Roxie stay over at her place tonight while they were at the wedding. It made sense to him, so he grabbed her chicken, her blanket, and some of her food.

Sometimes, having a dog was like being a parent. It was a lot of responsibility, but he couldn't imagine not having her in his life. He was so glad no one had ever claimed her. Some moron's loss had been his gain. Roxie was his dog now, and no one was going to take her away from him.

She looked at him as he straightened his tie in the mirror.

"How do I look, Rox?" he asked.

She cocked her head to the side, her ears perking up.

He grinned down at her. "Yeah, I thought so, too. Pretty fucking awesome."

He loaded Roxie in the truck, then drove over to Megan's house and went to the door.

Megan answered wearing a robe.

"Wow. I mean wow. You look amazing," she said as she looked him up and down.

"Thanks."

"And I'm sorry, I'm not quite ready yet. Come on in and make yourself comfortable. I'll only be a few more minutes."

"Okay."

He got Roxie and all her things situated, then took a seat at Megan's kitchen island.

She had some kind of tower of cream puffs sitting on a plate in the center of the island. He was tempted to take one, but they were covered in powdered sugar, and he was wearing a dark suit. The combination could be disastrous, so he'd better not. But later, after he got out of this suit? One of those cream puffs had his name on it.

Deciding to avoid temptation, he got up and went into the living room, picked up the remote, and took a seat on the sofa. He turned on the TV and surfed until he found the sports channel. There was a baseball game on. The St. Louis team was playing. Roxie, who'd mastered the art of jumping on his sofa, decided to join him. He waited, giving her a minute to navigate the height of Megan's sofa, but after assessing the situation, she leaped up beside him with ease.

"Atta girl," he said. "I knew you could do it."

She settled in next to his side and they watched the game together.

Okay, she went to sleep while he watched the game.

St. Louis had the bases loaded with one out in the fourth inning when Megan came out.

"Okay, I'm ready."

He really wanted to see this inning play out, but then he turned his head and saw Megan, and he forgot all about baseball.

He stood and went over to her. She wore a copper-colored dress with tiny straps at her shoulders. The dress

hugged every one of her curves all the way down to just
below her thighs, making him want to scope out her curves
with his hands.

He swept his hands down her arms. "You are beautiful."

"Thank you. I'm sorry it took me so long to get ready."

"You're worth the wait. I mean, come on. Look at
you."

He caught the blush of her cheeks. Cute.

"Well, thanks. And look at you. You clean up well."

"I'm going to admit that I hate wearing suits."

She pressed her palms against his jacket. "It doesn't
show. It's like you were born to wear them. And I like this
tie. It's very colorful."

"Thanks. I had to go buy a new one just for the wedding. I couldn't find the other one I had."

She cocked her head to the side. "Just one?"

His lips curved. "I don't have much need for dress-up
clothes, so yeah, just one."

"You chose well," she said, sliding her hand down his
tie. "Let's go watch our friends get married."

They drove to the church, and Brady filled her in on
his day.

"So was the guy happy about his bike?" she asked.

"Yeah. He seemed really pleased with the work. I'm
finishing up the demon and barbed-wire one this week."

"I can't wait to see how it turns out."

They arrived at the church and parked.

"Chelsea said they were lucky to get the church on such
short notice, but someone cancelled at the last minute, so
the reverend was able to accommodate them."

"I guess lucky for Chelsea and Bash, and maybe
unlucky for whoever decided to cancel their wedding?"
Brady said.

"This is true."

They went inside, and Brady had to admit, it looked
beautiful. Flowers were set up at the altar and alongside
the pews. He couldn't name them, but they looked pretty.

They found a spot up near the front and took a seat next to Sam and Reid.

It wasn't long before the church was crowded with people and music started playing.

The reverend came out to stand in front of the congregation. Then Bash came out, with Carter standing next to him.

Megan took his hand as Jane walked past their pew, and everyone stood when Chelsea made her way down the aisle.

Megan squeezed back tears as she watched her friend make her way to the front of the church. Chelsea looked beautiful in her simple beige lace and silk dress. Then again, when didn't Chelsea look stunning? Her hair was swept up into an intricate design, and the bouquet Sam had designed for her was lovely.

The way Chelsea and Bash looked at each other was as if there were no other people in the church.

As it should be.

Megan sighed as she took her seat.

The reverend made the ceremony simple, talking about commitment and values and cherishing one another, and always being willing to communicate. Megan skirted a glance at Brady, who seemed to be listening hard to the reverend.

Then Chelsea and Bash said their vows, and before she knew it, her two friends were married and sharing one very sweet kiss before everyone, who clapped for them.

They made their way down the aisle as everyone cheered.

Megan looked over at Brady. "Wasn't that wonderful?"

He nodded. "Not too bad. Over in a hurry, just the way a wedding ceremony should be."

She laughed. "Spoken like a true man."

They got in her car and drove the short distance to Hope Community Hall for the reception. She was glad they wouldn't have to drive far tonight.

"Not much on the outside," Brady said. "But they did a good job decking it out for the wedding."

"I've been to a wedding here before," Megan said after Brady helped her out of the car. "It's all about the decorations. And when I delivered the cake earlier today, the décor looked amazing. Sam did such an amazing job with the flowers and the team who did the tables really worked hard to make it look elegant and inviting. Des brought in a couple who do set design in Hollywood, and wow, did they do incredible work. I think everything came together perfectly in such a short period of time."

"It probably helps that Chelsea has such talented friends."

She smiled over at him. "We loved helping." They all had, from Molly and her mother, Georgia, to several of Chelsea and Jane's teacher friends. It had been a labor of love to put this together in record time.

She hoped Chelsea was pleased with the result.

He held his arm for her and she walked with him to find their table. They were sitting with Sam and Reid, and Molly and Carter, along with Deacon Fox and Zach Powers.

It should be a fun table.

Megan excused herself to go check on the cake. She'd left it in the hands of the community center employees, who assured her they'd set it up in the right place, but since she'd spent the better part of yesterday baking and frosting all the layers and setting every flower in perfect position, the last thing she wanted was for something to have happened to it.

She found it in its rightful position on its own table, looking breathtakingly beautiful—and she didn't mind at all being so proud of it. It was four layers of creamy buttercream frosting and vanilla cake with vanilla cream layers. Very traditional, but it's what Chelsea had asked for, and Megan had happily smiled her way through creating it. She also put peach and yellow roses on it, and she really hoped Chelsea and Bash liked it.

Of course, it was dessert, so Bash, being a man, would like it. Appearance-wise, it was Chelsea she had to please.

When a set of arms went around her waist, she knew it was Brady, especially when he said, "So, when's dessert?"

She laughed and laid her head against his chest. "After dinner."

"Cake looks amazing. I know it'll kick ass."

"Of course it will."

Once the wedding party got there, everything swung into action. Dinner was served, and it was spectacular. They ate roast beef and chicken and pasta and three different kinds of salad. There was wine and champagne, and Megan had so much fun chatting with everyone at their table. Of course, she'd known all these people for years, except for Zach, who was new to the Hope area, so they all spent some time talking to him.

"How has your first year been teaching at Hope High, Zach?" Megan asked him.

"Good. I've settled in. The kids here are all great, administration is good to work with, and the football team is shaping up."

"I've caught a few games," Deacon said. "Looks like you're whipping them into shape."

Zach nodded. "Working on it. I think we've got a chance to make state, if not this year, then next. We might be a small district, but that doesn't mean we won't fight hard."

"That's the kind of dedication Hope High needs," Carter said. "You can take them there."

"Obviously I'm going to have to catch a game," Megan said. "I haven't been to one since high school."

"Yeah, you should all come," Zach said. "The more alumni who show up, the more people who are there to root these kids on. I'm surprised Jane and Chelsea don't badger you about it, since they teach at the high school."

"I'm surprised, too. Chelsea especially is good at badgering."

"Badgering about what?"

They looked up to see the beautiful bride standing at their table.

Megan grabbed her hand. "Congratulations. You're gorgeous."

She beamed a smile. "Thank you. Now what am I badgering you about?"

"We're talking about the football team and how everyone should show up for games in the fall," Zach said.

"Oh, right. Well, football isn't really my thing, but I fully support Hope High's team, so Zach is right. You should all go to the games. *We* should all go. We could tailgate."

"A lot of the parents do that," Zach said. "It's fun."

"Clearly I'm missing out on a big social aspect of Hope's community," Molly said. "And a chance to do some marketing."

Carter, who had his arm around Molly, rolled his eyes. "My wife, always in work mode."

"Hey, somebody's gotta grow our business, buddy."

Carter leaned over and kissed Molly's cheek. "And you do it so well."

Megan got up and hugged Chelsea. "The wedding was beautiful. And so are you."

"Thank you. I feel like I'm floating on a cloud. I'm kind of shocked it all came together so perfectly."

"Of course it did. It was kismet. You two are meant to have good luck in your lives."

Chelsea rubbed her lower stomach. "I think this kid is going to bring us good luck. It was all about timing, and I guess the timing is right, you know?"

Megan nodded. "I do know. And I'm really happy for you."

Chelsea's eyes glittered. "Do not make me cry. I have like eight pounds of mascara on, and if it starts to run we're going to have a disaster on our hands."

"Okay. No crying for you. Did you see the cake?"

"I did. It's perfect and looks delicious. Thank you again."

"It was absolutely my pleasure to make it for you and Bash. Where is your husband, by the way?"

"I think he's having a cigar outside with some of the guys to celebrate being a married man. Or maybe a shot of tequila. One or the other. Quite possibly both. All I know is I'll be the one driving us home tonight."

Megan laughed. Then Chelsea got pulled away by Jane, who mumbled something about dancing, so Megan made her way back to her table. By then the music had started up, so they all watched Chelsea and Bash—who was inside now—dance together.

She was so happy for the two of them, and Chelsea really did look like she was floating on a cloud.

Once the bride and groom dance was over, the DJ told everyone to get up and dance. Megan turned to Brady.

"I'm going to get a refill on my wine. Do you want another beer?"

"I'm good right now. Thanks."

She headed over to the bar. While waiting in line, she turned to see Brady in deep conversation with Deacon and Zach. For some reason, that made her smile.

For someone who not too long ago kept mainly to himself above Carter and Molly's shop, Brady was coming out of his shell.

That was a good thing. A very good thing. And if he could break that cycle of being unsociable, then maybe there was hope for other things as well.

While Brady congregated with the guys, she found herself at a table with her core group of friends, along with Loretta, who had become a good friend of theirs as well.

"Where's your little girl tonight, Loretta?" Emma asked.

"She's with my parents, who will no doubt spoil her endlessly, feed her too much sugar, and let her stay up all night long. Which means I'll get her back tomorrow overtired and cranky."

Des laughed. "Grandparents' prerogative, I suppose."

"Sure. Which then will make me miserable. And Hazel, too."

"Of course."

Megan noticed Loretta's gaze shifting occasionally to where the guys were crowded by the bar. She didn't know a whole lot about Loretta and Deacon, other than that they were high school sweethearts who had broken up not long after they graduated. And then Loretta had gotten married to some other guy and had moved to Texas until her divorce.

"So how are you and Deacon getting along now that you're back in town?" Chelsea asked.

Leave it to Chelsea to dig right in.

"Oh, we're fine, I guess. I don't really see him much other than the occasional run-in at the grocery store or through town."

"So it's not awkward between the two of you?" Emma asked.

Loretta gave a sigh. "Define *awkward*. I mean, we were together for four years in high school. We thought we'd end up together forever. Until we didn't. And it ended badly. So I'd say there's awkwardness."

"Maybe you both need some closure," Jane said.

"Maybe. Or maybe the opportunity for closure passed a long time ago. I don't think he even wants to speak to me anymore."

"Have you tried talking to him?" Megan asked.

"Not really. I mean, it's in the past. Why reopen old wounds?"

"So you can close them and move on," Molly said. "Trust me—I left a lingering hole in my relationship with Carter for years. And it festered for a long time with neither of us being able to move on. Which was fine when I was gone, but once I was back in Hope, our past needed to be addressed."

"And look at them now," Megan said with a smile.

Loretta looked horrified. "I just got out of a relationship. I'm not looking to start another one. Or reopen an old one."

Chelsea shrugged. "You never know what might happen until you and Deacon have an actual conversation. And no one's saying you're looking for anything, honey. Only that it might be time to bury the past and look toward your future."

Loretta's gaze drifted over toward Deacon again, and Megan could swear she saw a slight look of longing on Loretta's face. Then again, Megan wanted all her friends to be happy, so she might have imagined it.

"You might be right about that," Loretta said. "Putting

the past to bed once and for all is a good idea." She pulled her focus back on the women and smiled. "But not tonight. Tonight is a night of fun and partying and celebrating Chelsea and Bash."

Chelsea grinned. "Well, I'll drink to that. If I was drinking, which I'm not, except for sparkling water."

Megan lifted her glass of wine. "To Chelsea and Bash." They all toasted.

Chapter 24

BRADY HAD TO admit that weddings or any type of mass social event just weren't his thing.

But he was having a good time. The music was kicking it hard, the food had been great, and he was enjoying the company of people he now thought of as his friends.

All in all, not a bad night. Plus, he had a beautiful woman by his side. Or, at least, mostly by his side. Since Deacon and Zach had come solo, they took the opportunity to grab all the women and take them out onto the dance floor. Which meant Megan as well, who didn't seem to mind, since she'd told him she loved to dance.

Right now she was arms-up on the dance floor, swaying her hips to a hard, driving beat with Deacon. And as long as those guys knew to stay hands-off with her, he didn't mind her dancing with them, especially since dancing wasn't his thing.

But he did notice that every once in a while she'd look over at him and smile. So he knew her attention was on him. And that worked for him.

Sam plopped down in the chair next to his. "So why are other dudes dancing with your woman?"

"I'm not much of a dancer."

"Neither is Reid. Doesn't stop him from getting up there and shaking his groove thing with me. Or with anyone else. Look at him up there dancing with Des right now. He's a total doofus."

Brady searched the dance floor until he found Reid. Sam was right. Dude did not know how to dance. In fact, he kind of looked like he was having a stroke up there.

"Yeah, well, he's a braver man than I am, then."

"Uh-huh. And at some point Megan is going to have some random guy's hands all over her."

"Nah. I trust Deacon and Zach. And Megan."

"Sure you do. But she loves to dance. And I wasn't talking about Deacon or Zach or any of the guys we know and trust. I meant some random drunken dipshit who's not in our trust circle is going to notice she's alone and available and maybe not be so trustworthy." Sam patted his shoulder. "Food for thought, Brady."

"Yeah, thanks."

He studied Megan out on the dance floor. So far, nothing had happened. But maybe . . .

He finally got out of his seat where his butt had been warming the chair for the better part of an hour. He shed his suit jacket, loosened his tie, and made his way through the throng of dancers.

Deacon at least had some rhythm. He tapped him on the shoulder.

"Cutting in."

Deacon grinned and wiped the sweat from his brow. "Perfect timing. I need a beer and some air."

Deacon grabbed Megan's hand and pressed a kiss to the back of it. "Thanks for the dances, honey."

Megan grinned. "Anytime."

Brady stepped in front of her, and Megan arched a brow. "You sure you're up for this?"

"You sure your feet aren't sore yet?"

She wound her hand around the back of his neck. "I could do this all night."

"Okay, then, dancing queen. Let's do this."

He did his best to keep up, but the woman had moves, and he had four left feet. But Megan didn't seem to notice. She danced around him, nestled up next to him, and seemingly had a great time just being with him.

So maybe he'd just been an asshole and too self-conscious, because Megan apparently didn't care that he couldn't dance for shit. And when the music slowed to something romantic, he pulled her close.

Now this part he could do. He swept his hand down her rib cage and over her hip, letting his fingers rest just above her butt.

Megan tilted her head back to look up at him. "Taking liberties, Mr. Conners?"

"You bet your gorgeous ass I am, Ms. Lee."

"You know, I have had quite a bit of wine to drink, and while I've danced some of it off, it's entirely possible I might be slightly inebriated."

His lips curved. "Fortunately for you, I've only had a couple of beers, am stone-cold sober, and intend to take full advantage of your inebriated state. Once I make sure you get home safely."

"How gallant of you. In a fairly self-serving way, of course."

"Of course." He let his hand drift lower, and since the dance floor was crowded, no one noticed when his hand drifted over her butt and drew her closer to what was fast becoming a serious erection problem.

Her brow arched up. "Hmm, a preview for later?"

"You could say that."

"You have my full attention."

He decided it would probably be a good idea to give himself some distance from Megan's hot body before the dance ended, so he stepped back and made the dance a lot less intimate. By the time the music switched to something fast-paced, Megan said she was ready to cool off and get something to drink.

"More wine?" he asked after he walked her back to their table.

She shook her head. "I think I've had more than enough wine. Some sparkling water would be great."

"I'll be right back." He leaned down and brushed his lips over hers.

She tasted so good, and when she lifted up as if she wanted more, he thought about letting the kiss linger.

But now wasn't the time or the place, so he reluctantly created some distance between them.

But soon enough, this wedding would be over. He'd take her home and remove that damned enticing dress she wore, and then he'd have her naked and underneath him. Or over him. He didn't much care, as long as the two of them were alone and he was inside of her.

He filed that visual away for later.

Chapter 25

IT HAD BEEN a stellar night. Megan's friends had gotten married, she had been there to witness it, and she'd had one of the hottest dates there—in her opinion.

And best of all, the cake had turned out perfectly. Chelsea had raved about it and Bash had pronounced it delicious, and as long as the bride and groom loved it, she was happy.

Though she also noticed that Brady had eaten two pieces. She was beginning to suspect he had a demon sweet tooth, especially when he shrugged out of his suit coat when they got back to her place and immediately grabbed one of the pieces of croquembouche pastry and popped it into his mouth as he took Roxie out back.

She laughed, then kicked her shoes off and stepped into the kitchen to grab the open bottle of wine. She poured herself a glass and took a sip. When Brady came back in with Roxie, she asked him if he wanted a glass of wine or something else to drink.

"Just water for me. Thanks."

She poured water into the glass she'd filled with ice, then handed it to him.

"These things are good," he said, grabbing another pastry ball from the tower. "Also, it looks really hard to make. They're like cream puffs, right?"

"Sort of. And I'm glad you like them."

He swallowed, then took a sip of water. "I like everything you bake."

"That's quite a compliment to a baker."

"Just being honest."

She leaned against the counter and sipped her wine, unable to keep herself from staring at him. He'd loosened his tie and unbuttoned the top button of his shirt. He'd also rolled up the sleeves of his white shirt.

She was so used to seeing him in jeans and T-shirts. He was sexy enough in those. But in a white button-down shirt and a tie? The man was devastating.

And the way he looked at her, with that incredibly direct, I'm-going-to-eat-you-alive kind of smoldering gaze, made every female part of her quiver in anticipation.

"Something on your mind?" he asked.

"Several things, actually."

He swept his finger down the outside of the glass.

"Have I ever mentioned how much I like your hands?" she asked.

"Uh, no. But go on."

"You have elegant fingers. Still, extremely masculine. But the art you create with your hands is magical. And the things you can do to my body with those hands is also quite magical."

He laid the glass on the island and came around it. Despite the fact that this wasn't the first time they'd been alone together, she noted the way her heart rate sped up, the dizzying breathlessness that came over her whenever he got close to her. Brady had a way about him that simply wired her up and made her neurons fire hot for him.

Just him. It had never been hot and passionate and so incredibly sexual for her with anyone but Brady.

And yet, when he brushed her hair away from her face, there was also a tenderness, an emotional yearning that had a lot more to do with her heart and a lot less to do with her sexual cravings.

She was in so deep with this man that it was dizzying, overwhelming, intense. She felt like she was stepping too close to an extremely dangerous fire. And yet all she wanted to do was let it consume her, especially when his lips touched hers.

Like wildfire, an explosion of heat enveloped her in a passion that was out of control.

And suddenly, she couldn't get enough of his mouth, his tongue, the touch of his hand along her back. She leaned into Brady, raking her nails along his arms, moaning with her need to have him.

He crushed her to him and deepened the kiss. It was sweet torment, to feel this close to him, to have what she wanted, but it only served to ratchet up the blinding tension that made her crave that fulfillment she so desperately needed.

He kissed her jaw, then blazed a trail of hot kisses along her throat and toward her shoulder. When he drew the strap of her dress off her shoulder and nipped that area with his teeth, she felt dizzy with the effects of the spell he wove over her.

"I've thought about getting you out of this dress all night long," he murmured against her skin. "About what you might have on underneath it."

"Something special."

With a low growl, he swept her into his arms and carried her into the bedroom, then stood her next to the bed. He turned her around so he could draw the zipper down on her dress.

It pooled into a heap at her feet and Brady held her hands while she stepped out of it.

"Holy shit," he said.

When she'd bought the dress, she'd known none of her everyday underwear could go with it. The copper metallic dress needed something special, so she'd found dark copper–colored underwear, but it sure was barely there—it was just a demi bra and thong panties.

"Stand right there and don't move. I need to just . . . look at you for a few minutes."

Under normal circumstances she'd feel ridiculous standing there in her underwear modeling for him, but as he watched her, he began to unbutton his shirt. She had to admit, she didn't mind watching the reveal of his skin button by button.

She finally stepped up and undid the last few buttons herself. She had to get close to him, had to feel that blast of heat that always seemed to emanate from his skin. She breathed in the masculine scent of him, then spread her palms over his shoulders and drew the shirt down his arms.

"I might want you to wear my shirt later," he whispered, bending down to draw his tongue across her neck. "While I have you bent over the sofa."

She shivered at the visual. "I think we can arrange that."

He undid the buckle of his belt, then unzipped his pants and let those fall. His boxer briefs followed, and he was gloriously, beautifully nude.

"But for now," he said, pushing her back on the bed. "I need to worship this new underwear of yours."

She scooted to the center of the bed. "I'd rather you take it off."

"Yeah, we'll get there." He skimmed his fingers over the tiny scraps of lace at her hips. "You bought these to torture me, didn't you?"

"To please you. I thought you might like them."

He nipped at her hip bone, pulling the strap up with his teeth before letting it fall back in place. "Oh, I like them."

He made his way up her body, sliding his tongue around her belly button, then kissing her rib cage and shoulders before teasing the swell of her breasts with his tongue. He put his mouth around her nipple, silk fabric and all, and sucked—hard.

She let out a yelp of pure unadulterated pleasure as he

kept sucking her nipple until she thought she might have an actual orgasm from him doing that.

And when he stopped, he teased the bud with his fingers while she fought to catch her breath—and her sanity.

He pulled the cup back. "Such a flimsy little piece of fabric. If I'd known you were wearing these while we were at the wedding, I'd have taken you outside, lifted your dress, and had you right on the balcony."

Her sex quivered. "I'd have enjoyed that."

His brows arched. "Filing that piece of information away for some other time."

She was aching for him, and as she swept her hand across his jaw, he took one of her fingers in his mouth and sucked. She quaked, inside and out.

"Brady."

"Yeah."

"I need you."

"What do you need? My mouth on you like this?" He bent and dragged his tongue across her nipple, then drew it into his mouth, slowly sucking on her until she whimpered.

He dropped down beside her, letting his fingers map a trail from between her breasts over her stomach. "Or do you need my hands on you, like this?"

He slipped his hand inside her underwear to cup her sex.

"You're so hot and wet down here. Do you need me to make you come, Megan?"

"Yes." She needed that more than anything. She was so in tune to him, to the way his hand moved over her, the sound of his voice, that this wasn't going to take long. Like, probably in an embarrassing way, she'd go off in a matter of seconds.

And as she suspected, he'd no more than brushed his hand over her a few times, using his expert fingers to find her clit and rub it as if he'd known her hot button like a best friend, and she was going over the top with a wild cry. She quivered against him while he murmured hot and sexy words against her ear, prolonging the exquisite pleasure.

While she was recovering from that blast of euphoria, Brady pulled off her bra and panties, licking her breasts and her sex, making her feel warm and languid and ready for more.

He kissed her, and she rolled over on top of him, needing him to feel that same passion he coaxed out of her every single time.

She leaned over on the nightstand and grabbed a condom. "Ready for a ride?"

His lips ticked up. "Saddle me up, babe, and let's go."

She put the condom on him, and then slid down on his shaft, her nerve endings still on fire after that amazing orgasm he'd given her. Her sex gripped him tightly and she took a few seconds to enjoy the feel of that, watching Brady's eyes darken.

"Yeah. I like that, too," he said, sweeping his hands over her thighs.

She rocked forward, an explosion of sweet sensation threatening to make her topple into yet another climax.

She stilled, waiting. This time she'd make him come with her. She leaned forward, lifting off him just enough to tease him a little before sliding back down on him again.

He tangled his fingers in her hair and brought her forward for a blistering-hot kiss that sent her tumbling over the edge. She moaned against his lips as she came, firing even hotter and faster with her climax as she took in his answering groans. She held on to his shoulders as he thrust into her and released, shuddering against her.

She settled against his shoulder, coming down off that incredible high while listening to the sound of his breathing. She could stay like this all night, just lying on top of him, letting his hands tenderly roam over her back.

They finally disengaged and cleaned up. Brady went to check on Roxie, while Megan got water for both of them.

"Is she okay?"

"Sound asleep on her blanket. With her chicken under her chin."

Megan handed him a glass of water. He took two long gulps, then set the glass on the coaster on the nightstand.

He pulled her against him and Megan settled in next to him.

"Don't forget about round two in my shirt."

"Trust me—I haven't forgotten about it."

They both fell asleep before round two.

Chapter 26

BRADY WOKE UP to an empty bed. And it was still dark outside.

What the hell time was it, anyway? He reached over on the nightstand, but his phone wasn't there.

Oh, right. It was in his suit coat pocket, which was somewhere in Megan's living room.

He went into the bathroom and, when he came out, grabbed a pair of jeans from the bag he'd brought over last night. He put on the jeans and made his way into the kitchen.

Now that wasn't something he expected to see at—he glanced up at the clock on the kitchen wall—six in the morning on a Sunday.

There was Megan, dressed in his white shirt from last night. It hung low on her thighs, and she had the sleeves rolled up past her elbows. And damn if she didn't look sexy as hell with her hair pulled high up on top of her head. Flour covered a wood cutting board, and she was humming to herself and rocking back and forth as she rolled some dough with a rolling pin.

Oh, she had earbuds in, and her miniplayer was clipped to the front of his shirt while she worked away.

He leaned against the doorway for a while to watch her. She rolled, sprinkled out more flour and rolled some more, then stirred something in a bowl.

Damn, the woman was hot, especially when she bent over to pull a pan out from one of the cabinets in the island.

He grinned. She had great legs and a really fine ass.

His dick got hard.

She stopped to take a sip of coffee, then went back to rocking out and rolling flour.

When she twirled, she stopped suddenly and pulled her earbuds out.

"I didn't see you standing there."

He pushed off the doorway and moved into the kitchen. "I was enjoying the show. Nice shirt."

She grinned. "I thought you might enjoy that."

"You know I do. And do you bake every damn day?"

"Pretty much."

He swiped flour from one of her cheeks with the pad of his thumb, then brushed his lips over hers. "It's early."

"I know. That's why I tried not to wake you."

"You didn't. But I'll take a cup of coffee now that I'm awake."

"Cups are in the cupboard to the left of the sink."

He pulled a cup down, then brewed himself a cup of coffee and came over to stand beside her.

"What are you fixing?"

"Apple turnovers. I thought those sounded good for breakfast. I'm going to do eggs and sausages, too. And I'll cut up some fruit."

His stomach grumbled. "You don't have to cook for me. Or bake for me."

She lifted up on her toes to kiss him. "But I want to. Plus, I'd bake even if you weren't here."

"Good to know. What can I do to help?"

"I'll cut the dough into triangles. You can spoon this stuff in the middle."

"Okay." He washed and dried his hands, then waited for Megan to cut the dough into triangles. Once she did, she walked him through how much to put into the center.

"Good," she said. "Not too much or I won't be able to close them, but not too little. We want them bursting with apple goodness."

He leaned into her. "You're making me hungry."

She lifted her gaze to his, then smiled. "That's the idea."

Once he finished, she put another triangle on the top of each one, then crimped the edges. She brushed the pastries with egg and put them in the oven. After she washed her hands she said, "Now, while those are cooking I can slice fruit and start cooking the sausages."

"I'll cook the sausages."

"All right."

They worked together, and he had to admit, this wasn't too bad. In the not so recent past he either didn't eat breakfast at all or had a piece of toast.

But lately, he waited until about ten or so and went to the bakery to get something Megan had baked.

She was spoiling him for really good bakery items.

As he monitored the sausages, the smell from the oven assaulted his senses—in a spectacular way.

"Those apple turnovers smell really damn fine, Megan."

She was slicing bananas to go into the fruit salad she was making. "They do, don't they?"

By the time he'd made eggs for them, she had poured juice and set the table, and the turnovers had come out of the oven looking crisp and golden. It was all he could do not to pounce on the plate when Megan took them into the dining room. Fortunately, Roxie had finally managed to drag herself off of her blanket, so he forced his attention away from the turnovers and took Roxie outside, then fixed a bowl of food for her and set it down in the kitchen.

"We're ready to eat," Megan said. "I assume you're hungry?"

"I assume you don't want any of those turnovers because they're all mine?"

She laughed. "Come on."

The first thing into his mouth was a warm, heaping bite of apple turnover, covered in butter.

"Oh, God," he said after he swallowed. "I don't know how men aren't beating down your door to marry you."

She lifted her fork to her lips, her eyes twinkling. "I admit, I've had a few proposals."

"Really?"

She nodded. "Mr. Springwater asked me out for coffee. I told him his wife wouldn't appreciate him seeing other women."

When Brady frowned, she gave him a tilt of her lips. "He's eighty. He said she wouldn't mind as long as he brought home one of my lemon cakes every time he and I had coffee together."

He laughed. "I see."

"Yes, and Timmy Caruthers asked me to marry him as well, but since he's only nine I told him he should wait until he's at least eighteen, then maybe ask me again."

Brady pointed his fork at her. "See? I told you. You're crazy popular."

"With the prepubescent and geriatric sets."

"I don't know about that. I think you're pretty popular with the thirty-year-old set, too. You've noticed me following you around, haven't you?"

"This is true. But I think you're just after my baked goods."

Brady leveled a hot stare at her. "I'm after your goods—that's for sure. The baked ones are just a bonus."

He saw the flush on her cheeks. Good. She needed to know he wanted her.

They finished breakfast and sat at the table for a while chatting and sipping coffee. Finally, they got up and piled the dishes in the sink.

"Those can wait," he said. "I have an idea that's been in my head since last night."

He took her hand and led her to the sofa.

"I'm pretty sure I dreamed about this last night. Woke up sweating. And hard."

He teased his fingers along the buttons of the shirt, tucking a finger between the buttons to feel her soft, silken skin and the fast beat of her heart against her breast.

Then he slipped the top button open and slid his hand inside to cup her breast. Her breath quickened, and his dick responded.

He brushed the crest of her nipple with his thumb.

"You're like butter here," he said, teasing her nipple. "Soft and supple, melting when you get hot."

She shuddered, her gaze riveted to his. "I melt a lot of places when you touch me."

His lips curved. "Yeah, I know. I've had my tongue on some of your melty spots."

He drifted lower, getting down on his knees. He raised the shirt, so damn happy to find she hadn't worn underwear this morning. He put his mouth on her, sweet and tart here. She spread her legs for him, giving him access to her.

He loved the way she moved against him, letting him know what gave her pleasure. And, man, he loved how she responded, the way she moaned and reached for his head and how she got lost when he put his tongue on her. There was nothing he liked more than a responsive woman, and Megan was that.

And when she came, she shuddered hard against him, so lost in her own pleasure she had a death grip on the back of the sofa when he rose up to take her mouth in a hot kiss. She slid her hand in his hair to hold tight to him, to twine her tongue with his, to let him know that she liked what he'd done and that she wanted more.

So did he.

He turned her around to face the sofa, pulling the shirt away so he could kiss the back of her neck. "You know what you are, Megan?"

"Mmm. What am I?"

"You're like the sweetest dessert." He gently nibbled on the back of her neck. "And no matter where I taste, it's like I can't wait for the next bite, the next lick of you. And when I have it, all I want is more."

She leaned her head back against his chest. "Take more."

He pulled out the condom he'd tucked into the pocket of his jeans, unzipped them and shoved them down, then pushed her over the back of the sofa and lifted her shirt. He spread her legs with his knee and eased inside of her, letting himself feel every inch as he slowly entered her.

Now it was his turn to shudder as her heat surrounded him, her body quivering around him as he began to move.

He reached around and undid another button, spreading the material aside so he could cup her breasts while he drove into her. And then he was lost in her, in the sensations and the sounds she made while the two of them were joined. It was all he could do to hold on, to keep from coming as she backed against him, pulling him deeper inside of her.

He gripped her hip and, using his other hand, bent her forward so he could drive deeper, giving them both what they needed. Then he slid his hand down to find her clit and take her over the edge again.

This time, when she cried out, he went with her, shuddering against her back as he rode out his orgasm.

Spent, he rested against her, feeling the warmth of her body and her deep breaths against his cheek.

He finally disengaged and dashed into the bathroom. Megan followed, then took his hand and led him back to bed.

"I work six days a week," she said. "And unless you have something to do today, I can't think of anything better than spending a couple more hours with you in my bed."

Even if he had a to-do list eight miles long, Megan inviting him into her bed would be at the top of that list.

"I've got nothin'," he said, climbing in next to her and watching as she undid the rest of the buttons on his shirt.

Chapter 27

IT WAS A hot and sunny Saturday afternoon. Brady and a bunch of guys were over at Reid and Sam's new house. At basketball earlier that week, Reid had mentioned he was falling behind on the construction, so everyone volunteered to help him pick up the pace. He told them he had it covered, but hell, no one had anything urgent to do on a Saturday, so why not?

The one thing Brady always enjoyed was being outside and doing things with his hands. And Reid had done so many things for so many people that when he stepped outside early Saturday morning, he found himself with a lot of company.

Reid's brothers Luke and Logan were there, along with Will, Carter, Bash, Zach, Deacon, and Brady, and about ten other guys from around town.

"Well, hell," Reid said, staring at all of them. "If I was a tearing-up kind of guy, I might just cry."

Sam was there, and she did get teary-eyed. She laid her hand on Reid's arm and looked out over the gathered crowd. "I'll do all the crying. And I made coffee and stopped for baked goods this morning from Megan's bakery. So help yourselves."

"Yeah, but don't help yourselves for too long," Reid said with a smile. "Now that I've got all these bodies, I'm putting your asses to work."

HVAC, plumbing, and electrical had all been set, along with framing, so at least that had been done. They spent the first half of the day putting up drywall and doing taping and mud in most of the rooms. Brady had worked on construction sites before, so he knew the drill. He'd brought his tool belt and his hammer and drill, so he went wherever Reid needed him.

Having such a large crew helped them check off a lot of items on the to-do list during the first half of the day.

They broke for lunch. Sam had gone for pizzas, so they all gathered in what was a dirt and gravel patch now but what would eventually be the backyard. They grabbed whatever folding chairs or coolers were available, and sat and ate.

"You have no idea how much this means to me that you're all here," Reid said as Brady sat across from him wolfing down his second slice of pepperoni.

"So you've mentioned about twenty times," Brady said. "You'd do the same for any of us, so you don't have to keep thanking us."

"Really," Carter said. "And someday Molly and I are going to work on that addition on our place, and we'll definitely be calling you."

"You know I'll be there for that. Or for anything any of you need."

"Keep making promises and you'll be in debt to these jokers for the next forty years," Sam said, nudging him with her elbow.

Brady laughed.

"Oh, speaking of," Reid said. "Brady, I don't know if you noticed it on the way over here, but there's a great spot of land for sale a few blocks to the south of us."

"Can't say I did."

"Would make a great place to build a house. And there's commercial property for sale only a mile or so east of that on the main road. I happened by it not too long back. It looks like it's a former auto shop. Space-wise, it seems perfect for what you need and it might be worth taking a look at for your future auto paint shop."

"Trying to steal away my best auto body guy, Reid?" Carter asked.

Reid shrugged. "Nope. But you know Brady had mentioned that he wanted to start up his own business someday."

"I did. But I don't know if I'm there yet."

Reid shrugged. "Sure. Just thought I'd mention it."

He actually had the money saved. He could lease property now and get started. Or he could do as Reid suggested and go take a look at the land. He had ideas for building his own place. Lots of ideas. He didn't know what was holding him back.

Because this was your and Kurt's dream, and Kurt's not here.

The thought was always in his head.

The problem was, Kurt was never going to go into business with him. Not now, not ever. And the sooner he got over it, the sooner he could open his own place, start working on and painting bikes, and follow his own dream.

Carter came over and sat next to him. "Hey, you know I was only kidding, right?"

Brady lifted his gaze to his boss and his friend. "Yeah, I know that."

"You know I'll never try to hold you back. I knew when I hired you that I'd only have you on a temporary basis. And while I think you're the best body guy I've ever had, the minute you want to get out there and start your own business, I'll happily recommend you to my customers."

Because that's who Carter was. Which was why Brady liked him so much. "Thanks. I appreciate that. I just don't know if I'm ready yet. Or where I'm going to start my business."

Carter frowned. "You'd stay in Hope though, right?"

Would he? "I don't know. I haven't thought that far ahead."

The thought of being here—where he and his brother had grown up, where they'd talked up all those dreams—caused an ache in his gut. The idea held promise, but it also hurt so damn bad every time he thought about it.

Reid mentioning the land where he could build a house wasn't something he had ever considered, though. He shifted, looking around at the exterior of the house where Reid and Sam were building their dream—their future.

He could have the same thing if he wanted to. A house. A family. A woman he could spend forever with. A business he'd dreamed of his whole life.

And he could have it all right here.

His brother would never have those things. But did that mean he couldn't?

Between going to Chelsea and Bash's wedding and then spending the day working on Reid and Samantha's house, he realized he'd made friends. He'd finally pulled himself out of his self-imposed isolation, and he'd developed some solid friendships.

There were couples in his life that he'd surrounded himself with who were happy and forging a future for themselves. But beyond that, he'd realized that lately he'd been happy, and that was something he hadn't allowed since Kurt had died.

He was digging in and making a life for himself here in Hope. Something Kurt could have had if he'd chosen the right path.

But Kurt hadn't chosen to walk that path.

Brady stood and dumped his paper plate in the trash, then took out a toothpick and slid it between his teeth.

These were some deep damn thoughts, and for the past couple of years since Kurt had died, he'd preferred not to think at all. It had been safer that way.

But now, as he stared at this great house with all these people around him who laughed and shared their lives and happiness with each other—with him—he realized he could build a life here.

With Megan.

As soon as the thought entered his head, he wanted it out of there.

Not yet. He wasn't ready for all this yet. He couldn't be. He might never be.

But just as he was about to push it all out of his head, Megan came through the doorway to the backyard.

Her smile was like a thousand watts of warmth, obliterating all that darkness mulling around in his head. There was never anything forced or fake about her. She always seemed so genuinely happy to see her friends.

She'd had it rough with her family, too, so she'd found a new family in these friendships she'd made. Yet she never seemed bitter about it. He didn't know how she managed it, but she always seemed happy. Content. She'd built an amazing life here in Hope.

"Hey, you loafers," she said. "I spent all morning at the bakery, thinking you were all out here in the heat sweating your butts off, only to find out you're kicking back and eating pizza?"

Sam laughed and went over to hug her. "There's plenty left."

"Great, because I'm starving. And also, I brought dessert for after the barbecue tonight."

Megan made eye contact with him and sent him that special smile that always seemed to hit him midway between his heart and his gut.

Yeah, there was more between them than just physical attraction. Sure, he always wanted her, but it was a lot more than just sex now. He wanted to talk to her, to be with her, to hold her hand and tell her about his day and hear about hers. He wanted to talk to her about what Reid had mentioned, to get her take on it and hear what she thought about it. There was no one else he wanted to talk to about it except Megan.

And that's when the realization hit him.

Shit. He was in love with her.

He wanted that house with the dog and the fence and the big backyard and the future and the happily-ever-after.

And he wanted it with Megan.

But he didn't *want* to want it with Megan.

He didn't want the commitment or the feelings or to fear the possibility of losing someone he cared about ever again. Because if you cared deeply about someone, they could hurt you. They could leave you.

He couldn't risk it.

And he didn't want to think about it anymore today.

So he grabbed his hammer and went back to work.

Chapter 28

MEGAN AND HER friends spent the remainder of the afternoon and evening moving around the house doing what
they could to help. A lot of that consisted of hauling trash
and sweeping, though she'd been given an opportunity to
do some sanding.

And now her shoulders ached like a million tiny needles
were poking them.

But at the end of the day, they'd made a ton of progress.
Walls were in place, and they had started to lay floors.
There were also cabinets in the kitchen, and Sam was so
happy she had cried several times. Megan had finally
pushed her out the door and the two of them had played
with Not My Dog and Roxie in the backyard.

"This has been so helpful," Sam said as she threw the
tennis ball and Not My Dog went running for it, Roxie
loping behind. "With us being so behind on the house
building, I was starting to get worried."

"You can't help the guys being busy with work. And
besides, work is good for Reid's business, right?"

Sam nodded. "It definitely is. Great for business, not so

great for building our house. And with winter and early spring being so wet, we got even more behind." Sam looked around. "But today, with all our friends showing up, wow. Everyone has saved our butts. I was beginning to think we were never going to finish this house."

"Of course you are. The major parts are done. Now it's just the smaller details."

She nodded. "I'm just so grateful."

Megan noted the tears welling in her best friend's eyes. "If you cry again, I'm going to toss this tennis ball at your head."

Sam laughed as she looked down at the gooey tennis ball Megan had just pulled out of Not My Dog's mouth. "Yuck. Okay, I promise, no more crying."

"Good."

Sam dragged in a deep breath. "Let's talk about something else, then. How about you and Brady?"

"How about that?"

Sam gave her a knowing smile. "So things are going well?"

"They're going very well. We see each other a lot. It's good between us."

Sam reached over and gave her arm a squeeze. "I'm so glad, honey. You deserve to be happy."

"I'm definitely happy."

"So . . . anything of a more permanent nature for the two of you?"

Megan shook her head. "I think Brady is more of a right-now type of person. And I don't want to push him. We're solid, as far as I know. And I'm fine living in the right now with him."

"But you want more."

Megan looked over at the house. "I want this. I want forever with him. I love him."

Sam shot a frown at her. "Hey. You said you didn't want me to cry."

Megan laughed. "Sorry. I've never said it out loud. I'm

not sure I even realized it until just now. So you, my friend, are the first to know."

Sam pulled her into a hug. "Your secret is safe with me."

Megan hugged her back. "Thanks. I just hope it works out for us. I know he feels the same. It just feels that way to me, you know?"

"I do know. But men . . . they take a while to come around sometimes. So give him time."

"I intend to. Like I said, things are great between us right now, and I'm content to leave them that way."

And she hoped they stayed that way.

But in the meantime, she was going to continue as if nothing had changed, even though in her heart, everything had changed. She even looked at him differently when he took a break to grab a drink. She met him out back and brushed her lips across his.

"Hard day?" she asked.

"Not really. Kind of fun, actually."

"Sure, building a house is something everyone does on the weekends."

He laughed. "Yeah, but it's something different."

She rubbed her hand up and down his arm. "Builds muscles. Though you already had those."

He gave her a smile, then went back inside to work. She left him alone and spent time with Sam and Molly and the other women, catching up on their lives.

At the end of the workday, some of the guys went out and grabbed barbecue for dinner, and they set up outside, where Sam and Reid had constructed a fire pit. They had plenty of chairs and soda, beer, and water for everyone, so by the time the barbecue had arrived, everyone had a spot to sit and eat.

Megan had set aside a chair for Brady, so after he filled his plate, he joined her. He was unusually quiet, but she chalked that up to him being tired—and probably hungry— after a long day.

She leaned into him. "I brought dessert."

He was digging into some ribs, so he just nodded and kept eating. When he didn't ask, she did.

"Aren't you going to ask me what I brought?"

He took a long swallow of water. "I figured it was something good."

She grinned. "It is. I think you'll really like it."

"I'm sure I will. These ribs are good. I think I'll go get a second helping. You want something?"

"No, I'm fine. Thanks."

She watched him wander off to the serving table, refill his plate, then get waylaid by Deacon. So he stood there, ate, and talked. She finished her meal and dumped her plate in the trash, then went to find Sam, who was in her makeshift sorta-kinda kitchen, just staring.

"What are you doing?"

Sam looked over at her as if she just got caught doing something she shouldn't. "Imagining."

"The cabinets look amazing."

"They do, don't they? I've already got the completed kitchen in my head. And thanks to everyone who came today, we have walls. Soon I'll have flooring and counter-tops and bathrooms."

Megan put her arm around Sam. "It won't be long now. I can already picture your shiny kitchen. And can I say I'm super jealous of all your cabinet space?"

Sam turned to her. "Your kitchen freaking rocks. I love your stove and your amazing island."

"It does. But I can still covet yours."

"Thank you. I covet it, too. And someday soon—not soon enough, mind you, but soon—it'll be done."

Megan laughed, and they went outside. She searched for Brady, but didn't see him. He was probably off with one of the guys, inspecting their work.

"I heard there was dessert," Luke said. "And I don't mean to be pushy or anything, but Emma texted."

Megan's lips curved. "And she wants to know when you're coming home?"

"Something like that."

"Then we need to get to dessert pronto. Can't keep your wife and baby waiting."

Megan broke out the raspberry tarts and the peanut butter chocolate cupcakes she'd made, making sure she set a couple aside for Brady.

He came back outside with Reid and Deacon about ten minutes later. Fortunately, she'd made enough of the desserts that there were plenty left for them.

"I was afraid I'd missed these," Reid said, hugging Megan, "and then I'd have been pissed."

"I made sure to guard them against second and third comers. But Luke had to leave, and I packed him a cupcake for Emma."

Reid bit into one, then made a moaning sound. "Allowable."

Brady snatched a cupcake as well and polished it off in about three bites. But he didn't gush about it like he typically did with her desserts.

Not that she expected praise or anything. She didn't. He obviously enjoyed it, since he all but inhaled it, and that was good enough.

She wandered off to help Sam clean up the remnants of dinner. The party was breaking up, so they folded up the chairs and put them away in the storage shed, then carried off the trash and put it in the back of Reid's truck. By the time they finished, only Reid, Deacon, and Brady were left.

Megan grabbed a bottle of water and took one of the few remaining seats in front of the fire pit.

"I mentioned to Brady that I saw a commercial spot for sale not far from here," Reid said to her. "I thought it might be a good spot for him to consider for his painting business."

She looked over at Brady. "Oh, that's interesting."

"Yeah," Brady said.

Which was all he said, so she didn't say anything more until they found themselves alone at her place later.

"What did you think about Reid's suggestion?" she asked as they curled up on the sofa together.

"His suggestion about what?"

"That commercial space."

"Oh. Not much."

"So you're not interested?"

"I don't know. I don't want to talk about it."

Wow. Was he ever cranky. Maybe he hadn't gotten enough sleep the night before, or he'd put in a hard day's work today. Whatever it was, she decided not to push him on anything tonight.

Maybe tomorrow he'd be in a better mood.

Chapter 29

MEGAN FINISHED UP at the bakery for the day. She closed up, cleaned up, then took the day's receipts to the bank.

She stopped in at Emma's house to visit her and the baby and stayed for a few hours.

"Are you anxious to get back to work?" she asked.

Emma looked at the gorgeous baby in her arms. "I do miss the vet clinic, my staff, and all my furry patients. But I have to admit it's going to be hard to leave Michael when it's time to go back. The only good thing is having the nanny here, and living so close to where I work, so I'll be able to come home at lunch and nurse him and visit."

"I think you'll do fine. And you still have some time at home."

Emma nodded. "I'm lucky that I have a great doctor taking care of the clinic while I'm on maternity leave. At least I don't have to worry about that part. But for now, I'm going to enjoy every second I have with this little guy."

After Megan left Emma's, she ran a few more errands and stopped by Loretta's bookstore to look for a few titles she'd had on her list. The place was busy, which was a good sign.

"Business is booming, Loretta," she said as the two of them shared a cup of coffee on one of the sofas in the back.

Loretta smiled. "Things are going well. I'm happy with the business. Someone bought the old secondhand store next to me, and I hear that's going to be renovated soon."

"Oh, really? What are they going to do with it?"

"I haven't heard yet. But hopefully whatever it is will drive new customers to the bookstore."

By the time she left the bookstore, it was late. Late enough to stop by Carter's shop to see Brady. And okay, she might have planned her day to coincide with the end of Brady's workday. Their conversations over the past week had been short. She'd invited him over for dinner last night, and he'd said he had work to do. Not unusual, of course, since he often did night work on motorcycles, but it was more his tone of voice than anything that concerned her.

Something was bothering him, and she wanted to make sure he was okay.

She went in through the front door. Molly and Carter were there, and it looked like they were about to head out.

"Big plans for tonight?"

"Oh, yeah," Molly said. "We have a hot date at the grocery store."

"Hey, it's pasta night," Carter said. "I love pasta."

"See?" Molly said. "It's all about the romance."

"You bet it is. Oh, how about garlic bread? We're making garlic bread, right?"

Molly rolled her eyes. "Let's go, Carter. Now I'm really hungry. See you later, Megan."

Megan laughed. "You two have a great night."

She made her way back to the shop. Roxie greeted her. Brady had trained her well, and now she was off leash and didn't wander beyond the perimeter of the garage.

"Well, hello, sweetheart. What are you up to today?"

She swooped Roxie up into her arms and cuddled her close, then made her way over to where Brady was sitting by the old metal desk in the corner of the garage.

"Paperwork?" she asked.

He looked up at her. "Oh. Hi. Yeah. Totaling up the bill for this one."

She looked over at the finished product, a dark blue Ford pickup that, to her, looked brand-new, even though it wasn't. "You can't even tell it had any body work done."

"That's the idea."

She waited while he worked on his numbers. Then he finally turned in his chair and looked up at her.

"So . . . what's up?" he asked.

"I just came by to see you. Maybe you want to have dinner?"

"Sorry. Someone's bringing a bike by tonight. I have to start on it right away."

"Okay." Something was definitely off. He was being gruff. He hadn't gotten up to hug her or kiss her, and that was typically the first thing he did.

She thought about leaving, but maybe he'd just had a rough couple of days. She could smooth it over. "You need to eat. I could grab something for us and—"

"I'm fine. I really just need to move this car out, sweep the place, and get ready for the bike."

In other words, *You're in my way, Megan.*

"Oh. Well, okay. I guess I'll get going. See you later?"

"Sure."

She went over to him and leaned down to brush her lips across his, depositing Roxie in his lap. "Call me, okay?"

"Yeah. I'll walk you out so I can lock the door behind you."

She made her way to the front door and turned to face him. "Is everything all right, Brady?"

"Everything's fine. Just busy, ya know?"

"Yes. Of course. I'll talk to you later."

She walked out the front door, turning to wave at him while he locked it.

He didn't smile. Just locked the door and closed the blinds.

Okay, then. That felt like a definite shutdown. And it made her stomach knot up.

What was wrong with him? With them? She didn't remember saying or doing anything to upset him.

But now she was upset. And she needed him to open up to her, to tell her what was bothering him.

Maybe tomorrow morning, if he didn't stop into the bakery for coffee and a roll, she'd steal a few seconds away and bring something to him.

And then they'd talk.

Because they really needed to talk.

BRADY MADE HIS way back into the garage. He rolled the Ford into the parking lot and texted the customer that his truck was ready to be picked up. Then he went back into the garage and started to clean up.

Roxie had climbed onto her blanket in the corner, and he could swear she was glaring at him.

Yeah, he'd treated Megan badly, and he'd been cold to her. But he needed some distance so he could figure out these weird feelings that had surrounded him ever since that day at Reid's.

He felt like the walls of this town were closing in on him and he couldn't breathe anymore. All these thoughts of buying property and land and houses and committing to Megan and settling down were only making it worse.

He needed his freedom, to make his own choices. When and if he settled down and set up his own business and found a woman to love, it was going to be on his own timeline. And that just wasn't now. He wasn't ready yet. There were still too many questions in his head that needed answers.

None of those thoughts you just had made sense. You know that, right?

He shook his head. Even the conversations he had with himself were driving him crazy.

He took a toothpick out and shoved it between his teeth. He really wanted a cigarette right now.

No, what he really wanted was to be sitting on the dock by the lake fishing.

With Kurt. Kurt would be able to tell him what to do.

He straightened and looked over at Roxie, who was asleep. Not that she'd be able to offer any advice even if she was awake.

And Kurt wasn't here. He wasn't ever going to be here to advise him about whether his decisions were the right moves or dumbass moves. Hell, even those last couple of years before he'd left town, Kurt hadn't been there for him.

So why, in his head, did he think his brother held all the answers?

Convenient, probably. Because his brother wasn't available, so if he couldn't go to his brother for the answers, then he didn't have to make any decisions.

At least he'd gotten that part of tonight's self-analysis right.

But as confused as he was right now, it stood to reason that this wasn't the time to make any serious life decisions.

He knew what he had to do.

Chapter 30

IT HAD BEEN a busy morning, but Megan managed to gather up an apple fritter and an extralarge cup of coffee and, with Stacy handling the post–morning rush crowd, she headed down the street to Carter's shop.

She ran into Molly, who told her Brady was in the garage.

"He's not painting or anything? I notice Roxie is in here."

She shook her head. "No, you're safe to go in there right now. He's just beating something up with a hammer, so it's too loud for Roxie out there."

"Great. Thanks."

She walked in to find Brady banging away on a fender with a rubber hammer. The sound was deafening. She went over to him so hopefully he'd notice her and stop.

He did, looking up at her and frowning. "What are you doing here?"

She held up the cup and the bag. "I thought you could use a break. You didn't come in this morning, so I brought you coffee and an apple fritter."

He frowned. "Just . . . put them on the desk."

Wow. No improvement in the mood yet. "Okay."

She went over and set them on the desk, and he went back to hammering, which made her ears ring.

Did he think she was just going to drop those off and leave? She went back over to him and stood there, enduring the endlessly loud hammering.

Fortunately, he stopped and stood. "What, Megan?"

"Why are you being so mean?"

"I'm not being mean. I'm working."

"I've been here before when you were working and you were never mean to me. So why now?"

"I'm busy. I've got a lot going on."

She tilted her head to the side. "Come on, Brady. Something's going on with you—with us. We need to talk about it."

He looked toward the door leading to the shop, then back at her. "Fine. But not here and not now. How about I come over to your place after work—maybe like six o'clock. We'll talk then."

"All right. I'll see you tonight."

She waited, but he didn't kiss her, didn't hug her, and didn't thank her for bringing him the coffee and the apple fritter.

Now she'd spend the rest of the day anxious about tonight, about what they were going to talk about.

But at least they were going to talk, so that was progress.

Chapter 31

MEGAN HAD SHOWERED and changed clothes before Brady was supposed to come over.

She'd also spent the afternoon nervously pacing her house. After she left work for the day, she'd baked two pies, one cheesecake, and a batch of chocolate chip muffins, then thoroughly scrubbed her kitchen.

She debated whether or not to lay out the baked goods for Brady. He'd been wretched to her lately, so he really didn't deserve anything.

Then again, maybe there was something on his mind and he just needed time to sort through it. And what better way to sort through a dilemma than with a slice of cheesecake or a muffin?

In the end, she decided to offer a spread of cheesecake and muffins—an obvious cure-all for anything. She also put a ham in the oven to warm, along with some sweet potatoes. He might be hungry. He probably was upset about something and wasn't eating well. She could at least feed him.

After she stared at herself in the mirror to check her jeans and peach silk blouse, she realized her hands were shaking.

Calm. Down. It's just a conversation, and no matter what's wrong, we're going to fix it. Together.

She took a deep, cleansing breath and felt a lot better.

Brady knocked on the door. She went to answer it. He was freshly showered and looked amazing, as always.

She looked around him. "Where's Roxie?"

"She's at my place."

"You could have brought her."

He shrugged. "She's fine at home."

Okay then. "Would you like something to drink?"

"A beer would be good."

She went to the refrigerator and grabbed a beer for him, then poured herself a glass of wine. She handed him the beer and he took a seat at the island. "Rough day today?"

He shrugged. "Average."

She took a seat in the chair next to his, took a long, courage-inducing swallow of wine, then laid her hand over his. "Tell me what's wrong."

"Nothing's wrong."

"Something is definitely off. You haven't been calling me. You haven't stopped in at the bakery, or come here to the house. There's been nothing, Brady. No contact of any kind."

"I've been busy."

She refused to let him brush this off. "Your attitude toward me is different. You aren't affectionate with me and you haven't been for more than a week now. You can talk to me, Brady. I'm a grown woman and I can handle whatever it is."

He took a couple of swallows of his beer, then set it on the counter. "Okay, fine. It's not working between us."

His words sliced through her like a knife in her heart, but she held steady. "What's not working?"

"This. You and me. I'm not meant to have a relationship.

I've been giving it a lot of thought, and I need to make some changes."

Her earlier confidence that she could handle whatever this was started to fade. "What kind of changes?"

He stood and paced back and forth in front of her. "You know, people seem to think they know me. But they don't. I had a plan, and it was a good one. I was happy being alone. I want to save money to start my own business. But I don't know when that's going to be or where that's going to be. People can't dictate those terms to me."

Now she was just confused. "What people are you talking about, Brady?"

He raked his fingers through his hair. "Just . . . people. Trying to give me ideas, trying to force me to set down roots, establish relationships. Make friends. I don't need permanence in my life. I just need to be left the hell alone."

He'd finished with a raised voice. She didn't even know this person who was standing in front of her yelling at her as if she and some random, faceless, nameless "people" were the cause of all his perceived problems. She only knew that whatever was bothering him, it was bothering him in a major way. "I'm sorry, Brady, but I don't exactly know what you're talking about. I can see you're upset. Let's have some dinner. I made a ham and sweet potatoes. We'll talk this through and figure out what's upset you."

He whirled on her. "I don't want any goddamn dinner. What I want is for everyone to leave me the hell alone. I'm not upset. I'm done. I'm done with you and I'm done with everyone else who has a plan for my life."

She blinked, shocked at the anger he was directing at her. "What? What plans? I haven't had any plans for you. Why are you so angry at me?"

"I'm not . . . I'm not angry. I'm just . . . I need to get out of here, Megan. Kurt and I had plans, and you saw how those worked out. I can't do plans. I can't do looking forward into the future."

Oh. She suddenly had an inkling of the problem. "So you're feeling things for me, and you're forming friendships here, and that scares you because you're afraid of losing it all just like you lost Kurt."

He stared at her for what seemed like an eternity before he answered. "That is not what I said. This has nothing to do with Kurt."

She wasn't buying it. She saw anger on his face, but there was pain in his eyes. "Doesn't it? Maybe it's time to separate the rest of your life from the past, to let go of your brother and look toward your future."

She got up and went over to him and laid her hand on his arm. While the words he'd said to her had hurt, she understood it was coming from a place of deep pain. He was scared of all his feelings, and she wanted to help him. "I'm here for you. I understand the pain you feel. But until you talk it out with someone, those feelings aren't ever going to go away."

He looked down at her, and for a moment, she saw the softness, the tenderness in him, and for just that split second, he was the man she'd fallen in love with.

But then those beautiful eyes of his hardened.

"You can't fix everything with a fucking muffin, Megan. And some things can't ever be fixed. So why don't you just leave me the hell alone and let me live my life the way I want to."

Okay. That was enough. "I didn't say I was trying to fix anything. And certainly not with a muffin. That was insulting, Brady."

His only response was to shrug.

"You're going to stand there and tell me you don't care about me. At all."

He didn't say anything. He gave her nothing in the way of a reply. Not even a shred of hope for the two of them.

She took a step back. He'd completely shut her out. Despite her offer to help, he'd decided he didn't want her support. He didn't want her love.

He didn't want her.

She folded her arms in front of her, pulling her own hurt and emotions in, because she'd be damned if she'd fall apart in front of him. "You can't keep running from your feelings, Brady. Eventually you're going to have to face them. You're going to have to face how you feel, and all those painful emotions you've kept locked away. And maybe someday when you're ready to do that, you're going to need someone who cares about you to be there with you. And maybe because you've spent so much time fighting so hard to keep yourself locked up tight and running from everyone who cares about you, when you finally fall flat on your face and need support, you'll be alone.

"And I'll feel really sorry for you when that happens, because I can't think of anything worse than being alone with all of those feelings you might actually have to admit to someday."

All he did was look at her. Emotionless, his stare like a deep, black hole of nothingness.

"Get out, Brady."

He turned and walked out the door, taking all her hopes and dreams with him.

Only when she heard his bike rumble down the driveway did she release the tears she'd held back.

BRADY THREW HIS keys on the kitchen table. He wasn't even pissed. He was just . . . empty.

He grabbed a beer and went to the sofa. Roxie hopped on his lap, and he absently stroked her back.

He'd done the right thing tonight. He'd let Megan go. She might hurt now, but in the long run, she'd be better off without him. And he'd sure as hell be better off without her.

Without anyone.

He didn't need all these people who kept pushing him to be someone he wasn't. He just wanted to crawl inside of himself and forget. He was tired of hurting.

He'd hurt enough over the past couple of years. All he wanted to do was forget about everything, forget about Kurt, and just live his life as if his brother hadn't existed. The problem was, this whole damn town and everyone in it wouldn't let that happen.

They all wanted to talk about Kurt, remember Kurt. They wanted him to talk about Kurt and remember Kurt. And if they didn't want him to remember Kurt, then they wanted him to get over Kurt. And because of that, the giant hole in his heart wasn't closing.

He should have never stayed here after Kurt died. He'd known it was a mistake, but because of his parents, he'd stayed and taken that job with Carter. And then he'd made an even bigger mistake by making friends and falling in love with Megan, who'd opened him up and opened old wounds that wouldn't close anymore.

He didn't want to be open and honest with his feelings. He'd felt a lot better when he was closed up tight, refusing to feel.

Feeling things hurt. They hurt so damn bad he wasn't sure he could make it through a day feeling everything he did right now.

Seeing that look in Megan's eyes when he'd shut her down hurt so damn bad he ached with the pain of it. And he hadn't felt pain like that since . . .

Hell, this pain was even worse. And there was only one solution to that.

Leaving.

He had to get away from Hope, from everyone who wanted him to relive the most painful moments of his life. He had to escape his parents, who refused to put away their memories of Kurt, as if the collections of photos they'd put up on the mantel and walls would bring their son back to life.

And most important, he had to get away from Megan, whose love suffocated him and made him open his heart in a way that made him bleed out the emotion and depths of feelings he'd fought so hard to keep locked up tight.

Yeah, he had to get the hell out of this town right now, so he could lock down those feelings and once again go stone-cold.

He'd feel a lot safer that way.

Chapter 32

"TO THE COLDHEARTED bastards of the world. May they all rot in hell."

Megan raised her glass to Chelsea's toast, but her heart wasn't in it. It had been eight days, nine hours, and . . . she refused to even look at her watch anymore to calculate the minutes and seconds since Brady had dumped her. She'd done enough clock-watching, hoping like hell he'd show up at the bakery or her house and beg her forgiveness.

He wasn't coming back, and she was just going to have to get over it. The best way to do that was with her friends. The girls had insisted she had to leave her house and go out with them.

"And may they all get STDs," Sam added, then hiccuped out a giggle.

"Atta girl," Chelsea said. "I'm enjoying this new inebriated side of you, Sam. I'm especially enjoying it because I'm sober when we go out."

"Thank you," Sam said. "I figure I have to pick up the slack for your lack of drinking while you're pregnant."

"I knew I could count on you." Chelsea smiled, then frowned. "Wait. Did you just call me a lush?"

Emma laughed. "I think she did."

Jane giggled. "I'm just going to take pictures so we can text them to Sam when she has a hangover."

"I'll especially enjoy those," Sam said. "Reid likely will as well."

"Either way," Emma said. "We're drinking to all the losers we've all dated. We're better off without them."

"Megan is definitely better off without He Who Shall Not Be Named," Molly said. "Also known as He Who Left Without Notice."

"Hear, hear," Sam said, hoisting her margarita. "To the deadbeat boyfriend and employee. No, wait, we're not toasting him, are we?"

"We definitely need to monitor Sam's margaritas," Jane said to Megan. "Though you need to be drinking a lot more."

"I do, don't I?" Megan took a long swallow of her wine. "Men suck."

"Well, sometimes they suck in all the right ways," Chelsea said with a wicked smile.

"Chelsea," Emma said. "Now is not the time to talk about great sex."

"Oh, right. Men are pigs."

"As one of the species you hate, I'm sorry," Bash said, coming over to their table. "But I'm just checking on refills and to see if any of you want to order dinner."

"We're drinking dinner tonight. Thank you, Mr. Bartender," Sam said, slurring most of that entire sentence.

"Uh-huh. Okay, then."

"Better bring menus over, babe," Chelsea said. "And alert Reid that Sam's on a tear."

Bash laughed. "I'll do that."

They'd been at it for about an hour and a half. Megan had nursed two glasses of wine in that time frame. What she should be doing was getting shit-faced with her friends, but so far, she was still sober, which was sad.

"Your sad face is killing my buzz, Megan," Sam said, then ordered a round of tequila shots for everyone.

"Oh, Lord," Emma said. "No shots for me. Megan, you'll have to do mine."

"None for me, either, for obvious reasons," Chelsea said.

"I'll pass, too," Jane said. "I have to pick up Tabitha from dance class in an hour."

In the end, Sam had taken Emma's shot and Megan had taken Chelsea's. After two shots of tequila, Megan was much more in the spirit of the evening. Then Loretta and Des showed up, so Megan had a couple more shots of tequila.

"I just don't understand him," Megan said now that she was unburdened of her sobriety. "I loved him. I was going to tell him I loved him before he went all brooding and angry on me."

"Sometimes men get scared when they start to have feelings," Molly said. "I think we all went through it."

"And sometimes they're just jerks," Loretta said. "And there's no hope for them."

"Well, this is true," Emma said. "There are relationships that are salvageable and some that aren't. I thought for sure Brady was the right one for you."

"We all did," Chelsea said. "I'm so sorry it didn't work out."

Megan nodded, then took a sip of her wine. "Me, too. But I'm better off without him. I don't need a man in my life who doesn't want me. I want a man who loves me, who will move heaven and earth to have me."

"Amen, sister," Loretta said, lifting her glass of wine in a toast.

Fortunately, dinner arrived, and it took the edge off of Megan's fuzzy head. By the time they got to dessert—a decadent triple-layer cake—Megan felt a lot better. But she still let Reid drive her home, laughing as Sam sang one of her favorite songs from the Top 40. In the wrong key.

"Thanks for the ride, Reid," she said.

"Anytime."

"Love you, honey," Sam said, waving to her over the front seat.

"Love you, too, Sam."

She went inside the house and changed into shorts and a tank top, then fixed a large glass of ice water, already feeling dehydrated from all the alcohol. She sat at the island and went through the day's mail. Then she looked up and saw the cheesecake she'd made earlier.

She pushed the mail to the side and rested her chin on her hands.

Cheesecake. Brady loved cheesecake. Out of all the sweet confections she'd made, he'd pronounced it his favorite.

She wondered where he was now. Was he happy?

She wasn't happy. She missed him. He'd hurt her—broken her heart, actually. But she still missed him. You didn't fall out of love with someone just because they broke your heart.

This healing was going to take some time.

She swiped her finger through the edge of the cheesecake and took a taste, not bothering to brush away the tears that slid down her cheeks.

Bastard. Someday she'd stop crying over him.

Chapter 33

BRADY SAT IN his one-room efficiency in Denver, scrolling through the apartment rentals.

He had a line on a job that looked promising. He'd interviewed at an auto body shop this morning, and the owner told him he'd probably have an offer for him this afternoon, but he'd promised his wife he'd interview her nephew, so he had to go through the motions. But the guy said the nephew didn't have a quarter of the experience or skills that Brady had, so Brady knew he had the job. Which meant he'd have to find a place to live. This efficiency hotel was fine for an interim, but he'd need at least a studio apartment, which would likely be cheaper anyway, from what he'd seen in the apartment rentals section of the real estate ads he'd reviewed.

He put his laptop aside, stood and stretched, then took Roxie for a short walk. He breathed in the cool, crisp air.

Yeah, Denver would work out. He didn't know anyone here, and that suited him just fine. Plus, he liked the mountains. He'd been here before. He and Kurt had come here one January to ski with some friends. They'd had a great time.

He took Roxie to a nearby dog park and let her run loose

with some of the other smaller dogs. She was having a blast, so he picked a bench and sat, keeping a close eye on her. So far, so good. He'd like to find a place near a dog park. Watching Roxie play with the other dogs made him realize she needed some companionship.

He didn't, but his dog definitely did.

He stared up at the mountains, remembering the year he and Kurt had come here. He'd been eighteen, fresh out of high school. Kurt had been twenty, and they'd packed up their car, along with two other friends of Kurt's. They'd rented a one-bedroom condo, mostly crashing on the floor and couches, and skied their asses off.

Hell, that had been fun. He'd been on a lot of fun adventures with his brother. Camping trips and canoeing and hunting. Except for the one year he'd found Kurt facedown and passed out, stoned out of his mind, when they'd taken a summer vacation in Fort Lauderdale. God, he'd been scared to death that time. But he'd been able to rouse his brother, who'd told him it was no big deal.

Yeah, no big deal. He'd believed him then. And so many other times when Kurt had told him to mind his own business, that he could handle the addiction.

There'd been good times with Kurt. And some shitty times, too.

It struck him right then that no matter where he went, no matter how many places he traveled to—his memories of Kurt would always travel with him.

He'd never get his brother out of his head. Those life experiences he'd shared with his brother—the good and the bad—would always be with him.

He hadn't left Hope because of Kurt. He'd left Hope because of himself, because he was afraid to lose what he'd built there.

Friendships. Love.

Megan.

That fear had become a real, tangible thing. And now he was afraid he'd really lost everything he'd built, everyone he cared about.

He looked up at the clear blue sky, at the mountains, at the beauty of the landscape, and suddenly that landscape shifted. All he could see was the warmth of a beautiful smiling face, gorgeous brown hair, and melting brown eyes.

He called to Roxie, and they headed back to the efficiency. He dug through his things and found a brand-new sketch pad, then pulled out a pencil. He tore the wrapper off the sketch pad, the ideas coming fast and furious now. He propped his feet on the coffee table and started drawing.

When his phone rang, he glanced at the number, then ignored it and kept drawing.

He had to get these images out of his head and onto paper. Then, he had to get back to Hope.

And hope like hell it wasn't too late to make things right.

Chapter 34

IT WAS A crap day. Megan had been up all night, because the thunderstorms blowing through town had been furious. First, they'd knocked out the power, and then the thunder had been so loud it had kept her up. By the time the power had come back on, it had been an hour until she was due to get up and go to the bakery, so she went in early, hoping the power was on at the bakery.

Fortunately, it was, so at least she had a head start on her baking for the day. She was more than ready by the time the bakery opened. And apparently everyone coming in was as cranky as she was, because they wanted coffee and pastries in a hurry. She and Stacy had their hands full until there was enough of a lull for Megan to start cleaning up in the back. By the time they put out the closed sign, they both looked at each other in utter exhaustion.

Stacy helped her clean the kitchen, then Megan ran to the bank, and she had nothing in mind other than falling facedown in bed and sinking into oblivious sleep for at least an hour. She was certain she'd feel a lot better after a nap.

The rain had settled into a steady downpour—minus the thunder and lightning—so she planned on letting the sound of it lull her into a lovely sleep.

What she hadn't planned on was seeing a motorcycle in her driveway, or Brady standing on her porch.

She got out and ran to the porch. "It's raining."

He smiled at her, the first smile she'd seen from him in what seemed like forever. "Yeah, I noticed that."

"You're all wet."

He reached out and grasped a tendril of her soaking wet hair. "So are you."

"Why are you—never mind. Let's go inside."

She unlocked the front door, and he followed her inside. She turned to him. "Wait here."

She threw her purse on the island, then went into the bathroom to grab two towels. When she came out, she threw one at him. "Dry off."

She did the same, shrugging out of the jacket she'd hastily thrown on at the bakery. Not that it had done much good. She was still wet. And now she was cold.

And mad. "What are you doing here, Brady?"

"I came to see you."

"All the way from . . . wherever it was you left Hope for?"

"I was in Denver."

"Long drive just to see me."

"You're worth it."

She frowned. "Don't be nice to me."

"Ohhkay. Why not?"

"Because you weren't nice to me the last time we were together."

"I know. About that . . ." He reached for her and she backed away.

"You hurt me."

He had the decency to look ashamed. "I know I did. I'd like to talk to you about that."

She used the towel to dry her hair. "I don't know if I want to talk to you anymore. The last time didn't go so well."

"Please, Megan. I have a lot of things to talk to you about."

She supposed she had to make a decision about that, rather than let him stand there dripping wet on her tile floor.

"Fine. I'm going to go change clothes. Dry off and I'll make some coffee. Providing you don't have any criticisms about me making coffee."

"No. I'd like some coffee. Thanks."

"I'll be right back." She started to turn away, then stopped as a realization hit her. "Where's Roxie?"

"She's at Carter's shop. I stopped there first, so Molly's watching her."

"Good to know. I just wanted to make sure you didn't dump her, too."

He looked down at the floor, then back up at her. "I guess I deserved that."

"Yes, you did."

She went into the bedroom and changed into dry clothes, then headed into the bathroom for a quick blow-dry of her hair. She knew she was leaving him out there a lot longer than she should, but the hell with it. He'd dumped her and left her. If he had to wait ten extra minutes while she dried her hair, that wasn't too much to ask, was it?

She came out and he was sitting at the island nursing a cup of coffee.

"I made one for you, too," he said.

"Good to see you still remember where everything is."

"I remember everything about you, Megan. And I was only gone for a couple of weeks."

An eternity to her broken heart, but she wouldn't mention that to him.

Even with his hair slicked back and wet, he was a force of sexy male. In some ways, it was good to see him. In others, it was traumatic, because if he'd come back due to some crisis of conscience and he wanted to apologize for his behavior in order to get some kind of decent closure, it was only going to rip her heart out all over again. She didn't think she'd be able to handle it.

But she supposed she'd only know if she asked. "Okay, Brady, why are you here?"

"First, to apologize for the way I treated you in the days leading up to and on the day I left."

She wanted to wince. This was it. This was his apology and his closure. She braced herself.

"Okay. Is that it?"

"No, that's not it. There's a lot more. I went to Denver so I could start over, forget about everything here. Forget Hope. Forget the friends I made."

She waited.

"Forget you."

Okay, that hurt more than she had expected it to.

"And? Did you?"

His lips curved in a wry smile. "Hell no. It only got worse. I was trying to run away from everything I felt. Everything I cared about. Everything I loved."

She'd been studying her coffee, but when he said *love*, her gaze snapped to his. "What?"

"While I was there, I started thinking about Kurt, about the good times—and the not so good times. At first I thought I was trying to get away from all the memories I had of him. Then I realized I'd never be able to escape the legacy of my brother, because no matter where I am, Kurt is always going to be a part of my life."

"Of course he is. You can't erase those memories, Brady. The good ones or the bad ones."

"I know. It took me a while, but I finally came to grips with that. I also came to the realization that I just have to let it go. I have to let him go."

Well, that was something. "I guess that's a good thing?"

"It is. But in the meantime, something else happened while I was in Denver."

She frowned. "What happened?"

"I was sitting in a dog park with Roxie, and suddenly the only images in my head were of you. So I went back to the hotel where I was staying and I got out a blank sketchbook. I want you to take a look at what I drew."

She cocked her head to the side. "You made sketches?"

"Yeah." He pulled a sketchbook from his backpack and handed it to her.

She flipped open to the first page and saw a penciled drawing of her face. Uncannily, it looked exactly like her.

She glanced up at Brady. "You sketched. You told me you never sketch."

"I was inspired. You were suddenly in my head and you were all I could think of. All these images hit me at once and I had to get them down."

He motioned with his head to the sketchbook, so she flipped to the next page. Her at the bakery behind the counter. Waiting on customers. She kept flipping pages. Her sitting on the grass by the lake. Here at the house. Playing with Roxie.

They were incredible. Page after page of sketches of her. Some were just random drawings. Her face. Her smiling. Her laughing. But others were incredibly detailed. Her dancing at Chelsea's wedding, one of her wearing his shirt—and only his shirt. She blushed at that one. She'd never seen anything like these.

When she got to another page, it was pictures of cars and bikes. He'd drawn the side of a car with dents, then another one of it smoothed out.

She looked up at him.

"I was trying to figure out what was wrong in my life," he said. "When I work on a car that's been damaged, I can see perfectly how to fix it. How to smooth out the dents and the damage."

She flipped to the next page and she saw a man's body, bent over and broken, the limbs not in the right places.

"That's me, Megan."

His voice had gone soft.

"I've spent all these years railing about my brother— about how fucked up his life was. All I could see was this wall with Kurt on one side and me on the other. Turns out he and I weren't so different. He might have had an addiction to drugs, but I'm messed up, too, just in a different way."

When he looked up at her, she saw so much pain and misery on his face it took everything in her not to go to him and wrap her arms around him. But she held back, knowing he needed to give voice to what was inside of him.

"It took me a long time to figure out that I'm the one who's broken, Megan."

Her heart did a small leap. She looked again at the sketch, then at him. "What do you mean by that?"

"I'm a master at fixing cars. But I can't fix myself without help. I need you. I screwed this all up. I spent so much time isolating myself after Kurt died, thinking that if I held it all in I'd be fine. And then you and everyone else pulled me out and made me start living life again, and I thought if I could do that without feeling anything, I'd be okay.

"But the problem was, I couldn't do that without feeling, because you made me feel things I'd never felt before. I never even realized I was falling in love with you until it was too late, and once I did realize it I got scared and I ran away from you as fast as I could. I didn't want to feel that deeply, and because of that I hurt you. I don't have enough words to say I'm sorry for that."

Her heart pounded as she listened to him talk. He hadn't come back for closure. He'd come back to tell her he loved her. But could she trust him? She'd told him when he left that at some point he'd need her and she wouldn't be there for him.

Was she really the type of person who could walk away when he was this vulnerable?

Then again, she'd been vulnerable, too. She'd laid out her heart to him, and he'd stomped all over it. He'd not only stomped all over it—he'd kicked it on his way out the door.

She looked down at the sketches. "These are amazing, Brady. Thank you for drawing them."

"They poured out of me. Every feeling, every emotion I'd tried to hold back for so long, I suddenly couldn't hold them inside anymore. Because of you—because of how I feel about you."

She was trying so hard to stand firm, to keep her own emotions in check.

She delayed by flipping through the sketchbook. There, on the last page, was that man with the broken body, lying on the ground. And above him, was an angel—an angel who looked a lot like her. She was reaching for him, their fingers almost touching.

"I'm not complete without you, Megan. I need you."

Tears filled her eyes as she lifted her gaze to his.

"I love you," he said. "I'm so sorry I hurt you. I'm sorry I left you. I'm not whole without you. Please forgive me."

No, she wasn't the kind of heartless person who could walk away from a broken person who needed her.

He loved her. And she wasn't complete without him, either.

She laid the sketch pad on the island and slid off the chair and stepped between his legs. His arms came around her, and she'd never felt anything better than the warmth of his embrace.

"God, I've missed holding you," he said as she laid her head on his chest.

"I've missed you, too." She put her arms around him.

He smoothed his hands over her back, and she nestled in closer, breathing in his familiar scent. She might never move away from him. For the first time since he left, everything felt right again.

"I love you, Brady."

He pulled back and he looked at her. "I love you. I mean those words. They're not ones I take lightly, because I've never said them to another woman before."

She shuddered in a breath, and then he kissed her and she felt those same dizzying heights she always experienced when his mouth was on hers. It was like being lost somewhere magical, where only the two of them existed.

They didn't need to say anything as she led him to her bedroom. They undressed and got reacquainted with each other's bodies, taking their time to run their hands over each other.

And when he entered her, it was with their gazes locked on each other, with such intimacy it took Megan's breath away. She knew then that Brady was fully there with her, his fingers entwined with her as he moved against her in slow, fluid movements. He took his time in such a sweet, sensual way, and when she climaxed, he kissed her, groaned against her, came with her. It brought tears to her eyes and he kissed them as they rolled down her cheeks.

After, he stayed locked within her.

"Good tears, I hope?" he asked.

She smiled up at him. "Yes. Good tears."

They stayed entwined together in bed for a while, their legs draped over each other.

"What are you going to do now?" she asked.

"I talked briefly with Carter. We'll talk more tomorrow. I already apologized for leaving and explained that I needed to get my head right. Because Carter's a great guy, he told me I could have my job back. He hasn't hired any-one to replace me yet."

She smoothed her hand up his arm. "That's great."

"Yeah. But I think it's time for me to move on, so I'll take the job back for now. But I'll let Carter know it's only tem-porary. I want to look at that building Reid mentioned."

"The one you wouldn't discuss with me when I asked you about it."

His look turned serious. "Yes. I'm sorry. That was kind of the catalyst for my panic and my running. Thinking about the future. About who I wanted to be. Where I wanted to be. But mainly you and me. Reid also told me about a plot of land near where he and Sam live that's for sale. A place where I could potentially build a house. And that got me to thinking about you and me and forever."

Her breath caught. "What?"

He traced her bottom lip with his thumb. "Don't look so surprised, Megan. That's where we're headed. At least that's what I want. Is it what you want?"

She swallowed past the suddenly arid desert in her throat. "Yes."

"Then I'll go look into that plot of land. I mean, I guess *we* should do that. If that's what you'd be interested in doing. I know you have this place. We could live here for now. Provided you're interested in having me here."

She rose up to kiss him. "I'm very interested in having you here. But this place isn't big enough to raise a family. And I want a family. With you. If that's what you want."

The look he gave her melted her heart. "That's what I want, too. You, me, Roxie, and a lot of kids. Kids who like cheesecake."

She laughed. "Sounds like a good plan."

He sat up. "This kind of sucks as a proposal, Megan, but what I'm saying is I want to marry you. I want forever with you."

She'd gone from the depths of sadness to the heights of happiness. She sat up and faced him. "Actually, it's kind of a perfect proposal. And yes, I'll marry you, Brady."

He dragged her onto his lap and kissed her; the kind of kiss that was filled with love and promise. They had their start, and the future looked better than ever.

Now they'd take it one step at a time.

Chapter 35

SINCE HE'D BEEN back in town, Brady had a lot to do. And a lot of apologies to make.

And it was time for some honesty if he was going to live his life the way he wanted to from now on.

Megan had been first, because she was the most important person in his life.

Now he stood at the doorstep of his parents' house. This conversation wasn't going to be easy, but it was necessary.

His mother gave him one of her happy smiles when she opened the door.

"Brady! I'm so surprised to see you," she said as she stepped aside to let him in. "I didn't know you were back in town for a visit."

When he'd left Hope, he'd stopped over at his parents' and had a very short, very abrupt conversation with his mom and dad, telling them he was moving on. It had been uncomfortable and he hadn't stayed long. And like most of the issues in his life over the past couple of years, he hadn't dealt with it well at all, and he knew his parents had been hurt by his leaving.

He'd hurt a lot of people when he'd left.

That changed today.

"I'm not back for a visit, Mom. I'm back permanently."

His mother's eyes widened. "You are?"

"Yes. I need to talk to you and Dad, though. Is he around?"

"He's in the backyard. Let's go outside."

She slipped her arm in his, and this time he didn't move away. He leaned into his mother and laid his hand over hers. "Yeah, let's do that."

His father stood when he walked outside.

"Brady."

"Hi, Dad. We need to talk. All three of us."

They obviously sensed it was a serious discussion, because his mother pulled up a chair at the patio table next to his dad, and the two of them grasped hands.

"What's going on?" his dad asked.

"I think it's obvious to both of you that I've avoided you since Kurt died."

His mother looked away for a few seconds, but nodded. "Yes. We know."

"The reason for that is that I didn't want to acknowledge his death. I avoided dealing with it, just like the two of you have avoided dealing with it."

His father opened his mouth to object, but his mom squeezed his hand to silence him.

"Whenever I walk into this house, it's like walking into a Kurt shrine. Pictures of him on the mantel, on every wall. It smothers me. I don't know how you handle it."

He saw the tears gathering in his mother's eyes. He knew he was hurting her feelings, but this was something he had to get off his chest.

"We miss him," Mom said.

"I know you do. So do I. But here's the thing. We're always going to miss him. There's a giant hole in our family and keeping his bedroom the same way it was when he was a teenager isn't going to bring him back. Nothing is ever going to bring him back or change the person he became because of the drugs. He's gone. But we're not. We have to start living our lives again. You know Kurt would want that for us."

He waited, until his father nodded. "I feel awful. Your mother and I used to go out together all the time. We had fun. We felt alive, until Kurt . . . well, you know."

Brady nodded.

"It's like time stood still after Kurt died," his mother said, "and we don't know how to move forward now."

He leaned forward and clasped his mother's hand. "I know it's hard. I screwed up so many things in my life because I stopped living, too. But here's the thing. I have friends now. And a woman in my life that I'm in love with."

His mom's face brightened and for the first time, he saw a genuine, happy smile on her face. "You're in love? Brady, I'm so happy for you."

He smiled, too. "Thanks. I'm pretty happy about it, too, but I really screwed it up with Megan, because I fought that happiness. I didn't want it. I was afraid of it."

"Because you were afraid of losing someone you loved again," his father said.

Brady nodded. "Yeah."

"Oh, no," his mother said. "Did you fix it with her?"

"I did. She's an amazing woman with an incredible capacity for love and forgiveness. I'm a really lucky guy."

"I can't wait to meet her," his mother said. "When you're ready."

"You will. But first, I need the two of you to start living again."

Now he saw the tears in his dad's eyes. "I need the two of us to start living again, too, son."

His dad stood and pulled his mother up. Brady stood, too, and for the first time since Kurt died, the three of them shared a hug.

This time, it wasn't a hug filled with grief and hopelessness.

This time, it was a hug filled with hope for the future. For all their futures.

Chapter 36

BRADY FELT CLEANSED after the conversation with his parents. He thought they felt better, too. They told him they hadn't realized how they hadn't moved on from Kurt's death.

He knew he'd hurt their feelings, but he loved his parents and told them he wanted them to live again. They'd had a really long talk and they'd all shed some tears, along with sharing some great stories about Kurt. In the end, he felt like it had helped. At least he hoped it had. He wanted his parents in his life. He knew everything wasn't going to change overnight. His parents weren't going to change overnight. Neither was he. But it had been a good first step. They'd work on it together.

He'd also sat down with Carter and Molly and apologized for cutting out on them. They were both understanding, and Carter told him he had a job as his body guy for as long as he wanted it, but when he was ready to open up his own place, he'd appreciate some notice next time. Brady laughed and promised him he'd get plenty of notice before he set up shop in a new place, and he'd find Carter someone to replace him before he left.

He felt a lot better about things now.

There was only one thing left to do, and it was the most important thing.

He and Roxie had moved out of the apartment above Carter's shop and into Megan's place. It felt a little odd living with someone. He'd never done it before, but at the same time, sharing a home with Megan felt right.

Everything about being with Megan felt right.

There was just one thing that wasn't settled yet, and he intended to rectify that tonight.

Brady and Megan were going to meet with their friends at Bash's bar for drinks after work.

He finished up early, went home and let Roxie out back to play while he took a shower. Megan had said she had to run some errands, so she wasn't home yet. He played with Roxie for a while, then Megan got home, jumped in the shower, and got dressed.

Roxie was all settled in Megan's place as well. She had her favorite chicken—of course—as well as other toys, and her new dog bed was in their bedroom. To Roxie, home was wherever they were, so she was good.

Megan came out of the bedroom dressed in a pair of tight black jeans and a black silk tank top. The silver chain she was wearing dangled between her breasts. And she wore a pair of heels that accentuated her legs. Her hair lay in soft waves against her neck, and he got an instant erection.

"Woman—are you trying to get us to stay home tonight?" he asked.

She frowned. "What?"

"You look sexy as hell, and all I want to do now is peel off those clothes you're wearing and lick you all over."

She grinned. "That's a tempting suggestion. I'm okay with staying home."

He laughed, then pulled her against him and kissed her enough to let her know how much he appreciated everything about her. But he had plans for tonight—at least the earlier part of tonight—that didn't include taking his woman to bed.

"Dinner and drinks with our friends first."

With a sigh, she took a step back. "If you insist."

She grabbed her jacket, since it was a little cool out with a threat of rain. He grabbed his jacket, too, and they headed out in Megan's car to the bar.

Their friends were already there, so they pulled up chairs next to Reid and Sam.

Bash was working the bar, but his assistant manager was also there, so he took a break to sit with them.

"I miss wine," Chelsea said, laying her hand across her stomach. "It's a rough life cooking a baby."

"Poor you. I'll drink for you," Megan said, lifting her glass to take a sip.

"That was just mean, Megan."

Megan winked at Chelsea.

"Des called me and said that she and Logan can't make it," Emma said. "Benjamin has a cough, so they're staying home."

"I hope he's okay," Molly said.

"He's fine. But they don't want to be gone in case he ends up sick."

"Understandable," Carter said.

They all sat and drank for a while, talking about work and what was going on outside of work. Once everyone was there, Brady decided it was time.

He stood. "So I'd like to do this in front of friends."

They all gave him his attention. Megan looked perplexed.

Good. He wanted her to.

"As you know, it was a hard road for me after my brother died. I didn't want to associate with anyone and I pretty much kept to myself. But thanks to all of you, who kept after me and forced me out of my shell, I now have the group of you who I call my friends. Thank you for your patience, and thank you for being there for me."

"Hey, we're nothing if not persistent," Deacon said with a grin.

"And annoying," Zach added.

Bash laughed. "What are friends for?"

Brady smiled. "And because you're all special to me, I wanted you to bear witness to me proclaiming my love for this woman." He looked at Megan, who smiled up at him.

"Without Megan, I wouldn't have become the man I am today. I wouldn't have been able to exorcise the demons of my past. I wouldn't have been able to make friends, to be able to love as freely as I have. I love you, Megan, and I want to spend the rest of my life proving myself worthy of you."

He pulled the ring out of his pocket. Megan's eyes widened as he kneeled in front of her.

Brady heard the collective gasps from their friends, but his eyes were only on Megan as he took her hand in his.

"Will you marry me?"

Her eyes had filled with tears. "Yes. I love you."

He slid the diamond ring on her finger, then pulled her to stand and planted one very hot kiss on her. Their friends applauded and cheered.

When he pulled back, she said, "You know I didn't need a ring."

"Yeah, you did."

"Well, it's sure a sparkler."

He smiled at her. "So are you."

She kissed him, then looped her arms around his neck. "I've got you now, Brady Conners."

"Yes, you do. Don't ever let go."

READ ON FOR A PREVIEW OF
JACI BURTON'S NEXT PLAY-BY-PLAY NOVEL,

Rules Of Contact

COMING SOON FROM HEADLINE ETERNAL.

FLYNN CASSIDY SAT at one of the corner tables of Ninety-Two, his new restaurant in San Francisco.

They'd opened just two weeks ago and so far, things were going well. Right now one of the major entertainment media outlets was doing a feature on the restaurant, so he had to be present for it. Which meant camera crews and bright lights and a lot of damn people in the way of regular business. He had already wandered around and apologized to his patrons, who seemed to take it all in stride. Hopefully the crews would get all the film and sound bites they wanted and would get the hell out shortly.

"This is so thrilling, Flynn."

He dragged his gaze away from the camera crews and onto Natalie, the woman he'd been dating the past two weeks. She was a looker, for sure, with beautiful auburn hair that touched her shoulders and the most incredible green eyes he'd ever seen.

"Yeah, *thrilling* isn't the first thing that popped into my head when the crews showed up today."

Natalie grabbed his hand. "Oh, come on. Who doesn't want to be on TV?"

Him, for one. As a defensive end for the San Francisco Sabers football team, he'd had plenty of cameras and microphones shoved in his face over the years. But since the restaurant was new, he couldn't turn down some publicity for it. So he'd done the interview, and now he just wanted to stay out of the way while the film crew got their overview shots of the restaurant.

"Do you think they'll want to get some film of the two of us together?" Natalie asked. "You know, kind of get some background on your personal life, like what you do on your time off away from football and the restaurant, who you're seeing, stuff like that?"

Warning bells clanged loud and hard in Flynn's head. He'd gone down this road with more than one woman, and had ended relationships because of girlfriends who were way more interested in the limelight than in him.

So lately he'd made sure to steer clear of any woman who had an entertainment background. No models, no actresses, no one he could suspect of chasing face time in front of a camera. He'd figured since Natalie was a financial analyst, he was safe.

But seeing her gaze track those cameras like a vampire craving blood, he wasn't sure career choice had much to do with someone needing popularity and limelight in her life.

"Maybe we should move to one of the more prominent tables, Flynn," Natalie said. "You know, that way we might be in one of the camera shots."

He bit back a sigh. "I don't think so."

She pushed back her chair and stood. "I'm going to go to the bar and get a drink. You know, all casual-like, and see if maybe they notice me."

He leaned back in his chair. "You do that."

This relationship was doomed. Just one of the many Flynn had seen go down in flames in the past couple of years.

Maybe there wasn't a woman out there who was interested in him. Just him. Not Flynn the football player. Just Flynn the guy.

He shook his head, mentally notched up another failure, and took a long swallow of his beer.

SINCE THE ORDERS had slowed down and she had the kitchen under control, Amelia Lawrence washed her hands in the sink and tried her best to hide, avoiding the cameras. The last thing she wanted was to be on television. She was head chef at Ninety-Two. This whole publicity thing was on Flynn and she didn't need to be interviewed, filmed, or in any way noticed.

But as she did her best game of hide-and-not-be-sought, she also spotted Flynn's new girlfriend, doing her best job to try to be seen by any of the camera crew.

Oh no. Not another one of *those* kinds of women.

She'd worked with Flynn for the past couple of months, even before Ninety-Two had opened. And in that time period she'd seen him go through no less than three women, all of whom seemed to be way more interested in his prowess as camera candy than anything else.

She felt bad for him, and felt nothing but disdain for the women who couldn't appreciate what a fine man Flynn Cassidy was.

He was supremely tall and ridiculously well built, with a thick mane of black hair and amazing blue eyes. She could spend at least a full day doing nothing but appreciating his tattoos. And who didn't love football? Plus, the man had fine culinary taste. When he'd hired her, they'd spent several weeks arguing over the menu for the restaurant. She had to admit he had good ideas.

So did she, and she appreciated that he listened to hers. But the bottom line was that it was his restaurant and his call on the menu. But in the end they'd blended both their ideas, and she loved the way it had turned out.

So why couldn't the man find a decent girlfriend? He kind

of sucked at it, actually. If she were a native of San Francisco, maybe she could help him out, but since she'd only moved here recently from Portland, she knew only a handful of people. Her only ties here were a friend from college and her friend's husband. Otherwise, she was pretty much alone here.

Just the way she wanted it.

She still thought she could find better women for Flynn to date than the ones he'd been parading in and out of the restaurant lately. She could spot posers a mile away. Maybe she could offer her service to Flynn.

"Orders up."

She focused her attention on the incoming orders, on directing her staff, on minding her own business, and not on Flynn's idiot girlfriend, who was currently preening for the cameras.

With an eye roll, she dismissed the woman and set about making scallops.

Because Flynn Cassidy was decidedly not her problem. And no matter how much she felt sorry for him, she wasn't going to get involved in his personal life.